The black ink spiraled over his left pectoral like a segment of conch shell sliced down the center.

Phoebe was having trouble focusing on the tattoo itself. The flesh beneath it was kind of spectacular. She tried not to drool. "What's it mean?"

"It's an *ehecacozcatl*. A wind jewel that belongs to the god. It's sort of a family coat of arms."

"Your family's ancestry is Aztec?"

"Maybe. Probably not, but who knows? The Diamantes like to say so." Rafe flashed another of those smiles that were beginning to do funny things to Phoebe's stomach. Because *stomach* was the organ involved. Sure.

Rafe started to settle onto the floor in front of the coffee table.

"You're keeping the pants on?" Phoebe had to resist rolling her eyes at herself. The words had just jumped out. "I mean—you said the fabric gets in the way."

He answered as if she weren't a complete loon. "I figured going fully skyclad would be a little presumptuous."

About the Author

Jane Kindred is the author of the Demons of Elysium series of M/M erotic fantasy romance, the Looking Glass Gods dark fantasy tetralogy and the gothic paranormal romance *The Lost Coast*. Jane spent her formative years ruining her eyes reading romance novels in the Tucson sun and watching *Star Trek* marathons in the dark. She now writes to the sound of San Francisco foghorns while two cats slowly but surely edge her off the side of the bed.

Books by Jane Kindred

Harlequin Nocturne

Waking the Serpent

WAKING
THE SERPENT

JANE KINDRED

978-0-373-13977-4

Waking the Serpent

Copyright © 2016 by Jane Kindred

For questions and comments about the quality of this book, please contact us at CustomerService@Harlequin.com.

® and ™ are trademarks of the publisher. Trademarks indicated with ® are registered in the United States Patent and Trademark Office, the Canadian Intellectual Property Office and in other countries.

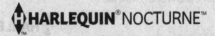

HARLEQUIN® NOCTURNE™

www.Harlequin.com

Printed in U.S.A.

Recycling programs
for this product may
not exist in your area.

978-0-373-13977-4

Waking the Serpent

Copyright © 2016 by Jane Kindred

Printed in U.S.A.

Dear Reader,

Although I grew up in Tucson, Arizona, I never visited the northern part of the state until I'd graduated from college and moved away, and then only briefly. It wasn't until I decided to set my little series about magic-touched sisters in the town of Sedona that I took the time to discover it for myself.

If there's anywhere in the West where magic exists, Sedona is that place. It's easy to imagine that the veil between the worlds of the living and the dead is thin among its otherworldly rock formations in hues that run the gamut from the brash tones of a shiny copper penny to the rich, earthy decadence of a dense red velvet cake.

Waking the Serpent pays homage to that sense of magic, as well as to Sedona's quirky individuality. I like to think my heroine, Phoebe, nicely represents the latter, while my hero, Rafe, contributes plenty to the former. I hope you'll think so, too.

Wishing you unexpected magic,

Jane Kindred

Chapter 1

Hello vertigo and free-floating anxiety, my old friends. Phoebe let the familiar nausea-inducing miasma wash over her as the lights in her Sedona ranch house flickered and went out. The latter might be reasonably explained by the summer storm rolling over the desert, downed power lines, the fact that the old house had bad wiring, maybe— if it were anyone but Phoebe. But she'd driven around the bend of reasonable and onto the unimproved county road of completely certifiable a long time ago.

The dead and Phoebe had an uneasy truce. She'd given up trying to ignore them, because looking like the crazy lady who occasionally talked to herself was infinitely preferable to public outbursts worthy of an exorcist. She agreed to help them find justice, or closure, or peace—as long as they backed off when she told them to.

The electrical activity of a rainstorm actually brought them out. Or gave them energy to manifest, anyway. They'd been mumbling about her all day, the spectral aura of a migraine telling her somebody wanted in.

The shade trying to step in right now was new at it,

making the room swim around Phoebe in gut-churning waves.

Phoebe stood over the couch with a death grip on the back of it, teeth clenched to keep from losing her lunch on the faux leather upholstery, trying to focus on the room through the dark bob of her ponytail swinging in front of her eyes. "For the love of Mike. Just step in already. The damn door's open."

As if in contradiction to her statement, the kitchen door slammed behind her, yanked by the air being sucked through the house in the wind tunnel created between the front entrance and the screen door opening onto the back porch. There was nothing better than the smell of petrichor stirred up by an oncoming storm. Phoebe had left the doors open to let it clean out the house and freshen things up. Given her housekeeping habits—and Puddleglum's litter box habits—any little bit helped.

The storm-dark sky visible through the windows in front of her lit up for an instant with a horizontal bolt of lightning, and the answering crack of thunder came swiftly.

"I think he set me up." The uncertain murmur had come from her own lips. The shade was in.

"It's okay." Phoebe spoke aloud, though it wasn't necessary. Someone else talking through her was bad enough without answering in her head. She had *some* mental dignity left. "You can talk to me. You're safe here."

"Here?" The answering voice seemed youngish but Phoebe couldn't get a handle on the gender. "Where's here? I don't know where I am."

From experience, Phoebe knew it was better to prevaricate a bit. Especially with the newly dead. "You're at the hospital. Do you remember what happened to you?"

Her heart began to hammer—the shade's fear—as the

answer came. "I was supposed to meet someone. But I… Something went wrong. Oh, God. Why is he here?"

Phoebe had to center the shade in the present before panic took over and it got stuck on a loop at the moment of its death. "Why don't we start at the beginning, hon? Can you tell me your name?"

"I…I can't… I think… I'm not sure."

"That's okay. Don't worry about that right now. Do you remember who you were meeting? Where were you supposed to meet?"

"I got a message, and I… He isn't supposed to be here. Oh, my God. He set me up."

Before Phoebe could bring the shade back to center, her throat began to tighten as though a pair of strong, gloved hands had closed around it. Fantastic. A violent murder and the shade was going to relive it inside her. There was no use fighting. She had to let the shade go through it—let it make *Phoebe* go through it—before it would release her.

Her lungs, however, were harder to convince. They fought like hell. Adrenaline shot through her bloodstream, a last-ditch, futile attempt at fight-or-flight, as Phoebe stumbled backward, hands convulsing at her throat. Before she could lose consciousness from the air being squeezed out of her, however, the back of her head hit the hardwood floor, beating it to the punch.

Rain spattered the entryway through the screen door as the storm broke at last. Phoebe lay and listened to it for a moment without moving. She hadn't felt the shade go. But, like being blackout drunk, it had left her with a serious hangover. The ungrateful little wretch.

Howling at her like a Klaxon from the coffee table, her cell phone announced there wouldn't be time to indulge her headache.

Phoebe crawled around the couch and jabbed the speaker

button to let it know who was boss. "This had better be good." Her voice sounded like she'd been gargling kitty litter.

"Ms. Carlisle? Phoebe Carlisle?"

Phoebe cringed at the booming, deep baritone. "Yeah, you got her. Who's this?"

"I was given your name for representation."

Her stomach gave a little lurch of protest at his volume and Phoebe pressed her fingers to her temples. "I'm a public defender. If you need an attorney and you can't afford legal assistance—"

"Jesus. I don't need a fucking Miranda recitation." *Wow. Charming.* "I need a lawyer. Now. I'll pay your standard hourly rate."

Despite his rudeness, Phoebe's ears perked up at the sound of money. Being an assistant public defender wasn't exactly a high-paying gig. But she wasn't about to let this jerk get the upper hand. She needed to be the one in control of any potential client relationship. She'd refused clients before when she knew their anger issues—or their woman issues—were going to prevent that. Which didn't help the pay situation any, but it was where she drew the line.

"How about you stop swearing at me and tell me what kind of lawyer you—"

"I don't have time for sweet talk. I'm at the Yavapai County Jail. Rafael Diamante."

The line went dead while Phoebe's mouth worked, poised on a pointless rebuke of her potential client. *Rafael Diamante.* Why was that name familiar? She'd seen it somewhere in her newsfeed this morning.

Phoebe pulled up the browser on her tablet and thumbed through her feed until she found the post from the *Sedona Red Rock News.*

Local Businessman Brought in for
Questioning in Mystic Murder.

Barbara Fisher, a self-described psychic medium
who offered palm and tarot readings from her residence on Cedar Road, was found strangled in her
home early this morning. An anonymous Sedona
PD source confirmed entrepreneur Rafael "Rafe"
Diamante was discovered at the scene—apparently
intoxicated.

Unless two people had been strangled in Sedona this
morning, the victim had to be Phoebe's step-in. And Rafe
Diamante—Phoebe had seen his name on signs all over
town: Diamante Construction and Excavation. He owned
half of Yavapai County. Why he would want Phoebe to
represent him, she couldn't fathom. Was this some kind of
joke? Common sense and her conscience told her to stay
far away from this one. Representing the accused killer
of someone whose shade she had just hosted had to be a
pretty big conflict of interest. But neither common sense
nor her conscience was in the driver's seat of her Jeep as
she headed to the county lockup in Camp Verde.

Chapter 2

Rafe Diamante wasn't at all what she'd expected. Waiting for him in an interrogation room, Phoebe had been picturing a man in his sixties with a beer belly and a receding hairline. Apparently she was thinking of his father. This Rafe Diamante was perhaps thirty, tall, hard and lean—a fact accentuated by the white T-shirt hugging his abs—his skin a deep coppery brown, as though he worked the construction sites himself. Far from a receding hairline, he had a rich, dark head of hair with a wavy curl to it, tied back in a short ponytail, while penetrating brown eyes glowered at Phoebe from under some serious eyebrows. Damn. He could excavate at her place any time.

When he spoke, the illusion of hotness was shattered. "You're Phoebe Carlisle? Un-fucking-believable."

"I beg your pardon?"

"You're a goddamn Girl Scout."

Dropping the hand she'd extended when he was escorted in, Phoebe sat across from him, taking her tablet out of her bag and flipping the cover open before making a point of tugging her bouncy ponytail tighter behind her head. "I made Cadette, actually. But the uniform doesn't really fit anymore and I got stuck on the goddamn deportment badge."

Diamante wasn't amused. "Do you even have a law degree?"

"Mr. Diamante, I'm an assistant public defender. You don't get that position without having a law degree and having passed the bar. But I'm quite certain you're aware of that. You're the one who called me, if you remember."

He folded his arms—such an impressive display of his biceps she almost expected him to beat his chest—and deepened his glower. "You were recommended to me."

"So you said. I have to confess, Mr. Diamante, I don't understand why you wouldn't already have a lawyer who represents your family and your business—someone who I'm sure has the requisite gray hair to satisfy your age requirement. And a penis."

The corner of his mouth twitched and his glower warmed as if he would have smiled if he wasn't concentrating so hard on being on the offensive—a tiny sign he might not be a complete douche. "I can't use my family's lawyer. It's complicated. But I can certainly afford exceptional legal counsel. Your recommendation, however, involved a specific unique skill."

It was Phoebe's turn to stifle a mouth twitch. "What skill would that be?"

"I was told you're…" Diamante paused and the tips of his ears turned an adorable pink. "A step-in."

Her amusement at his boyish blush dissipated instantly. Phoebe flipped the cover back onto her tablet as she rose. She remembered now why his name seemed familiar. It wasn't just the construction signs. The outline of his pendant was visible under the shirt—she'd been thinking it was some kind of saint medallion. It was a pentacle. He belonged to her sister's coven.

"A step-in, Mr. Diamante, as you well know, is an unanchored shade. Not the vehicle. That's an offensive term for someone who does what I do, and I won't sit here and put up with your bigoted insults just because you've gotten yourself into some kind of metaphysical bind and can't use Daddy's money to get you out of it."

Phoebe turned on her heel and headed for the door, anger at Ione making the blood pound in her ears. Ione had never had any respect for her younger sister, imagining herself morally superior because she had the backing of a group of twelve equally uptight jerks behind her. And now she had the gall to tell this rich-boy witch Phoebe could defend him because he'd murdered a psychic?

"Wait. Ms. Carlisle." Diamante rose and came around the table, grasping for her arm before she could open the door.

Phoebe moved out of his reach with a smooth sidestep and turned the handle, facing him as she did a quick twist to go through the door. "I'm sure you won't have any trouble finding another lawyer with your charming personality." The multilayered insult was probably lost on him.

"Not one who can talk to the people I'm trying to help."

Phoebe paused. "What people?"

"The shades."

He was full of crap. "Exactly how would someone of your affiliation be helping shades? I think you're confusing 'help' with 'persecute.'"

"I don't share the majority opinion of the Covent."

The name always annoyed her. They couldn't just use "coven" like normal people. They had to be snooty about it.

Diamante was unconsciously rubbing the pentacle through his shirt—an unfortunately sexy quirk. "If you'd come back in and close the door, I'll be more candid. And I apologize. I didn't realize that was an offensive term." He looked annoyed, as though he'd never needed to apologize before. Which strained credulity.

Phoebe stepped back inside and shut the door, leaning against it with her briefcase in front of her as if to ward off any underhanded spell-casting. "All right. I'm listening."

"To the rest of the Covent, I'm a warlock. An 'oath-breaker.' I was working with Barbara Fisher to communicate with shades. It goes against the Covent's creed."

"No kidding." Despite her skepticism, Phoebe couldn't help but be intrigued. She hadn't pegged Diamante for a spiritual maverick. "If you don't mind my saying, you don't really look like the type to buck the system." If anything, he looked like the type who owned the system.

Diamante slipped his hands into his pockets. "My little brother died a few years ago. Broke into one of my father's construction sites to party after his senior prom and fell to his death trying to impress some girl. His shade visited me." He'd been glancing down as he spoke, but he looked up and met Phoebe's eyes. "I insisted on crossing him over. He didn't want to go. He seemed confused, not understanding he'd died, but I stuck to the strict doctrine and cast the crossing spell. I exorcised my own brother from the mortal plane. And he was sobbing and begging for mercy when he went."

"Jesus." It was an ironic exclamation in such a pagan context, but it was automatic from her years in the church. Not that she'd set foot in one recently.

"You have to understand, the fear behind the doctrine is real—shades are vulnerable to being manipulated by unscrupulous practitioners—"

"Like me, you mean."

Diamante sighed. "I didn't say it. But some people do take advantage of step-ins…" He paused, the pink returning to his ears. "Is it okay to call them that? The shades, I mean."

"Of course. If they're stepping in, that's what they are.

It's using the term to describe the person hosting the step-in that's offensive. The implication being the host has no soul of her own." Phoebe studied him as she relaxed her stance. Rafe Diamante was a marvelous bundle of contradictions. She'd never met anyone so thoroughly belligerent and sure of himself yet so quick to express self-conscious awareness of his own ill-mannered behavior. The pink-tipped ears were downright hot.

Diamante shrugged and took his seat once more. "Some people take advantage of them, and often for unsavory purposes. The Covent doctrine that it's unnatural for them to remain here is based on centuries of experience. Crossing them over is meant to be an act of kindness. But in practice, it seems to me it's an act of self-righteousness. After Gabriel, I knew it was wrong. Since then, I've argued against crossing a shade against its will. And I've been branded an oath-breaker."

Phoebe dropped back into her chair and set the tablet on the table, ready to take notes. "So you're out of the Covent, then."

Diamante's mouth opened but before he could answer, the door swung open, admitting a pair of well-dressed witches and a flustered desk officer.

The officer glared at Phoebe. "She said she was his legal counsel."

"Mr. Diamante already has legal counsel. We'll handle this, Phoebe. Thanks for coming by." Ione held the door open for her.

Phoebe rose, bristling. "*He* called *me*."

"This is a serious matter that requires an experienced legal team. We've got it covered." Her sister flipped her expensively straightened and ombréd hair over her shoulder as she took the seat opposite Diamante, all maternal concern. "Why didn't you call us, Rafe?"

The officer took Phoebe's arm. "Ms. Carlisle."

Phoebe cast one last glance at Diamante, who skirted her gaze. "Yeah, I'm going."

Chapter 3

Well, that had gone swimmingly. Rafe rubbed his hands over his face with a quiet groan. He'd actually called her a goddamn Girl Scout. And if she was a Girl Scout, he was having really inappropriate thoughts.

The golden-haired, overgrown frat boy who'd arrived with Ione Carlisle held out his hand when Rafe glanced up, an overly confident smile showing professionally whitened teeth. Rafe had seen him at the temple earlier that week when the Conclave had convened.

"Carter Hanson Hamilton."

Rafe shook the offered hand and tried not to roll his eyes. The name sounded like it should be a law firm all by itself.

"The Covent has me on retainer, Mr. Diamante. Don't worry—we'll have you out of here in no time."

Rafe glanced at the high priestess—impeccably dressed and professional, she couldn't have been more different from her sister. "I appreciate your coming down here, but I had things under control."

Hamilton answered for her. "I'm sure the younger Ms. Carlisle is a fine public defender, but you're not exactly the public, Mr. Diamante. You can't afford to make any mistakes here. The Covent takes care of its own." Hamilton was still standing, which irked him unreasonably.

Rafe got to his feet to meet him at eye level and leaned back against the wall with his arms folded—as if he hadn't just been found with a dead woman and brought in on suspicion of murder. "I wasn't aware I was still one of the Covent's own. Did I not just get slapped with a scarlet W?"

Ione spoke before Hamilton could cut her off again. "Rafe, the Covent has to take matters of doctrinal dissent seriously. We can't all follow our own brand of the craft. That's for Eclectics. As a respected member of the Sedona Coventry, you're held to a higher standard. But that doesn't mean we're going to throw you to the wolves when you're in trouble. Even if ignoring the wishes of the Covent is what put you there."

"Ione's right." Hamilton sat, leaving Rafe the only one standing. "This situation is a direct result of your oathbreaking, and I'm sure it's brought home to you just why the proscription against allowing shades to continue to occupy the physical plane is in place. But the Covent intends to stand by you. We're all unified on that front."

Rafe scowled. "Unified. Like you were when my apprentice spoke in support of my position at the Conclave."

Ione maintained a stern expression but the color in her high cheekbones wasn't all cosmetic. "You had a responsibility to Matthew—to groom him and guide him, not fill his head with false doctrine."

"He made one misstep and you dismissed him from his apprenticeship."

The stern look faltered. "It was a misstep in front of the entire Conclave, Rafe. If I hadn't responded swiftly and firmly, the entire Sedona Coventry would have been in jeopardy."

"Well, now he's missing. You know that, right?" Rafe glanced at Hamilton, but his expression was neutral. "He disappeared right after you all presented your unified front against him. So I guess the Conclave won't have to worry about my bad influence on him anymore."

"It's an unfortunate situation, but 'missing' is a strong word. I'm sure there's nothing to worry about. And I'd think that would be the least of your worries right now." Carter gave him a patronizing smile. "Luckily, I'm on your team."

Rafe stifled a snort. Yay. Lucky him.

Rain battered the car as Phoebe drove through Oak Creek Village, letting the rhythmic thump and whine of the windshield wipers pound out a sort of mantra to exorcise her anger at Ione. Her big sister had been upstaging her all her life. And what had she done to deserve Ione's scorn? Treated the dead like people and listened to them when they talked. Phoebe might be green, but she was a damned good lawyer, and Ione had no business swooping in to pat her on the back and usher her out like a precocious child.

Ione had imagined herself an adult—and the only adult—from the day Phoebe was born. Only four years Phoebe's senior, she seemed to think she'd raised Phoebe and their younger sisters, Theia and Rhea. Their mother would have begged to differ—if she'd been around to finish raising them, anyway.

The white open-work Gothic spires of Covent Temple rose out of the misty backdrop of a huddle of low clouds against the improbably red hoodoos scattered around Bell Rock and Courthouse Butte. The less dramatic geological formations among which the temple nestled couldn't be found on any tourist map. To the casual eye, the temple was effectively invisible, hidden by a glamour. But once seen, it teased with half-glimpsed visions, a mirage ever-approaching but never reached.

It tended to be more visible the more it was brought to mind, and Ione's slights had definitely brought the Covent and the temple to mind. Phoebe turned onto the brick-cobbled road almost without thinking, drawn by its presence. She'd never been inside. That was for the privileged few. But Diamante's status as an oath-breaker had piqued her curiosity. From what little she knew of Covent doctrine, branding a member of the Covent as a warlock required a convention of the Conclave. Which meant the regional Covent officials had either come here in person or convened magically. Either way, such a meeting ought to have stirred up the shades, but Phoebe had heard nothing of it.

The brick drive wound through the rocks, giving glimpses of the towers, but the rain was coming down hard now and Covent Temple didn't seem to want to be found. But just as she circled back to return to the highway, it rose out of the wall of rain ahead of her like Brigadoon on its hundredth anniversary.

Phoebe hit the brakes hard and the car whipped back and forth on the road, but the cobbled texture of the brick surface broke the swerve before she went into a tailspin. There it was, much smaller than it seemed from the highway, but gorgeously out of place with its shockingly white Gothic design. It was like coming upon the brilliant San Xavier Mission—the White Dove of the Desert—in the southern part of the state. She supposed its appearance had a similar purpose, if more arcane, visible in stark relief against its rugged surroundings for those who were meant to see it. The only difference was that the Covent didn't proselytize.

But something other than just the temple's aura had drawn her here. She sensed the ethereal tug of a shade but without the usual step-in immediacy. It had the same feel as the shade she'd encountered earlier, but this time it kept its distance, and its confusion and fear had receded. If it was Barbara Fisher, she'd accepted her fate surprisingly quickly. But why would Barbara bring Phoebe here? And why not step in and try to communicate?

A strong atmosphere of shade activity shrouded the temple as she drew closer, different from the shade that had prodded her here, prickling in the air with a soft electric vibration Phoebe couldn't fully tune in to. She'd never experienced anything like it. Shades often congregated around sacred spaces, but they tended to hone in on Phoebe when she was anywhere near them, like bees to their queen, and none of them here was trying to step in. There was something off about the feel of them, as though they were hovering between one plane and the next.

For a moment she felt a little flutter, a voice trying to manifest in her head, a held breath. She caught a name—Matthew—before something jolted her as if the shade had been yanked away as it tried to make contact. In the wake of the missed connection, her head throbbed with pressure as if she'd made a sudden change of altitude. Everything felt wrong. Whatever was going on at the temple didn't bode well, and it had Covent interference written all over it.

By the time she reached the semiprivate drive to her house, the uneasiness had faded and Ione's unbelievable stunt was playing musical chairs in Phoebe's head once more, with Phoebe metaphorically dumped on her ass. Leaving the wipers at half-mast, Phoebe switched off the engine and pounded her fists on the steering wheel with a loud, cathartic expletive. Thank goodness for the county zoning that kept her closest neighbors just beyond screaming distance.

Okay, Ione was out of her system. Done. She wasn't wasting another minute on her sister's crap.

In its place, however, the image of Gabriel Diamante— begging his brother for mercy as he was forced to leave behind everything he'd known—slid to the fore. She couldn't get it out of her head. Something about it triggered her, too close to the feeling of helplessness she'd experienced in the early days of hosting step-ins.

In the beginning, when she hadn't been careful about setting boundaries, she'd been paralyzed by the emotions of shades. If their deaths had been sudden and unexpected, they were often awash in anguish over what they'd lost and drowning in fear of the unknown. To force them to move on before they were ready was like holding their heads under water—killing them all over again. It was a prime example of the Covent's arrogance, and why Phoebe was willing to let the shades in. Someone had to speak for them. But letting them in had also meant opening herself up to an intimacy that wasn't entirely consensual.

She shivered, trying to dispel the feeling of violation, and swept her bag off the seat as she hopped out of the Wrangler. The leather briefcase seemed light. *Son of a—* Phoebe opened it, knowing full well what the missing weight was. She'd been so flustered, she'd left her tablet at the county jail. It had an encrypted password, at least, but what were the odds she'd ever see that thing again? It had all of her recent case notes, along with personal files— photos and videos she hadn't uploaded to the cloud for backup yet. A quick call to the jail confirmed the worst. The tablet was long gone.

It was definitely time for a drink.

Inside, Phoebe opened a bottle of Côtes du Rhône and poured herself an oversized glass, ready to curl up on the papasan chair and do nothing but sip wine and listen to the rain as the sky brooded with storm-induced dusk. Her head still pounded from the incident with the step-in; she might as well earn the hangover. Besides, tomorrow was Sunday and she could sleep in.

Halfway to the living room, her phone vibrated in her pocket. Maybe someone had found the tablet, after all.

"This is Phoebe Carlisle." She assumed every call was professional. Wherever she happened to be at any given moment functioned as her "office" much of the time.

"Phoebe, it's Di." Ione's given name was actually Dione. She'd dropped the D when she was younger, but the nickname had stuck.

Phoebe's thumb hovered over End Call.

"Don't hang up, Phoebes, I need to explain."

"Don't call me Phoebes like we're BFFs. We're not children anymore. And we're most certainly not friends."

Ione sighed into the phone. "I don't blame you for being angry, but that wasn't my call. Diamante Senior hired his own counsel for Rafe and he wanted it to go through the Covent so Rafe wouldn't refuse. And you have to recognize you would have been in over your head, anyway. The evidence is pretty damning, and there are a lot of people in the valley who'd love to see a wealthy business owner like Rafe take a fall. It's going to be a media circus."

"And you don't think I can handle a serious case. I get it. Thanks for calling."

"Phoebe. Do *not* hang up this phone."

"Oh, my God. You really think I'm twelve." Phoebe decided to act like it and clicked the button.

Predictably, the phone rang again. She put it in do-not-disturb mode and took her wine to the papasan chair, kicking off her heels and sinking into the soft cushion. The voice mail notification popped up a moment later. With a sigh, Phoebe played the message.

"Listen, Phoebe. This is about Rafe. I gave him your card when he started messing around with this step-in business. We may not see eye to eye, but I know you believe in what you do, and I think you can help him. Just… don't get too tangled up with him. He can be very charming."

Phoebe laughed out loud as the message ended. *Right. Mr. Charm.* It was exactly the nickname she would have given him. She couldn't decide what offended her more, Ione's dismissal of her as a serious attorney or assuming Phoebe was so gullible—or so desperate—she'd fall for any good-looking guy who said two words to her. Though, to be fair, Diamante was slightly more than just good-looking.

She was half considering calling Ione back to tell her off when the doorbell rang followed by a rap on the frame of the screen door. She took another big swallow of wine before opening the door and choked on the mouthful, coughing gracelessly as she stared at her unexpected visitor. Speak of the devil.

Chapter 4

Rafe Diamante, looking like Heathcliff out on the moors, narrowed his eyes with concern, reaching for the handle of the screen door. "Are you all right?"

"Am *I* all right?" Phoebe continued coughing up a lung. "Weren't you just in jail on a murder charge? How do you even know where I live?"

He held up her business card. "I promise I'm not stalking you, Ms. Carlisle. Your sister gave it to me."

Right. Ione. The jerk. The rain was coming down in sheets and Diamante was soaked to the skin.

"Sorry to show up unannounced. I called first, but your phone kept going straight to voice mail."

Phoebe unlocked the screen door and held it open. "Better come in before you drown."

Mr. Charm stepped in, wiping his boots on the welcome mat to avoid tracking red desert mud inside. "Before you go calling the cops to report a fugitive, they can't officially charge me with murder until the coroner's report comes back. My lawyer challenged the police on holding me without cause."

"Right. That *serious* lawyer." Phoebe took another sip,

trying not to stare at Diamante's pecs through the white tee plastered to them. Beneath the shirt, some kind of dark, patterned tattoo swirled over his heart beside the pentacle. She mimicked the motion of the art with her wine. "Can I get you a glass?" She took his shrug for ascent and headed to the kitchen.

When he remained standing, Phoebe waved the bottle at the rustic wood-frame couch in the living room. "Have a seat."

He cast a doubtful glance at the couch. "It's leather. I'm soaking wet."

Phoebe snorted as she came around the bar with his glass. "It's pleather. Don't worry about it. I can't afford anything real on my salary." She took the matching chair kitty-corner to the couch while Diamante sat on the edge of a cushion. "My sister said you needed my help with the step-ins. Why did you call me from county? Why not call your family? You can't really have wanted my representation."

"I wanted to deal with this myself. Without my father or the Covent using their influence to sweep things under the rug."

"What would there be to sweep under the rug?" Phoebe's eyebrows drew together. "You didn't actually kill Barbara Fisher?"

"I don't think so, no."

"You don't *think* so?"

"I'm…fuzzy on what actually happened. I remember driving to her house for the appointment last night, and I have a vague idea we argued. I can't remember what about. She gave me a cup of tea and I guess it must have been drugged. The next thing I can recall clearly is waking up feeling sluggish, like I'd been in a trance—with Barbara dead on the floor beside me and the cops breaking down the door."

"A trance. So you think maybe one of the shades…?"

"Stepped in and took over? I don't know. It's possible." His expression was pained. "I find it difficult to believe I could do something so completely against my nature under the influence of a step-in, but it's what the Covent has always argued. And someone had been controlling the shades—using them to control their hosts. So it could have been me they used this time."

"Do the police have any evidence? Besides circumstantial, I mean. Were there any prints on the body? Your hair?"

"I don't know."

"I can find out for you. I mean, your lawyer can."

"There were leather gloves lying on the floor next to her." Diamante's expression was grim. "They fit."

A shiver rippled along her spine. Gloves. Like the ones she'd felt closing around her throat when the shade possessed her.

She shrugged off the unpleasant memory with a flippant comment before she could stop herself. "So they won't acquit." Phoebe stared wide-eyed into her glass at her stupidity as she finished her wine. "Sorry. Sometimes I have an infantile urge to say whatever pops into my head." She set the glass on the coffee table and tried to act more like a normal person. "I'm still not quite sure how you expect me to help you, Mr. Diamante."

"Please—call me Rafe."

Phoebe returned his smile despite herself. "Rafe." Crap. He *was* charming. "I'm not a medium. I can't just call on a shade. They come to me on their own." It occurred to her she ought to disclose that one shade in particular had come to her this afternoon. But perhaps it would be better to keep that to herself. The shade hadn't stayed long enough to confirm it was Barbara Fisher or to give any indication of her killer's identity, but if Diamante—Rafe—had done it under the control of a step-in, Barbara could identify him. Which could make things awkward for Phoebe if he knew.

"But they trust you. The ones you've dealt with. As I understand it, you have something of a reputation with them."

"If you mean they know to come to me, I suppose they do. Or maybe they try several people until they find someone who's receptive. I don't really know. I've never asked."

"But the point is, they might come to you. The ones I was communicating with."

"I suppose so."

"And if they did, would I be able to talk to them? I mean, would you be able to talk to me—as the shade?"

Phoebe sat back. "They don't usually communicate with anyone else *through* me, just *to* me." Though that was more Phoebe's choice than the will of the shades. "Usually they come to me because they're confused and don't understand what's happened to them. Or because they want my help finding someone or something. I'm sort of like an afterlife private detective." She grimaced and added, "Except my clients are all pro bono."

"Well, I could pay you." Rafe finally took a sip of his wine. "I'll give you the same hourly rate you charge for legal consultation. And as you probably know from your sister, there are spells that can summon a shade."

Just as her inner accountant was getting excited, anger flared inside her. "You mean entrapment spells. So you can force them to cross."

Rafe had the grace to look embarrassed. "That's what the Covent uses them for, yes. But the spell can be cast merely to bring them here. It doesn't hurt the shade."

"Here. As in now." Phoebe narrowed her gaze. "That's why you're here."

He nodded and took another sip. "Time is of the essence if I'm going to stop him and clear my name."

"Stop whom?"

"Whoever it is that's manipulating them. Whoever wanted to retain that power over them so desperately he was willing to silence Barbara Fisher."

Phoebe studied his dark, intense eyes. Whether or not someone in Sedona was manipulating shades for nefarious purposes, Rafe Diamante obviously believed they were. And he seemed sincere in his respect for the shades' autonomy. Unless the summoning spell wasn't as harmless as he claimed.

"If you summon a shade and I find out it doesn't want to be here—if any of this summoning process is against its will—my 'consulting' with you will be over. Is that clear?"

Rafe nodded, holding up his right hand with his thumb over his pinkie. "Scout's honor." The sudden warm smile accompanying the gesture distracted her. It took her a moment to make the connection with the comment he'd made when they'd met at the county jail.

"Oh…you were actually a Boy Scout. I was kidding when I said I was in the Scouts. I'm afraid I was never a Cadette."

"Oh. Well, that's embarrassing." He dropped his hand to his side with an apologetic smile that was possibly even more endearing. "Sorry about my reaction earlier. I was having a pretty bad day."

"I imagine you were." It was impossible not to return the smile as she rose. "So what do you need for the spell?"

"I'm going to guess you don't keep an altar yourself." When Phoebe laughed, Rafe recited the ingredients without skipping a beat: "Three candles, preferably white, some incense—if you don't have any, I can show you how to make something serviceable with your spice collection—

a bowl of salt, a bowl of water and a libation." He tapped his glass. "We've got the libation."

Phoebe went to the kitchen and set out two condiment bowls. "Salt's on the bar. And I've got the candles and incense somewhere around here."

After fetching the supplies from the bedroom, she returned to find Rafe stripping off his shirt. A tattoo of a colorful winged serpent adorned his back, the ink in vivid shades of an almost iridescent blue-green and violet with a deep scarlet red down the breast of the creature, its wings spanning both broad shoulders.

Phoebe clutched the candles to her chest. "Whoa."

Rafe turned as he pulled the shirt over his head, ears reddening at the tips. "Sorry. I should have asked first. It's easier to spell-cast without fabric—and this fabric is freezing. But I can put it back on." He was halfway to doing it.

"No, it's fine. I should have offered to dry it for you anyway." Phoebe set the candles and incense on the coffee table and held out her hand to take the shirt. "It was just— unexpected. And I was admiring your tattoo."

"Oh. Quetzalcoatl." His expression took on an element of defiant pride, as if he expected to have to defend his choice of body art. "I forget he's there since I can't see it without a bit of acrobatics." He cast his gaze downward as he turned to face her. "The one on the front, of course, I'm much more aware of." The black ink spiraled over his left pectoral like a cross section of a conch shell.

Phoebe was having trouble focusing on the tattoo itself. The flesh beneath it was kind of spectacular. She tried not to drool. "What's it mean?"

"It's an ehecacozcatl. A wind jewel that belongs to the god. It's sort of a family coat of arms."

"Your family's ancestry is Aztec?"

"Maybe. Probably not, but who knows? The Diamantes

like to say so." Rafe flashed another of those smiles that were beginning to do funny things to Phoebe's stomach. Because *stomach* was the organ involved. Sure.

Rafe started to settle onto the floor in front of the coffee table.

"You're keeping the pants on?" Phoebe had to resist rolling her eyes at herself. The words had just jumped out. "I mean—you said the fabric gets in the way."

He answered as if she weren't a complete loon. "I figured going fully sky-clad would be a little presumptuous. I can work with this."

"But they're soaked. If I'm going to dry the shirt, I may as well dry those, too. Unless you're commando under there?" *Geez, Phoebe. Get a grip.*

Rafe smirked. "No, I'm not really the commando type." He emptied his pockets onto the couch and unbuckled his belt and the utility knife holster at his hip before reaching for the buttons on his fly. "You're sure this is okay?"

"Why wouldn't it be? They'll be dry in a jiff." There was something seriously wrong with her mouth. Or her brain. Who the heck said "jiff"?

As he bent to untie his boots and work them off before stepping out of the pants and handing them over, it was all Phoebe could do not to ogle his ass in the white boxer briefs. Maybe she ogled a little.

"Is it ohgle or ahgle?" Oh, my God. She'd said that out loud.

Phoebe escaped down the hall and opened the laundry closet to toss the wet things into the dryer, leaning back against the appliance to take a deep breath. When she returned to the living room, she managed to have a normal expression on her face. She hoped.

Rafe was clearing off the coffee table to arrange things for the spell—two candles in the top corners and the third in the center, with the condiment bowls holding water and salt on either side of his nearly untouched glass of wine.

Phoebe grabbed a box of matches from the pantry. "Anything else we need?"

"Just one or two things, but I've got them covered." Rafe took his knife from the holster and set it in front of the incense holder. "I use it as an athame in a pinch." He unhooked the pendant from around his neck and let the disc drop from the chain into his hand. "And this will do for the pentacle." He set it in front of the center candle. "My wind jewel tat can stand in for the image of the god. Do you have anything that can serve as a goddess image? It's not absolutely essential—"

"If we're having a god, we're having a goddess." Phoebe began to unbutton her blouse.

Rafe's dark brows twitched. "What are you doing?"

She reached the center button and showed him the silver-blue crescent moon that curled around her navel. "This should do, right?"

Rafe nodded. "That's nice work."

"Thanks." Phoebe slipped off the blouse and set it aside. "My little sister designed it."

"You don't really have to undress. It's mostly symbolic, helps me get my head in the right space."

She unzipped the back of her skirt and stepped out of it. In for a penny, in for a pound. "I wouldn't want you to feel weird being the only one undressed. Frankly, *I* feel a little weird being dressed when you're not. I think this evens the playing field. Or the spell-casting field." She still wore her bra and panties. It wasn't as if she hadn't worn skimpier bathing suits in public. Phoebe sat opposite him and tried to maintain an air of nonchalance.

Rafe struck a match, calling the guardians of the four corners as he lit the candles and incense in a counter-clockwise pattern. She'd seen all this before—had even done it, once upon a time, dabbling with witchcraft in middle school until it had become Ione's "thing." But the summoning spell was one she'd never witnessed.

Holding the makeshift athame aloft in his left hand and the wineglass in his right, Rafe began the invocation. "I call on Xolotl, brother of Quetzalcoatl, protector of the sun in its journey through the valley of the dead, and upon Mictlantecuhtli and Mictecacihuatl, Lord and Lady of the Underworld, to open the gates of Mictlan and usher forth the three souls who've visited this plane in recent days to share knowledge of the afterlife with me. Jacob, Lila and Ernesto, join us now and speak with us here." The black ink of his wind jewel tattoo seemed to glow with a pale blue luminescence as he spoke the words, but perhaps it was only the lightning flickering in the window at Phoebe's back. Thunder rumbled in the wake of the latest flash. A moment later, the electricity went out for the second time today, leaving them in the fluttering glow of candlelight.

The hairs on Phoebe's arms rose. For an alarming instant, she thought lightning was about to strike right through the roof, until she recognized the familiar tug. The shades had come and they were seeking entry—all three at once.

She'd never hosted more than one step-in at a time. When Phoebe opened her mouth to tell them to wait their turn, a wild laugh came out of it. Not her own.

Dimly, she heard Rafe asking if she was all right, but the shades were pushing her consciousness down, making her a sort of backseat passenger. There was no uncertainty as with the shade this morning, and even her own uneasiness felt secondary to the personalities of these shades. They'd done this before.

"Marvelous, darling." Her mouth formed the words in a husky, sensual purr. She sensed Lila as an older woman, pleased with the youthful body she occupied. "Though it's crowded in here."

"Step out, then, *chica*." Phoebe's voice this time was rough and deep, and heavily accented. *Ernesto*.

"You step out." Another masculine cadence, slightly amused, with a soft, Texas twang, challenged the first.

Phoebe was beginning to feel light-headed, and she must have looked it.

Rafe reached across the table and took her hands in both of his. "Let me speak with Phoebe for a moment."

She opened her mouth to assure him she was still there, but her breath seemed to be sucked from her across the table, and Rafe took in a deep, gasping inhalation, eyes wide, as one of the shades leaped from her into him. It was a first in her experience.

"What are you doing?" Ernesto protested with Phoebe's mouth. He swore in Spanish and then Phoebe felt a strange wrenching sensation. Lila was shoving Ernesto out. She thought she'd have more control now with only one shade to deal with, but instead of coming to the fore, she felt herself slipping deeper, her distress at the sensation all but subsumed by Lila's eminent self-satisfaction.

Rafe pulled her to her feet and drew her around the table. But it wasn't Rafe, of course. It was Jacob. "Care to dance?" Jacob's amusement sparkled in the dark eyes.

"I thought you'd never ask." She could swear she was hosting Kathleen Turner. Before she could try to wrest some control from the step-in, she found herself in Rafe's arms, arousal evident in the hard warmth against her thigh as he pulled her in tight. Rafe's lips were kissing hers and Phoebe's were ardently kissing back. She gasped into his mouth as his tongue prodded her open, his fingers drawing goose bumps along her skin, and she moaned as he pinched one of her nipples through the thin cup of lace. She was instantly wet, needing this man as she'd never needed anyone, desperate, lest he disappear once more and fade into the incorporeal shade of the man she loved but was denied. Too much time had passed since he'd been taken from her, too much time had been spent alone, and she would not allow this moment to be taken from her, as well. Jacob was hers and she meant to have him inside her, to experience the union she ached for finally.

Rafe's fingers slid down Phoebe's side as he kissed her, dipping inside the elastic of her panties. Phoebe begged with little moans into his mouth for him to go farther, to open her. Two fingers teased at the perimeter of her sex, one slipping toward the center and stroking like a warm knife against buttercream frosting on a springy cake.

Deep in her mind, alarm bells were going off. This wasn't her. It wasn't Rafe. Something neither of them had consented to was about to happen. Even if she couldn't deny wanting the body pressed against her, the desire flooding her decidedly her own, this wasn't right. She ought to be the one in control here. She was the mediator. Rafe was essentially at her mercy.

The panties dropped to the floor and Rafe slid down one bra strap and let the taut nipple peek out, just at the edge of the fabric.

He lowered his head, his breath against her breast. "God, I want you."

God, she wanted him, too. His mouth closed over the nipple, sucked between his teeth, his other hand prodding between her legs, fingers poised to enter.

"*No!*" The word tore out of her throat, even as she writhed with pleasure under the adoration of his mouth.

Rafe paused and lifted his head, confused.

Phoebe gritted her teeth. "Get out, Lila. Jacob, let him go."

Rafe's hands dropped away from her and he took a step back, doubling over with a sudden groan as if he'd been punched in the gut. The shade rushed out.

Phoebe heard herself screaming—Lila, anguished and mournful, a banshee's wail as she was torn from Phoebe's corporeal matter. For a moment, while the connection still held, she experienced the shade's desperate sorrow as her own. She felt like a heel as Lila left her. But that was only fleeting next to the full awareness flooding back to her. And just to help out, the electricity blinked back on, leaving them standing facing each other in the glaring light of the wagon-wheel chandelier.

"Oh, my God." The blood drained from Rafe's face as Phoebe tried to re-cover herself with as much cool, collected calm as she could muster—which was zilch.

Rafe grabbed an afghan from the back of the couch and threw it around her. "Phoebe, I—I swear to you, that wasn't my... I don't know what happened—"

"You don't have to explain. It was the shades. I've never felt any quite so...determined before." Her knees began to shake in the aftermath of the possession, quickly morphing into a full-body tremble, complete with chattering teeth. "I need to warm up." How ironic. She'd been plenty hot a second ago. "This happens sometimes, after."

"What can I do? What do you need?"

"Run a bath for me. Please." Her knees buckled and Rafe caught her, easing her to the couch. After gently setting her head on a pillow, he hurried down the hall, the sound of running water announcing he was doing as she'd asked. He stayed in the bathroom while the tub filled, too mortified, she supposed, to be in the same room with her. She had to admit, not looking at him right now was probably a really good idea.

When it was ready, he came to get her, dressed in his damp, steamy clothes fresh from the dryer. She was still unsteady, and she made a little yip of surprise when he swept her off the ground and carried her the rest of the

way, setting her on her feet only when he'd reached the
bathroom rug.

"Do you need any help?" He addressed the top of her
left ear.

"No. I've got this. Thanks. It'll just take me a few minutes to warm up."

Rafe nodded and stepped out, closing the door to give
her privacy. He'd also given her bubbles—lavender. That
was sweet. Phoebe dropped the afghan and her underthings
in a heap and climbed into the claw-foot tub, sinking into
the aromatic suds. It was impossible not to replay every
touch—illicitly received though they might have been—
as she lay back against the porcelain and closed her eyes.
Her body wasn't likely to forget it, even if she managed
to stop thinking about it. Even the taste of his mouth and
the smell of his skin lingered.

A sound carried from the front of the house—the click
of the front door closing. Damn.

Chapter 5

Rafe drove through the storm toward home on autopilot, his gut churning as his truck wound through the hills. What the hell had just happened? He was beginning to think the Covent was right about step-ins. If one could control him so completely, it was easy to imagine he'd been taken over by a step-in long enough to kill poor Barbara Fisher. Yet for this, despite being unable to take autonomous action, he'd been fully aware on some level—watching himself. Feeling every sensation.

And what sensations. Phoebe's skin against his had felt like the rain itself, caressing, enveloping, washing him clean. He knew it was Jacob's desire for Lila he'd felt, but it was impossible to extricate his own from the experience. He'd never wanted any woman so intensely. His cock was still stiff as a steel rod in his pants.

He could smell her on his fingers gripping the wheel, intoxicating and incredibly arousing. There was no way he'd be able to sleep tonight without relieving the tension. Yet the thought of what he'd done, lack of personal volition notwithstanding, was mortifying. How could he even think of taking pleasure in the memory?

The storm had passed over the valley by the time he
punched in his code at the gate to Stone Canyon. His
place was modest compared to the family home, but the
gated community always made him feel like an imposter.
Phoebe Carlisle's little cottage was much more his style.
Of course, if his lawyer couldn't get him acquitted of the
murder charge, he'd be living in an altogether different
gated community soon enough.

That ought to be what occupied his mind right now—the
very real possibility that he might spend his life in prison
for a murder someone else had committed, whether with
his hands or otherwise—not his inappropriate arousal at
being used as a vessel for another man's desire. How very
Freudian it all was, even without the puppet sex show he
and Phoebe had almost starred in. *Had* starred in. Things
had gone far enough to constitute one hell of a perfor-
mance.

He had to get her out of his head, and the scent of her
off his skin. As soon as he arrived at the house, he hit the
shower: cold and pounding him with the ultra-massage
setting. It was a temporary reprieve, but he needed to pull
himself together and take care of some business before
clients started backing out after hearing he was being
investigated for murder. God only knew what kind of con-
versations they'd already been having with Rafael Sr. The
fact that his father had sent his fancy lawyer to the county
jail to intervene but hadn't contacted Rafe himself spoke
volumes.

After drying off and getting dressed, he pushed down
the insanity of the entire day and dove into his business
communications to keep operations running smoothly.
He'd earned a reputation as a solid manager in the years
since graduating from college and taking on increasing
responsibility while Rafael Sr. concentrated on his politi-

cal career, and he knew he could count on the people in his employ.

In the beginning, the men and women on the ground at the Diamante sites had viewed him as some kind of pampered playboy amusing himself with his father's money, but he'd quickly proved himself and earned their respect. And when he'd taken his place in the Covent after earning that on his own, as well, through hours of mundane magical practice, the privileged connections available through the arcane community had also become his own instead of hand-me-downs from his father.

When he made his calls, he made a point of asking after family members and mentioning them by name before addressing the Fisher business, as if it were an unfortunate misunderstanding that would blow over by Monday.

Distracting himself with business worked until he collapsed into bed and closed his eyes. The scent and taste and texture of Phoebe rushed back at him as if she were lying right beside him. Worse than the ill-gotten knowledge of her body was the certainty that his desire for her was distinct and his own. This wasn't some residual effect of the step-in. And no amount of worry about the Fisher case or the business could seem to dampen it.

But it didn't matter, because the unfortunate incident with the step-ins wasn't going to be repeated. He'd have to clear his name without Phoebe Carlisle's help.

As he drifted off into a fitful sleep, the tattoo seemed to prickle under the skin at his back, as though Quetzalcoatl were moving.

The evidence of last night's debacle spread across the coffee table like a surrealist painting: *The Persistence of Memory* in encaustic. She'd let the candles burn down, too tired to come back to the living room after her bath.

Phoebe sighed and got to work scraping the spattered

puddles of wax off the table and the hardwood while Puddleglum looked on with disapproval at her apparent misplaced interest in something that didn't involve rectifying the travesty of the tiny spot of emptiness visible at the center of his otherwise full cat dish.

It was possible she was getting dangerously close to becoming one of those crazy cat ladies, providing motives and inner dialogue for Puddleglum as a sad testament to having no life. Nah. That was totally what he was thinking.

"At least you don't bolt in horror if you accidentally see me naked." Because there was nothing weird about having a one-sided conversation with her cat. Not that talking to herself was new. It had taken her until fifth grade to realize no one else had "guests" stepping into them to ask questions—out loud, through their mouths. She'd developed coping mechanisms, becoming a theater geek so she could pass off her random changes of voice and nonsequiturs as doing impressions or rehearsing lines.

Ione had teased her mercilessly, thinking Phoebe was just a weird kid, while the twins, Theia and Rhea, five years younger, were immersed in their own private language—and what often seemed to be their own private world. Then Ione had taken an apprenticeship with the Covent, leaving Phoebe to her own devices. Luckily, being on her own was something she'd always excelled at. She'd had to. By the time she went off to college, it had become second nature to have step-ins wander in and out—which wasn't exactly conducive to friendships or romantic relationships.

Despite the delicate balance on the edge of consent, she'd sometimes enjoyed the company. But she'd also resented it, being at the beck and call of the dead because no one else was ever listening. It had made her cautious about letting anyone get close. And it had also made her protective of the shades.

But the step-ins last night—she'd never experienced anything so overwhelming, never had one direct her own actions against her will. Though maybe the will part was the problem. Maybe she hadn't been entirely resistant on some deeper level. Or some not-so-deep level. She hadn't been touched, after all, since…well, in an embarrassingly long time. Or maybe it had been the wine.

And maybe she could come up with a million other excuses for being so easily controlled by Lila. The fact remained that her engine had already been revving for Rafe Diamante without the influence of the step-in. Lila had just stepped on the gas pedal. And floored it.

Phoebe opened the broom closet and chucked the candle viscera into the trash, cringing as she recalled how Rafe had looked as if he'd sobered up in the middle of a "coyote" date. "Yeah, well, you're not so hot, Rafe Diamante. Bet you were a dork in high school."

"Sorry?"

With a sharp inhalation, Phoebe swallowed the gum she'd been chewing to keep the morning-after nausea at bay, narrowly missing her windpipe. She whirled around to find Rafe Diamante standing on the other side of the screen door.

Chapter 6

Rafe's heart sped up a little just at the way she moved. This was starting to seem like a worse idea than it had before.

Phoebe stood poised in the open arch between the kitchen and the living room, limbs smooth and supple in a light-blue ribbed tank and a pair of curve-hugging cut-offs, the ponytail clipped high and swooping over backward. "How long have you been lurking out there?"

"Not lurking." He held up her tablet. "You left this at the jail yesterday and I forgot to give it to you."

"Oh. Wow." Phoebe came to the door and opened it to accept the tablet. "I thought I'd never see that again. Thanks. You've saved me a lot of time and aggravation." She held it awkwardly inside her folded arms, as if aware of the effect the skin-hugging fabric was having on him. "Did you want to come in?" It was obviously an invitation he was meant to refuse.

"No, I just came to…" He paused, distracted by what he thought he'd heard. "Were you talking to me just now? I thought you said my name."

"To you?" Phoebe gave him a look that said he was full

of himself. "I was just working with a step-in. Some dead cheerleader or something. She was kind of incoherent."

"Oh." Rafe ran a hand over the thick waves of his hair, kept manageable in a short tail at his nape. "Anyway, I wanted to apologize for what happened last night, and to make sure you were all right."

Phoebe stared him down. "Why wouldn't I be?"

Rafe pocketed his hands. She wasn't going to make this easy. "I should have stayed to see that you were. You were pretty shaky on your feet. And I think maybe I'm the reason things got so…weird." Her cheeks flushed pink and he hurried on. "I think it was the invocations I used."

"The invocations?"

"To the Aztec deities. The Lord and Lady of the Underworld. I think it may have created a double channeling— you channeling the shades and the shades channeling Mictlantecuhtli and Mictecacihuatl. They're more chaotic, passionate gods than the usual pantheon invoked in the craft. A lot of practitioners stay away from them because of the darker history they became associated with, but I've always felt drawn to their primal archetypes. I never thought their history mattered. I assumed the symbolism invoked by the deeper mind was important, and not the specific energy it raised. At any rate, I feel responsible, and I just wanted to say that." He reached into the back pocket of his khakis for his checkbook. "I still want to pay for your time last night. And don't worry. I won't be bothering you for any further help contacting the shades. I'll figure something out. What's your hourly rate?"

Phoebe's eyes darkened from periwinkle to violet and she pushed the screen door wide. "Don't write me a check standing on my porch." Her smile seemed forced. "People will talk. Come in and sit down for a minute. I'll get you a lemonade."

Rafe hesitated but decided he'd seem like more of a

jerk if he said no. He stepped inside, surveying the stained wood of the wax-encrusted coffee table as he sat on the couch while Phoebe went to the kitchen. "I should have put foil under the candles."

Phoebe grabbed some glasses from her dish rack and took a pitcher out of the fridge. "I should have put them out instead letting them burn down into a soup."

"You were in the bath. I should have put them out when I left."

"I—" Phoebe came around the bar with two glasses of lemonade and cocked her head. "Wait, whose turn is it again? Does one of us win a prize if we manage to be the most self-effacing?"

"I wasn't trying to be self-effacing—"

"Man, I don't have the energy for 'who's more defensive.' Besides, I think you'd win that one hands down."

Rafe scowled. "What's that supposed to mean?"

She smirked as if he'd proved her point. "You seem to be taking all of this personally, like your honor's in question. It was an awkward night, and it wasn't anyone's fault. Let's call it a learning experience and move on."

This had definitely been a bad idea. Rafe stood, feeling large and awkward in her cozy living room. "You can mail me an invoice."

"Jesus, Diamante. Just drink the damn lemonade. Fresh squeezed." Phoebe shoved a glass at him. He was out of his element here. "It's okay to be freaked out by what happened last night. It freaked me out a little, too. But let's not make any hasty decisions just because it was uncomfortable. You're facing a murder charge, and the evidence is stacked against you. If we set some ground rules for the shades next time we summon them, we can avoid any surprises."

The condensation-damp glass nearly slipped from his

hand. "Next time? You'd actually consider doing that again? Knowing the risk?"

"You said they wanted your help. It doesn't seem like they'd be deliberately contrary if we make the rules clear and tell them they have to abide by them to get what they want."

Perhaps the shades Phoebe was used to dealing with weren't contrary, but he had a feeling she hadn't dealt with any like these before. These shades had a history. That much, at least, Rafe could explain. As long as he could keep his mind off the soft slope of Phoebe's skin where the moon tattoo nestled above the hip-hugging panties she'd been wearing last night. And everything beneath them.

Rafe took a swallow of lemonade and cleared his throat. "You need to understand where these shades are coming from. There's been an increase lately in the number of shades who aren't crossing on their own. That was the source of my falling out with the Covent. They felt they needed to address it and I, of course, disagreed. But they overruled me and decided to convene the Conclave." He sat on the couch again and Phoebe sat beside him.

"To censure you."

He gave her a wry smile. "Censuring me was just a convenient bonus. They actually came for the ritual."

"What ritual?"

"A sort of wide-net snare—to cross every shade in the valley."

Phoebe made a noise of outrage. "Every shade? Shades they hadn't even encountered, who hadn't bothered any-one—they were going to haul them all in?"

Rafe nodded. "Regardless of how recently they'd passed or whether they had any unfinished business."

"That's barbaric."

"I don't disagree."

Phoebe's eyes, darkening again to violet, held the same

passionate intensity they'd had last night, though this time it was the passion of anger. She reminded him distinctly of a young Liz Taylor.

He realized he was staring. "They went ahead with the ritual, and I stood in the back of the temple refusing to be part of it." Gabriel's pleading had been fresh in his mind, and Rafe had been unwilling to leave, wanting to stop it from happening somehow, to keep his coven from doing to any other shades what he'd done to Gabriel. "You could feel the energy of the shades being drawn into the circle as the ritual began. It was palpable. I couldn't see or hear any of them like I had with Gabriel, of course. When he came to me, I could see the apparition because we had a blood bond. I'm sure you've experienced that with people you've known who've passed."

The terse shake of Phoebe's head surprised him. "I've never had that kind of visitation. Just the step-ins."

"Well, these shades weren't visible or audible, but the energy was like a pulsing wave. It was heavy and oppressive and I couldn't just stand there any longer and let it happen. As the rest of the coven began the crossing invocation, I raised my voice in objection." He hadn't meant to, but he'd called the shades to him, and he and Matthew had been surrounded. He didn't feel like describing that peculiar moment when the psychic energy in the temple had nearly overwhelmed him. It had seemed for a moment as if the shades were waiting for him to command them.

"So what happened?"

"I must have disrupted the coven's focus. The shade energy dispersed before they could cross them and the ritual was in chaos." Rafe shrugged. "Most shades, new ones, anyway, aren't aware there's a self-appointed after-life policing effort from the Covent. But they'd drawn in so many with this ritual the word is presumed to be out, and they've been having trouble raising any shades at all."

"That must be why." Phoebe looked thoughtful as she sipped her lemonade. "I drove by the temple yesterday. Something drew me there, the presence of a shade that seemed to want to make contact, except it didn't step in— maybe couldn't. And the air around the temple seemed full of shades, but none of them tried stepping in, either. Which, well…you probably can't appreciate how unusual that is. But I got the feeling they were caught in some half-way state. It was unsettling."

The idea was worse than unsettling. As much pain as it caused him to think about what he'd done to his brother, he'd hate to think of Gabriel's spirit being trapped.

Phoebe regarded him. "So that's when they branded you an oath-breaker."

He nodded. "The Conclave revoked my active status with the Covent and the right to practice ritual."

"Which you evidently ignored."

Rafe met the twinkle in her eye with one of his own. "Evidently."

"But the Covent's lawyer is still defending you. How's that work if you've been excommunicated?"

"It's not quite that severe. It's more like I'm on a meta-physical 'time out.' At any rate, their reputation is at stake if my association with them comes up in a murder trial. And the lawyer is actually my father's, which he thinks I'm unaware of."

Phoebe leaned her elbow on her knee with her chin propped in her hand. "Ione didn't think you knew."

He shrugged as he took a sip of the lemonade. "We all do a lot of pretending, I guess, so everyone gets what they want."

"So, after the ritual, you went to the psychic?"

Rafe nodded. "My apprentice left town without a word right after the ritual. I was worried about him and hoped she could help me find him."

"You have an apprentice?"

"Well, had, anyway. The Covent gave him the boot for not standing against me. Matthew's a freshman at the University of Metaphysics. He applied to the Covent as an apprentice after a summer internship. But no one there has heard from him since last week."

She was staring at him with an odd expression. "Matthew?"

"Yeah. Why?"

"I just…heard the name Matthew somewhere recently. It's probably nothing." The way she said it gave him a feeling of misgiving, but she didn't elaborate.

Rafe finished his lemonade and set the glass on the coffee table. "When I went to see Barbara Fisher, she couldn't help me with Matt, but she told me there were three souls attached to me, invoked by what I'd done at the Covent's ritual. She was able to channel them, and the shades appealed to me for help, claiming someone was compelling them to step into unsuspecting hosts."

"A necromancer." It was a label he hadn't thought to use. The idea was chilling.

"She could only channel them for short intervals. We had two more sessions, but the last was cut short. Barbara didn't channel shades the way you do." Rafe reached for his glass to cover the awkwardness conjured by the unspoken implication before remembering it was empty.

Phoebe jumped up. "Would you like another? There's plenty."

He accepted, glad of the distraction as she went to refill his glass. "Her method was fairly traditional. Tarot, and similar summoning spells to what I've used. So there was no direct communication, just her acting as an interpreter. She said she sensed the shades were being pursued by the man trying to control them. She was trying to get details about who he was, or where he was, but they went silent and she couldn't raise them again. But we were so close to something. I felt it. The shades had begun to trust me." Rafe glanced up as Phoebe brought him the lemonade. "I think we would have gotten a name that evening, before whatever spooked them. And I think that's why someone stopped Barbara from contacting them. Permanently."

Phoebe looked as if she was about to say something, but a loud clatter from the kitchen startled them both. A striped Siamese cat scrabbled at the window over the sink, eyes fixed on a large owl perched in the mesquite tree framed in the glass.

"Puddleglum!" She ran to the kitchen and pulled the cat away from the window, but it was the bird that caught Rafe's attention. The yellow eyes rimmed with ivory in the dark-brown face stared in at them boldly.

Puddleglum struggled out of Phoebe's arms and made a dash for the cat door. A moment later, the owl took off from its perch, the pale breast the only spot of color against the chocolate-brown wings as it flew away.

Phoebe examined her scored arms. "Dammit, Puddleglum."

"Interesting name." Rafe tried not to show his concern at the visitation by the bird. "He doesn't look like a marshwiggle."

Phoebe glanced up at him with a pleased smile. "You know the books."

Rafe laughed. "I don't live in a cave. Who hasn't read the *Chronicles of Narnia*?"

"Most men, in my experience. At least, not that they'd admit to. I'm more likely to get a positive response to Bilbo Baggins. My theory is the preponderance of strong females in Narnia. Or females at all."

Rafe blinked at her. "Wait, how did this happen? I thought we were sharing a nerd moment. Now I feel like I've had my feminism card revoked."

She cocked her head, setting the ponytail bobbing. "You have a feminism card?"

"A man can't be a feminist?"

"Of course he can." Phoebe studied him as if she'd just found a new species of his genus. "I just don't meet a lot of them who look like you."

Rafe raised an eyebrow. "Like me?"

Phoebe laughed. "I think I'm the one being sexist now. Never mind."

He couldn't help wondering what he looked like to her. A Neanderthal? Some kind of machismo-obsessed asshole? But the symbolism of the owl nagged at him, putting his ego on the back burner.

The owl was the nagual of Mictlantecuhtli, Lord of the Underworld, whom Rafe had invoked only last night to such spectacular and mortifying effect. The nagual could be a spirit animal offering protection or it could be the animal form of a sorcerer. He'd never heard of a single documented case of such a transmogrification happening literally, but such myths abounded. And with everything that had happened in the past twenty-four hours, he couldn't afford to dismiss the bird's appearance as coincidental.

He set down the untouched lemonade and rose. "I should probably get going."

Phoebe frowned. "I thought we were going to try to work with the shades to get some answers."

"We?" It was Rafe's turn to frown. "You said we'd need to set ground rules. I think one of those should be that I don't participate in the summoning. Whatever happened, whether it was my energy or the gods I invoked for the ritual, it doesn't seem wise for the two of us to put ourselves in that position again."

Phoebe's mouth set in a tight line. "Right. Because that would be horrible."

He didn't know what to make of that comment. Was she actually offended that he was trying to protect her from whatever had tried to use them last night? She couldn't possibly be willing to risk being assaulted just to help him channel a few shades.

"My lawyer is coming over this afternoon, anyway. I need to get back." Rafe went to the door and paused at the threshold, glancing over his shoulder at her. Bare arms and legs glistened with a light sheen of perspiration in the humidity. Rain was always in the offing this time of year. It made him wonder what she'd taste like with rainwater coursing over her skin.

Rafe cleared his throat. "I suspect the shades might seek you out now that they know you. If they do, let me know what you find out. I appreciate your help." He tried to smile amiably as he pushed open the screen door. "And the lemonade."

"Rafe."

He took a deep breath and turned back, sure she was going to press him on participating in summoning the shades.

"I remember where I heard the name of your apprentice. At the temple yesterday, the presence that drew me there. The name I got from it was Matthew."

Chapter 7

Rafe felt himself go pale. Hearing Matthew's name in connection with a shade unnerved him more than he cared to admit.

"Are you sure?"

Phoebe gave him an almost apologetic nod. "I couldn't get much else. It was like something was blocking the shade from stepping in. But that name—it was almost tangible."

He tried Matthew's phone once more on the way home, but this time he got a recording instead of Matthew's voicemail: "The wireless customer you are attempting to reach cannot be located."

The phrase had a terrible finality, and the appearance of the owl this afternoon took on an ominous significance. One of the things that had drawn Matthew to apprentice with Rafe was his interest in Aztec studies. Mictlantecuhtli and the underworld of Mictlan, in particular, had fascinated him. Born on the Day of the Dead, Matthew had identified strongly with the skull-faced god. And now Mictlantecuhtli's nagual was hanging about Phoebe's backyard.

Rafe glanced at the clock on the dash as he arrived at Stone Canyon to find Hamilton waiting for him. The lawyer was early. Hamilton waved to him from in front of the red convertible parked beside the gate and stepped up to the truck, sticking out his hand as Rafe rolled down the window.

Instead of shaking his hand, Rafe nodded and handed him a guest card for the gate. "Hamilton."

The lawyer flashed his improbably perfect teeth. "Call me Carter. It's better if we're on a first-name basis. And I hope I can call you Rafe?"

"Rafael." He wasn't sure why this guy rubbed him the wrong way, but something about him made Rafe want to be difficult.

Hamilton followed him up to the house and parked in front of it, admiring the décor as they entered and Rafe ushered him into the great room. "The construction business seems to be treating you well."

Rafe crossed his arms as he sat in the leather armchair. "We do all right. As I'm sure my father must have told you when he hired you."

Hamilton paused in opening his briefcase on the couch. "The Covent hired me, Rafael. I am acquainted with your father, of course."

"Of course."

Hamilton took a pocket voice recorder out of his briefcase like a flashback from the 90s and set it on the table between them. "Do you mind if I record this meeting? It helps me keep track of what we've agreed on." Rafe nodded and Hamilton hit the record button. "So, Rafael, in your own words, please tell me exactly what you recall from the night of July 29 and the morning of July 30."

For the dozenth time, Rafe went through the details he remembered.

Hamilton nodded as Rafe spoke, making notes as

Phoebe had, only his tablet was old school. "And how would you characterize your relationship with Barbara Fisher?"

"I'd met with her a few times prior. As a client."

"So it was cordial but professional."

Rafe shrugged. "Yes."

"There was no intimacy between you?"

"Intimacy?"

"I have to ask. Anything that might be relevant to the prosecutor's case is liable to come up in the preliminary hearing. I need to be sure there aren't any curveballs being thrown. I'm sure you'd prefer to avoid an indictment so we don't have to build a defense for a criminal trial."

"Right." Rafe's skin felt clammy. This was all beginning to seem a lot more real than it had yesterday.

Hamilton gave him a reassuring smile. "Relax, Rafael. I'm going to be with you every step of the way. I know it all seems pretty overwhelming now, but the evidence is purely circumstantial." He paused, waiting for Rafe to say something, then prompted, "You didn't have an intimate relationship with Ms. Fisher?"

"No. I barely knew her."

"So the police aren't going to find any of your DNA on her. Or in her."

"Jesus. *No.*"

Hamilton made a note. "You mentioned you thought the tea she gave you might have been drugged. Can you think of any reason Ms. Fisher would want to drug you?"

"No, of course not. She seemed like a very nice woman. Honest. Her abilities seemed genuine."

"But people aren't always what they seem. If she wasn't what she appeared to be, what reason do you think she might have to drug you?"

Rafe raked his fingers through his hair. "To rob me, maybe? Wouldn't be a very smart way to go about it, though, with a client in your own house. I don't know. What I thought, honestly, was maybe one of the shades was controlling her."

Hamilton paused. "You know that's not going to wash in court. The Covent might find it plausible, but the government rarely takes the word of a witch in such matters." He made a rueful face. "Going back to the Dark Ages."

"I know. I'm only telling you what I think happened. If you're going to defend me, I assume you want the truth."

"Of course. We just need to come up with something more plausible to the general public so shades and spells don't get brought up. People are generally okay with someone going to a medium for a reading, maybe even amenable to the idea that it's possible to contact someone who's passed on. But the minute you say 'shade' or 'possessed,' your credibility is shot."

Rafe nodded tightly. He knew all this. Which was why he needed to find out who'd killed Barbara Fisher—and find evidence tying the killer to the crime—before his case went to trial. "And if she *was* shade-walked...or I was...what then?"

Hamilton turned off his digital recorder. "If you say anything like that in court, I won't be able to help you. Your defense simply cannot be 'I was possessed when I killed her.'"

Rafe didn't flinch from the serious pale gaze. "Then I guess we'd better hope there's not enough evidence to charge me."

"Well, we may have a problem, given your answer about your level of familiarity with the victim."

Rafe blinked at him. "What's that supposed to mean?"

"The police have a witness who alleges to have seen you and Ms. Fisher together on multiple occasions engaged in behavior that didn't appear to be related to palm reading."

"What?" Outrage spiked in his blood. He leaned forward in his chair, his posture challenging, as if Hamilton had made the false accusation himself. "That's ridiculous. I only met Barbara Fisher a week ago, and saw her exactly three times, including Friday night—as a *client*."

"That's what the witness is implying. That you were a client of Ms. Fisher's—in a rather different sort of business."

"I'm not sure what you're getting at."

"Barbara Fisher operated more than one business out of her home. She also advertised her services on adult websites as a masseuse—for very personal massage, if you catch my drift. The police tracked IP addresses of her correspondents on the site—and one of them matched yours."

Rafe's hands clenched around the armrests. "That's impossible. I've never even been to any adult services websites—or any high-end masseuses."

Hamilton set down his pen and paper. "Then I'd have to conclude, Rafael, that someone must be setting you up."

Chapter 8

The weather stayed muggy all afternoon, with nothing but heat lightning to show for it, though the bolts of current across the sky made a pretty picture at dusk over the stone pylons of Cathedral Rock. The view from the back of the house was mostly obscured by newer housing developments, but even a little bit of a view could be spectacular.

A chime from her phone provided a welcome distraction—a text from Theia. She hadn't talked to either Theia or Rhea since they'd been home from college for spring break.

Had a dream about you. It wasn't the first time Theia had started such a conversation out of the blue. You were flying on the back of a snake.

Snakes don't fly. She typed the reply automatically, but Rafe's tattoo of Quetzalcoatl immediately came to mind, brilliant blue-green wings rippling over his shoulder blades.

This one did. It had feathers. A pause for effect was followed with, Maybe it was a boa.

Hilarious. Theia was studying zoology; maybe she could identify Puddleglum's bird. Speaking of feathers, Glum treed a bird earlier, some kind of owl. Dark brown, except for white on its chest and around its eyes. Is there anything like that around here?

Sounds like a spectacled owl. Not native this far north. Maybe somebody's pet got loose. Theia typed for a moment. Could be an omen. Anyone new in your life?

Phoebe hesitated, which was foolish, because Rafe wasn't in her life. No, no one new.

Well, there should be. You're going to get cobwebs up there.

Phoebe sent an eye-rolling emoji.

All kidding aside, I'd keep an eye out for someone untrustworthy entering your life. Maybe a client, someone bright and attractive who's not what he seems. Just be careful.

Phoebe hated how intuitive her little sister could be. After Theia signed off, she set the phone down and wiped the sweat from her temple. The evaporative cooler was useless in this humidity. She shut it off and opened the windows wide, letting the ceiling fan in the living room move the air around.

Phoebe was serving up Puddleglum's "beef and chicken feast" in the kitchen when the air grew heavy with the familiar aura of a step-in. She considered refusing it. Maybe it was time to start putting up some defenses. But if it was Barbara Fisher or one of the other shades who might have information about her murder, Phoebe needed the shade as much as it needed her. She'd go with her gut.

Phoebe sat on the couch, not wanting to take another fall. Her skin prickled with goose bumps as the shade began to step through into the same corporeal space. Some might dismiss the sensation as someone "walking over their grave," unaware a shade moved through them unable to find an anchor. Phoebe, on the other hand, had always been solid for them, a body they could merge with without displacing its usual occupant, as might otherwise be the case. And thus, a body they could communicate with, and through.

But this shade wasn't trying to communicate. It was trying to manipulate her physically. Though it seemed to be attempting to hide its identity, she recognized it now as the one she'd hosted the night before. For whatever reason, Lila had stepped in and wanted to control her.

Phoebe rose from the couch, her limbs directed by the shade, though she felt she could wrest control from her if she had to. Perhaps Lila wanted to show her something. For now, Phoebe would let her steer.

She walked to the back door and opened it, stepping out into the yard. She was only wearing flip-flops, but presumably, Lila wouldn't take her far. Unfortunately it was also getting dark and Lila hadn't stopped for a flashlight or turned on the porch light.

Phoebe continued walking toward the rear of the property. She hadn't been out here to deal with the weeds and briars in weeks, and she was beginning to brush against the spiky overgrowth of graythorn bushes.

A sound ahead of her in the brush sent a chill up her spine. She'd never encountered one on her property before, but the telltale maraca-like sound of a rattlesnake gave warning. And Lila was directing her right to it.

Phoebe tried to stop, but her feet continued moving forward. She dug her nails into her palms and gritted her teeth, slowing a little but still walking.

"*Lila.*" The sound of her voice seemed to shake Lila's hold, and Phoebe managed to stop herself in her tracks, though she couldn't yet persuade her limbs to turn back. "Lila, what are you doing? What do you want?"

"Stop fighting me." The throaty Kathleen Turner voice came out of her. "He wants you to go."

"Who wants me to go?" Her own voice was stronger now. She was breaking Lila's hold.

"Tloque Nahuaque. Lord of the Near and the Nigh."

The rattler sounded again, threatened in its hiding place.

Phoebe lowered her voice to a whisper. "Why? What does he want with me?"

Lila let out an exasperated sigh. "He wants you gone." The irritation apparently distracted Lila. Phoebe regained control, backing away from the brush before turning tail and hurrying back toward the house. Lila still lingered but she could sense the shade's frustration at having failed in her mission.

"Who is this Taloque…?" She couldn't remember exactly how the name went, though Lila had just used her mouth to pronounce it.

"Tloque Nahuaque." Lila sighed. "He keeps my Jacob from me."

"Maybe I can help you." She'd barely gotten the words out before Lila followed them with a sharp laugh. "If you don't try to force me to do things against my will, I can be much more helpful to you, Lila. It's what I do."

"You can't help me. The only way you can help is if you go. If you go, I get my Jacob."

"How do you know?" That seemed to give the shade pause. "Has this Tloque Nahuaque kept any promises to you or does he keep holding them out as something you'll earn from him eventually when he's decided to grant them?" She'd managed to reach the back door as she spoke, and Lila was no longer resisting her movements. Phoebe dashed inside and closed the door, locking it behind her. "Lila." She'd gone quiet in Phoebe's consciousness, but Phoebe could tell the shade was still there. "Has he done anything but exploit your need for Jacob?"

"Titlacauan commands us. We are his slaves."

How many names did this guy have? Phoebe leaned

back against the door, her hand still on the knob. "And if you could have your Jacob? If you could be with him… what would you do?"

She felt the shiver of arousal run through her, from the top of her head to her core, like a little shock of lightning.

Lila's voice on her tongue was full of both anguish and desire. "If I could be with Jacob as we were meant to be, just once, I could be at peace." With that, she was gone.

It was absolutely out of the question. Phoebe shouldn't even be thinking it. But if she offered an exchange— the evidence against whoever this Tloque Nahuaque or Titlacauan was, as the price for giving Lila what she wanted—wouldn't that be worth the minor inconvenience of being temporarily at the mercy of someone else's desires?

Of course, it didn't hurt that Phoebe was hopelessly attracted to the vessel Lila's Jacob had chosen to occupy. Phoebe covered her face with her hands and groaned. What was the matter with her? She couldn't make that kind of deal and involve someone else. What was she really thinking, anyway? That she could blackmail Rafe Diamante into having sex with her in exchange for exonerating him of a murder charge? How pathetic was that? She'd sunk to a new low.

When Phoebe checked her messages in the morning, her caseload had tripled. As the lowest on the totem pole at the Public Defender's Office, she had to take what she could get—especially if she wanted to have any hope of eventually removing "assistant" from the front of her title. That little word meant the difference between getting a mix of grunt work and the cases no one else wanted and getting to work serious cases that would challenge her. And it also meant the difference between people like Ione seeing her as some kind of glorified legal secretary and respecting her as an actual lawyer. Not to mention not having to always live hand to mouth.

After the forty-five-minute drive to the county courthouse at Camp Verde, Phoebe met with her first client, a scared eighteen-year-old kid charged with a DUI who'd spent the night in lockup, afraid to call his parents. Since it was his first offense, she managed to bargain the charges down to reckless endangerment. The prosecutor owed her one, and he was in a good mood.

Phoebe glanced at the time while she scheduled her next client consult and found it wasn't quite eleven. Not bad for a morning's work. She even had time to grab a scone and a latte.

Heading upstairs from the basement café with the latte in hand, Phoebe nearly ended up wearing the drink when she took a corner too swiftly and met someone else coming down.

She held the sloshing beverage out of the way as the lid popped off the cup and a dollop of foam hit the tip of an expensive Italian dress shoe. "Shoot. I'm so sorry. Let me get that." She'd knelt to dab her napkin on the mess without waiting for an answer, but an amused voice made her pause.

"That's really not necessary, Ms. Carlisle."

The face she glanced up into was familiar but she couldn't place it. Thirty-something and blond with soulful blue eyes, he looked like he ought to be on the cover of *GQ*.

Phoebe straightened with the napkin wadded in her hand. "Sorry—have we met?"

"Just briefly. Carter Hanson Hamilton." He held out his hand and Phoebe pocketed the napkin before extending hers, still not sure where she'd seen him before. He had a firm, easy grip. "I'm representing Rafael Diamante in the Barbara Fisher case."

"Oh." Phoebe pulled back her hand. Of course. She'd seen him yesterday when Ione had blindsided her.

"I hope there are no hard feelings. The Covent only has Mr. Diamante's best interests in mind."

"No, I get that, Mr. Hamilton. I do." She might as well be gracious. "I wasn't sure why he called me, anyway. He was probably in shock and just dialed the first number he found in his pocket."

"Please, call me Carter. And I'm sure you're selling yourself short. Your sister speaks very highly of you."

Phoebe couldn't contain the short outburst of laughter. "Ione? She did not. That's kind of you to say, Mr. Hamilton—Carter—but I'm not exactly the Covent's favorite person. As I'm sure you know."

Carter smiled. "You may not be the poster girl for Covent doctrine, but I think you may be wrong about your sister's regard for you. Blood transcends belief."

Phoebe regarded him quizzically. "You're not exactly what I expected from a Covent lawyer."

"And you're not exactly what I expected from an evocator."

"Evocator?"

"Evocation is the official name for what you do. Has no one ever applied the term to you before?"

Phoebe shook her head. "I've always called it 'stepping in.'"

"That's what they do, of course. Not what you do." Carter glanced at his watch. "I have some time before my next appointment. Care to join me for an early lunch?"

Phoebe looked down at her latte. "I just got breakfast."

Carter smiled. "Half of it's on my shoe. Toss it. I'm buying."

They ended up downstairs in the café again. The Camp Verde neighborhood boasted little more than the courthouse and county jail, a shooting range and an incongruously placed African wildlife park. Carter looked a little out of his element in his impeccable suit.

Phoebe tore open the little envelope of Caesar dressing to squeeze onto her salad. "Big spender. I'm impressed."

Carter laughed. "I thought about suggesting the promising-sounding Carl's Custom Meats, but it's a little too close to the wildlife park for comfort."

Phoebe grinned. "That's why I'm sticking to salad." She carefully speared a cherry tomato. "So, you're not from the local chapter, I take it."

"No, does it show? Not wearing enough crystals?" He winked and ate a bite of his sandwich, managing not to end up with mayonnaise at the corner of his mouth as Phoebe would have done. "I live in Scottsdale. I'm with the Phoenix chapter."

"And do they not have strict rules about consorting with 'evocators' in the Phoenix chapter?"

"They don't think highly of the practice, I have to admit. Though most who profess to have the ability are charlatans."

Phoebe paused with a hunk of romaine on her fork. "Do you think I'm a charlatan?"

"I haven't seen your work, so I have no basis upon which to make such a judgment. But your sister's talent as a witch is impressive. I imagine your talent must be every bit as much so."

"Well, I don't do it to impress anyone. I do it because I can, and people seem to need it."

"By people, you mean shades."

"You don't think shades are people?"

"I think they *were* people. But I think letting them cling to what they were can be dangerous. For both the shade and the evocator." He paused and looked up from his lunch, giving Phoebe a perfect million-dollar smile. "But I'm willing to keep my mind open to other possibilities." It was more than Ione or the rest of the local Covent had ever done. Carter took another meticulous bite while Phoebe pondered and chewed. "Have you ever encountered a hostile shade?"

"Hostile?" She swallowed her bite. "No, I wouldn't say hostile. A few who were angry and confused at first." And of course there was Lila, who'd tried to feed her to a snake last night to appease some Aztec god. "What do you think of Rafe's—Mr. Diamante's situation?"

Carter set down his sandwich and took a sip of his Perrier. "As his legal counsel, I have to believe he's sincere in his account of what happened. Whether his suspicions are correct about how it happened, I can't say."

"But you think it's possible. That a shade might have stepped into him without his knowledge."

"Possible? Absolutely. Whether such testimony would be admissible in court is another matter. Of course, everything Rafael has told me is confidential, so all of this is merely hypothetical, you understand."

Phoebe nodded and swallowed a mouthful of salad. "Of course. I didn't mean to pry."

Carter touched her arm. "I didn't think you were prying. Just reminding myself, really. You're easy to talk to. I find I'm forgetting myself." He regarded her for a moment. "Can I ask you something personal?"

Phoebe pushed lettuce around in her plastic clamshell. "Fire away."

"Is there a reason you aren't a member of the Covent? Other than the obvious philosophical differences, of course."

"Yes, there is." Phoebe smiled. "I'm not a witch."

"So you don't believe the animating forces of nature have a spiritual component."

"I've never been big on spirituality. I believe in science."

"Yet as an accomplished evocator, you work with spirit beings."

Phoebe shrugged. "I suppose I consider magic to be just another facet of science. The flip side, if you will. I don't attribute it to any god."

"Some might attribute it to the flip side of a god."

Her brows quirked upward. "The province of the Devil? Isn't that considered heresy in the craft?"

Carter laughed with genuine amusement. "No, of course not the Devil. I was thinking along the lines of a goddess. Inanna or Astarte, for instance. Lilith." He glanced at his conspicuously expensive watch. "I'm afraid I need to get back. But it was delightful talking with you, Phoebe—I hope I can call you Phoebe?"

He certainly had a way of making everything he said sound utterly sincere.

She smiled. "Of course."

Upstairs, Carter paused before they went their separate ways. "I hope we'll have a chance to talk again soon." He took her hand and brought it to his lips and Phoebe blushed, not sure anyone had ever kissed her hand before.

"Phoebe?" The surprised voice was a deep baritone. Phoebe looked up to find Rafe staring at the two of them, dark brows drawn together in mistrust. "What's going on?"

Carter let go of her hand and gave Rafe a placid smile. "Just lunching with Ms. Carlisle. We all have business in court today, as it happens."

Phoebe glanced from Carter to Rafe. "You have business in court?"

Rafe looked grim. "Barbara Fisher's death has officially been ruled a homicide. And I'm officially being arrested."

Chapter 9

Phoebe's face was slightly flushed as she studied Rafe, as if he'd interrupted something more than lunch. Her surprise at the news, at least, seemed genuine.

Hamilton filled in the details Rafe had left out. "I was able to get Rafael an immediate arraignment hearing on the condition that he come in on his own. This is just a formality. We'll be entering a not-guilty plea, of course. I'm completely confident he won't be spending a moment in jail."

Phoebe glanced from one man to the other. "I hope everything goes well."

"I'm sure it will." Rafe couldn't help adding with a touch of bitterness, "When you're my father's son, things usually do."

He couldn't get the idea out of his head that Phoebe's lunch with Hamilton was more than just business. Or had they been discussing Rafe's case? Was that why she was blushing? Was that guilt? What other reason would Phoebe have for meeting with Rafe's lawyer? He hadn't slept well last night; maybe he was imagining things. It was probably just a social meeting like Hamilton said. So why did seeing Phoebe Carlisle with Carter Hamilton fill Rafe with such misgiving?

If he had any sense, the legal proceedings he was about to face should be filling him with much greater misgiving. In twenty minutes he'd be standing in front of a judge for his formal arraignment on a murder charge. Every step of this seemed surreal.

He realized he was still staring at the two of them as if he'd caught them in flagrante. Rafe addressed Phoebe, trying to ignore the unpleasant conviction that he was somehow being punked. "Have you had any more contact with the step-ins?"

She cast a sideways glance at Hamilton. "Briefly. We can talk later, if you like."

Hamilton frowned. "If you have any information relevant to Rafael's case, it's important I'm kept apprised."

"I'll keep you apprised," Rafe interrupted. "If there's something I need you to know."

Hamilton's expression flickered with disapproval before settling back into the usual, neutral-yet-confident smile he must have learned in law school. "Of course. So long as there are no surprises that come up in the prelim. I don't like surprises."

"I'll call you, Phoebe." Rafe nodded to Hamilton. "I guess we'd better get this over with."

Rafe thought perhaps his father would show up for the arraignment, but as the judge read the charge of second-degree murder, Rafael Sr. was nowhere to be seen. Maybe he was avoiding the inevitable media swarm. Or maybe he just didn't give a damn. After all, he'd thrown his money at the problem and he expected it to go away.

With his plea entered and bail posted, Rafe had seen enough of courts and lawyers to last him indefinitely, but Hamilton was sticking to him like an annoying lapdog.

"You're going to need some help getting through the media gauntlet outside." Hamilton followed close behind as Rafe headed downstairs. "Why don't I have my car brought around to take you back to your place? I can have someone drop yours off later when things settle down."

"I'm parked around the side." Rafe pulled out the baseball cap he'd tucked into his back pocket and tugged it on as he headed for the exit. "I'm good."

"I'll follow you over, then." Hamilton was still at his heels. "We can talk about strategy."

Rafe sighed and turned around, palm in front of him to hold the lawyer at bay. "No offense, Hamilton, but all I want to do right now is have a drink. And maybe a smoke."

"I didn't know you smoked."

"I don't."

"I see." Hamilton gave him a patronizing smile. "We can't really afford to get complacent right now—"

"That's what my father is paying you the big bucks for. So why don't you go be lawyerly somewhere and I'll go do what my father thinks I do best—enjoy the fruits of his labor."

Hamilton was speechless for once as Rafe put on his sunglasses and pushed open the doors. The reporters waiting outside for their scoop weren't quick enough to identify him, focused on Hamilton trailing behind, and they mobbed the lawyer as he emerged, expecting him to precede their prey.

Rafe ducked out of the crowd and made a beeline for the side lot before they caught on. That was probably the last time that trick would work. In his rearview mirror, he saw one of the crews dash for their van to follow him as he pulled out.

As he drove toward Sedona, he remembered what Phoebe had said about being drawn to the temple when she'd come this way on Saturday. It would be empty today, and taking the private road to the temple grounds through the Covent's glamour would leave his pursuers wondering how they'd lost him.

Sure enough, when he turned toward the white pinnacles of the temple, the news van drove on down Highway 179 toward town—and Stone Canyon, where they wouldn't find him.

The oppressive feeling he'd noted during the ritual definitely still lingered as the tires of his Escalade rumbled over the brick pavement of the parking lot. The heaviness increased after he'd crossed the courtyard and entered the nave to approach the altar. If Matthew was dead as Rafe feared and his shade lingered here among those the ritual had trapped, perhaps Rafe could reach him with the conjuring spell.

Calming his nerves with a shot of bourbon from the flask in his pocket, Rafe set up the altar and undressed. He called the quarters first for protection, invoking Tezcatlipoca, god of night and invisible forces, as the Guardian of the North; Xipe Totec, god of force and rebirth, as the Guardian of the East; Huitzilopochtli, god of will and fire, as the Guardian of the South; and instead of Quetzalcoatl as Guardian of the West, he chose Chalchiuhtlicue of the Jade Skirt—goddess of rivers, seas and storms—for a more feminine aspect.

As he called upon Matthew's spirit to join him, however, the tattoo on his back began to itch. He thought he'd imagined it two nights ago as a hypnagogic hallucination at the brink of sleep, but now he felt distinct movement under his skin—the movement of a snake.

Rafe turned to look over his shoulder in front of the small mirror above the altar. In the flickering flame of the temple candles, the ink was undulating, the scarlet scales of the serpent's belly rippling over invisible terrain, reflected candlelight glittering off the teal and violet feathers as they fluttered in an unseen wind. Rafe touched his fingers to the ink. There was no doubt about it. Quetzalcoatl was moving.

He'd called on the guardians for protection. Maybe this vision of Quetzalcoatl's image was a message from his patron god. But he'd never heard of such a thing.

After taking a few deep breaths, Rafe collected a dried cutting from the century plant in the entryway and returned to the altar. Whatever was happening, it was clearly magic, and he needed to channel it before it got out of hand.

"I call on Quetzalcoatl, Lord of the star of the dawn." He pressed the thorns of the agave spine to his tongue, letting the pain give him clarity. The old way involved a more intimate body part, but Rafe was interested in symbolic sacrifice, not masochistic fanaticism.

As the blood rose around the thorns, he let it drip onto the dried edge of the spine, and then burned the clipping in the censer with the incense. "Invest me with your wisdom, O Ehecatl-Quetzalcoatl, god of wind and light. Accept my sacrifice—chalchiuatl from my own veins—as your divine sustenance."

Invoking the wind-god aspect of Quetzalcoatl seemed to make the wind rise outside, the inner doors to the narthex rattling as though moved by it, though the outer doors were closed and locked. Gooseflesh raised along his skin, the hairs standing up, and something rushed him, a shade stepping into him. He thought for an instant it was Matthew, after all. But he'd felt this presence before. *Jacob.*

Branches whipped in the wind outside Phoebe's front window as another monsoon storm began to brew above the brooding sandstone dome of Thunder Mountain. Over the sound of the wind, she heard the rumble of a truck on the gravel drive. Curled up in the papasan with a cup of tea and a paperback, Phoebe peered out, aggravated that

someone would interrupt her moment of quiet. The black
Escalade looked familiar, and it was definitely heading for
her place. Phoebe lowered her cup. That was Rafe's truck.

Puddleglum protested in his best throaty, mournful
moan when she moved him from her lap, but he wasted
no time taking her spot.

Phoebe set down the tea and went to the door, watching Rafe pull up in front of the carport. "What's up?" She
held the screen door open as he strode toward her with
purpose. "Everything okay?"

When he arrived in front of her, Rafe pulled her into
his arms and kissed her hard enough to have knocked her
on her ass if he hadn't been holding on to her.

With a sputter, Phoebe drew back from the unexpected
greeting. "Are you feeling all right?" His eyes had a glossy,
energized look.

"I'm wonderful." With his arms still hooked around her
lower back, he nuzzled her neck, making her shiver. "This
vessel has everything I need."

Not again. Phoebe peered into his eyes. "Jacob?"

His face fell, bottom lip protruding almost like a child's
disappointed pout. "You're not my Lila."

"No. And you have no business stepping into Rafe. If
you want to talk to me, you talk to me. You don't need to
do it through him."

Rafe's arms dropped away from her. "He was willing."

"I doubt that." Phoebe regarded him expectantly, but
Jacob only blinked at her through Rafe's eyes. "Well? Are
you going to release him?"

He folded his arms. "No."

Phoebe sighed. Better to keep watch on him here than
to leave Jacob on the loose with Rafe's body, doing who
knew what. "Then at least come inside."

Whether of his own volition or at Jacob's direction,
Rafe stepped into the house—barefoot, she noted—and

let Phoebe close the door. "Where's Lila?" He touched Phoebe's face, drawing his hand sensuously along her jaw. "She was here. Recently. You smell like her."

"I *smell* like her?" He meant Lila as she'd been in life, obviously, but Phoebe grimaced at the idea of smelling like the dead.

"You have the look of her, as well. Maybe I can draw her in."

Phoebe took a step back. "Or not. Why don't we just talk? You could tell me what you know about the necromancer who's been manipulating you. Rafe said you wanted his help to stop it."

Rafe's eyes regarded her. "Tezcatlipoca is very powerful, and he'll become more powerful still because of Rafael Diamante."

"Because of Rafe? Why? What does Rafe have to do with it?"

"He's a conduit." Jacob strolled farther into the house, touching the surfaces of things—the walls, Phoebe's knickknacks—running his fingers over them as if it were a luxury to be able to feel things through Rafe's skin. Which it probably was. Phoebe tried not to think about what else those fingers had touched at Jacob's direction.

"A conduit for what? Not for shades? Is he a…an evocator? Like I am?" It seemed unlikely Rafe could have gone this long without being aware of such an innate skill.

Jacob's eyes narrowed, studying Phoebe with renewed interest. "No. Not an evocator. A conduit for energy. He bears the mark of the ancients." Jacob began to unbutton Rafe's crisp white shirt with slow, sensuous movements.

"Jacob. What are you doing?"

He turned and continued down the hall. The shirt fell from his shoulders and slipped down his arms to the floor, revealing the magnificent tattoo of Quetzalcoatl, wings flexing as Rafe's arms swung easily with his gait.

Phoebe couldn't take her eyes off the ink. "Where are you going?" She raised her voice as he disappeared into her bedroom. Great. That was all she needed. Half-naked Rafe Diamante in her room, possessed by the shade of a smooth-voiced Lothario. "Jacob." No answer.

She followed him against her better judgment. If she could keep him talking, she might be able to discover the identity of the necromancer. In the dusky half-light of her room, Rafe—or Jacob, rather—reclined on her bed with his hands clasped behind his head. The position displayed his pecs to maximum advantage. Man, this guy was like a catnip mouse to her inner Puddleglum.

Phoebe leaned against the door frame. "If the necromancer is so powerful, why does he need Rafe's energy?"

"How do you think the powerful become what they are? By taking the power of others." Jacob ran Rafe's tongue over his bottom lip and Phoebe felt her own lips clamping shut on a frustrated mewl. "Come here and I'll tell you more."

"I'm not going to give you Lila. I can't, even if I wanted to. She's not here. I don't sense her anywhere nearby."

"I know you want this man."

Good grief. If Rafe was hearing this… Phoebe squeezed her eyes shut. Maybe he'd have another memory lapse with Jacob taking such complete control.

"Phoebe Carlisle." Rafe's voice sounded so ordinary as he spoke her name she thought Jacob had left him suddenly.

Phoebe opened her eyes and took a step toward the bed. "Rafe?"

"He desires you, as well."

"Dammit, Jacob. That's enough."

Jacob lifted Rafe's shoulders in a shrug. "I'm only telling you what this body is telling me." His eyes flicked downward and back at Phoebe, just enough to draw her gaze to the obvious erection in Rafe's jeans.

Phoebe yanked her gaze away, heat radiating off her skin. "I thought you wanted to tell me about the necromancer. Does he have a name?"

"Tezcatlipoca." *Him again.* "That's the name he calls himself. It's a stolen name. He imagines himself a god."

"And the reason he wants Rafe's power is because of Rafe's affinity for the Aztec deities? His family's ancestry?"

"His family's legacy." Jacob withdrew his arms from the headboard and leaned forward. "Come. I'll show you." She'd heard that one before. Jacob turned away, looking over Rafe's shoulder. "Touch the serpent."

Phoebe let out a sharp laugh. She'd *definitely* heard that one before.

Jacob smiled. "I don't mean anything by it. It's the source of his power."

Phoebe's eyes threatened to fall right out of her head, they were rolling so hard at the double entendres. But Jacob merely waited, his hands propped to one side as if in a yoga pose. Quetzalcoatl's feathery scales did seem rather luminous despite the low light in the room.

She closed the space between them, sitting on the edge of the bed so she could reach Rafe's back, and placed her hand against the tattoo. It was oddly cool, though his flesh was warm. And Rafe smelled like the coming rain. His muscles rippled under her hand. Only it wasn't muscle. It was the tattoo.

"What the hell?" Phoebe drew back, but Jacob caught her wrist and tugged her into his lap.

"The quetzal awakens, charmed by the evocator. And it will soon take flight."

"Let go of me, Jacob." She managed to rise onto her knees, straddling Rafe's muscular thighs as she tried to climb off and tangling her skirt in the process, but the grip on her arm was like steel. He pulled her down closer. Between her thighs, she could feel Rafe's heat against hers—nothing between Phoebe's flesh and his jeans but the thinnest of microfiber. "I don't think Lila would approve of this." Her lungs seemed to be having trouble taking in a full breath of air.

"I can't help what this body feels. What it desires." He bucked lightly against her, and Phoebe knew he could feel how damp her panties were. The last time she and Rafe had been this close, she'd been in the grip of Lila's control, unable to exert her own will. Now she had complete control over her own faculties. And she was moving in tandem with the gentle rise and fall of Rafe's pelvis.

What was she doing? It was one thing to have entertained even for a second the thought of bargaining her body to Lila in exchange for the necromancer's identity, or to have indulged in the fantasy of having Rafe at the mercy of Jacob's desire for her. But she couldn't participate in this—whatever this was—no matter how hard up she was.

Rafe's lips were against her throat.

"Rafe." Her voice came out hoarsely. "You have to tell Jacob to go." He paused in his caress. "I know you can hear me in there. It's your body. Tell him to leave."

His grip tightened around her wrist and he brought her in closer with his other arm around her waist. The dark eyes looked into hers. "He doesn't want me to leave. And neither do you."

There was a certain truth to the latter. Possessed by Jacob's shade, Rafe desired her. With Jacob gone, Rafe would recoil from her as before. Not only would he no longer be touching her like this, she'd feel like a fool for having let Jacob manipulate her into this position—mentally and physically—with Rafe aware of how she'd been responding. But that didn't mean she was willing to let it continue.

"Rafe. Throw him out." She placed her hand against the spiral conch shell tattoo on his chest. "You're stronger than he is."

Rafe's eyes shut tight. "Ehecatl." He breathed in deeply. "Go. Get out."

For a moment she thought Jacob was telling *her* to get out, but when Rafe's eyes opened again, Jacob was no longer peering out of them. But Rafe still held her.

"Rafe?"

"Phoebe…" He released her and pressed the heels of his hands to his eyes. "God. I can't—I don't know how to explain this. Again."

She slipped off his lap onto her hip, trying for casual. "You don't have to explain. Jacob and Lila are obviously determined to be together."

Rafe opened his hands like a book and peered around them. "Lila was with you?"

Phoebe's cheeks warmed. "Well…no. Not this time. She stepped into me yesterday, though, and tried to take complete control of me. She managed for a few minutes."

"But you're able to cast them out."

"So did you just now."

"Only with your help."

"I've been doing this for most of my life. I've had a lot more practice than you have. And Lila and Jacob are very different from any step-ins I've encountered before. Stronger."

Rafe regarded her. "I suppose our chemistry makes it easier for them."

Phoebe's heart skipped a beat. "Chemistry?"

"I mean—I don't think I'm imagining there's something between us."

There'd been very little between them a minute ago.

Jesus, Phoebe, don't say that out loud. Awkwardness was triggering her most inappropriate impulses: make an uncomfortable joke or climb back onto his lap. Or, you know, just stare at him for twenty minutes until *he* felt uncomfortable.

"I should go." Rafe straightened and glanced around the bed. "Where did he leave my shirt?"

"Or you could not go. And not look for your shirt." Inside Phoebe was desperately trying to throttle Outside Phoebe.

Rafe paused on the edge of the mattress. "Phoebe…"

"Sorry." She slipped off the bed past him and straightened her skirt, trying to will down the heat in her face. "I think I'm a little worked up."

"You don't think I'm worked up?" Rafe's gaze drew hers to the still-prominent bulge in his jeans. "And I'm not even sure if what I just did doesn't count as assaulting you."

"You weren't in control."

"Well, that's one excuse, isn't it?" Rafe headed down the hall to retrieve his shirt. He wobbled a moment, steadying himself with a hand against the wall when he stood, but hosting a step-in didn't seem to take it out of him as it did Phoebe. Maybe it was the level of mediation she provided, maintaining dual consciousness and facilitating communication instead of being a passive vessel.

Phoebe watched him pull on the cool white cotton over the warm hue of his skin—and the oddly animated tattoo. "What did Jacob mean when he said 'the quetzal awakens'? Did he mean Quetzalcoatl?"

Rafe paused in buttoning the shirt and turned to face her. "The quetzal? It's the name of a bird—the resplendent quetzal. It's where Quetzalcoatl's name comes from." He looked thoughtful. "I don't really know what he meant."

"But you know your tattoo is moving."

Rafe's fingers fell away from the middle button, nicely

displaying just a hint of his impressive physique from within the contrasting fabric. "That's the last thing I remember clearly before Jacob took over. You felt it, then. It really is moving."

"So it doesn't normally do that, I take it."

Rafe laughed, looking beleaguered as he ran his fingers through hair unencumbered by its usual elastic band—lost somewhere by Jacob, presumably—and pushed it back behind his ears. "No. Not normally. I was performing a protection spell when I felt it. I thought maybe it was some kind of omen from the god. So I called on Ehecatl—Quetzalcoatl's aspect as the god of wind—and that's when I felt Jacob step in."

As Rafe spoke of wind, the gusts that had been rattling the house all afternoon at last ushered in the storm. Heavy monsoon raindrops pelted the roof and through the screen door a wall of rain was visible. And largely nothing else.

Chapter 10

Phoebe gazed out at the deluge. "You don't want to drive in that." Even if it didn't hit him as hard, hosting a shade was the metaphysical equivalent of tying one on.

Rafe hesitated. "No, I suppose not."

"I'm always famished after a step-in. Why don't you stay for dinner? I promise not to do anything untoward."

"Untoward?" Rafe's smile was rueful. "If anyone's been untoward, it's me. Possessed or not."

Yeah, but you don't know what I was thinking. Phoebe turned and headed toward the kitchen to avoid giving it away with a blush. "I don't have anything fancy in the house, but there's pasta and sauce in the pantry." She checked the pantry to be sure, and glanced up at him as he came through the living room. "And I think I have a bag of salad."

Rafe gave her a quizzical smile. "A bag of salad?"

"It comes in a bag," she said defensively. "Pre-fab salads. I'm sure you've seen them at the store. Or do people like you not do their own shopping?"

His smile faded. "People like me?"

Phoebe waved her hand at his clothes. "People who can

throw on something casual like that and still manage to look like everything they own is…bespoke, I think is the word." He was still frowning at her. "Sorry, I wasn't trying to be insulting. I was mostly trying to be funny and self-deprecating." And failing miserably. "I'm sure you do your own shopping."

A reluctant and somewhat sheepish smile crept back onto his features. "I've shopped. I mean, I'm sure I must have at some point."

She couldn't tell whether he was teasing or not. Rafe Diamante was a hard man to read. A *difficult* man. Phoebe really needed to stop making unfortunate word associations in her head.

Though the rain hadn't let up by the time they'd eaten, Rafe had to admit that spending a relaxing evening with Phoebe Carlisle wasn't exactly a horrible time. She'd managed to dig up an old Scrabble board with real wooden tiles, and the two of them played on the coffee table where he'd inadvisably conjured their problematic shades two nights ago. Remnants of wax still remained, making the surface slightly bumpy under the board. He had to consciously avoid thinking about how that ritual had ended.

"What do you think it means that your tattoo is moving?" Phoebe laid down her tiles to spell "parabola" on his meager ten-point "sip" for ninety-five points.

Rafe rearranged the tiles in his tray. "I honestly don't know."

"Jacob said it was the source of your power."

He tried not to picture the moment Jacob had said that with Rafe's own lips, luring Phoebe to the bed. "I don't know what power he meant." Jacob had spoken of the Diamante legacy and Rafe didn't have a clue what that meant, either. He'd never heard of any family legacy, other than having a place of power in the Covent.

"But it's something the necromancer wants."

Rafe nodded. "And is willing to frame me for murder to get. Though I have no idea how that's supposed to work."

"Jacob and Lila seem to have a different agenda." Though she spoke casually, her voice was carefully controlled. "And who knows what Ernesto wants." She glanced up. "We could try to conjure him again. Might be more likely to get information from Ernesto alone than with the other two. And certainly less of a chance of something... unpleasant happening."

Rafe heard the hurt in her tone. It was time he addressed it. "You know it hasn't been entirely unpleasant for me."

Phoebe's smile was thin. "Not entirely?"

"What's unpleasant is not being in control. Not to mention the possibility of harming you." He set his tiles aside. "It's not that I'm not attracted to you." It was, in fact, the furthest thing from not being attracted to her.

"We don't have to do this, Rafe."

"I think we do. *I* need to say something to you, anyway. I've been with a lot of women."

"We *really* don't need to do this."

"But never anyone more than once."

Phoebe scrunched up her nose as if trying to figure out where he was going with this. He might as well get it over with.

"I have...intimacy issues. I've seen therapists about it off and on since I was a teenager." He skipped over the reason, hoping she wouldn't notice or wouldn't ask. "Basically, I don't get physically involved with a woman unless I never want to see her again."

Phoebe fidgeted with her tiles. "I see."

"I just ended up sounding like a creep, didn't I?"

She still wasn't looking at him. "Well... I don't know." When she glanced up, the periwinkle eyes were almost playful. "I guess maybe I'm trying to decide whether I should be flattered—or whether I should be wishing you never wanted to see me again." Her sly smile said she was cutting him some slack, after all.

Rafe grinned. "I'm kind of wishing I never wanted to see you again, too."

"That could be arranged." Phoebe winked and hopped up from the floor to refill their drinks.

He watched her as she moved about the kitchen, that ever-present ponytail swinging behind her. Rafe wondered how her dark chestnut hair would look down—tumbled about her bare shoulders. Dammit. He really needed to not go there.

"Maybe we could try to raise Ernesto."

Phoebe glanced across the breakfast bar. "You sure? I don't want you to do anything you're not comfortable with."

Which was what made her so comfortable to be around, he realized. "Yeah, let's do it. I'm good."

They cleared off the coffee table and gathered the tools for the ritual once again—both of them skipping the sky-clad symbolism without discussing it. The tattoos, after all, were still there, visible or not.

Rafe was careful to call the usual guardians of the directions, not wanting any unpredictable elements this time. He wasn't certain what had provided the opening for Jacob to step into him earlier—though the ritual bloodletting probably had something to do with it—but he wasn't taking any chances.

The magic tingled in the ink at his back as before; as though the guardians he called upon were animating it, amplifying some power in his blood he'd never been aware of. For the moment it seemed benign enough, but he needed to talk to his father and find out what this legacy was. Of course, he needed to talk to his father about a number of things.

Rafe sighed and began the invocation. "I call on Xolotl, brother of Quetzalcoatl, protector of the sun in its journey through the underworld and its return from Mictlan." He wasn't about to give Jacob and Lila an opening by mentioning the rulers of the underworld again, so that would have to do. "Allow the shade of Ernesto to join us here that we may communicate with him. Speak through Phoebe, Ernesto, and tell us what you would have us know." He wasn't leaving room for any misunderstandings here. The shade was welcome to enter Phoebe, who knew how to handle it. Entering Rafe was off the menu.

Phoebe closed her eyes and breathed in, expectant, but after a few moments of silence except for the rain pelting the roof, she opened them again. "I don't feel anything."

Rafe tried again, calling once more on Xolotl and Quetzalcoatl. The tattoo made a definite undulating motion through his skin when he spoke the latter's name. He found himself rising to his feet, agitated by the movement. "Ernesto," he began, but Phoebe clutched the edges of the coffee table, chest rising and falling with deep, rapid breaths beneath her soft cotton shirt.

She looked up with a start, the gray undertone in her eyes shifting to brown as though they were no longer her own. "I am bound by the quetzal." The voice and accent clearly weren't her own. "What do you want of me?"

Rafe studied her face. "Ernesto?"

"I have come as you commanded."

Commanded? He'd never commanded any sort of spirit before and certainly not a shade. "Why do you say 'commanded'? I called you, but I have no authority over you. I merely asked to communicate."

"You are the quetzal."

"What does that mean?"

"You walk between Teteocan and Mictlan, the abode of the gods and the abode of the dead. I serve Tezcatlipoca, but I am bound by the quetzal."

Rafe decided to take another tack. "You say you serve Tezcatlipoca. You mean the necromancer who calls himself by the god's name. Who is he? How does he compel you to serve him?"

"Rafe." Phoebe's eyes looked normal again and her voice was her own. "Why don't you let me talk to him? It's a little unnerving being questioned by you and having someone else answer. Plus, he seems to be afraid of you."

Rafe sat on the couch, taken aback. "Okay."

"I fear only Tezcatlipoca," Phoebe's guest insisted.

"Why? What does he hold over you?" If she thought it was unnerving to have someone question a shade occupying her, she ought to watch herself have a conversation with herself sometime. Ernesto didn't answer. "Lila told me he kept her from Jacob. Has the necromancer threatened someone close to you?"

Rafe could see Ernesto hesitating with Phoebe's features. "He means to send me from this plane. My family— I won't be able to protect them."

"Maybe we can protect them," Rafe offered. "If you tell us who they are, give us some details about yourself so we can find them and keep them safe for you."

"No!" Phoebe lunged across the coffee table at him, arms braced against it in a threatening posture, as though the person wielding them was accustomed to having more substantial musculature. "You leave my family alone, quetzal."

"I don't mean them any harm—"

"Titlacauan will have your power. And he will use it for harm."

Rafe didn't care for the conviction the shades seemed to have of his inevitable defeat. He opened his mouth to say, "Over my dead body," but thought better of it. Words had power, after all. But the necromancer wasn't coming anywhere near Rafe's power—whatever it was—if Rafe had anything to say about it.

"We won't let anyone harm your family." Phoebe's voice was soothing and her threatening pose relaxed. "We just want to know what power the necromancer has over you so we can weaken him."

A spiteful laugh followed this declaration. "You will not weaken him. He will weaken you."

There were questions Rafe couldn't leave to Phoebe. "Ernesto, why did you and Lila 'attach' yourselves to me, as Barbara Fisher said, if you thought I couldn't do anything to help?"

Phoebe sat back on her heels, rubbing her eyes as if the step-in tired her. Rafe wondered if there was a limit to the time she ought to give the shade.

"The Fisher woman was a weak evocator," Ernesto replied. "We meant to warn you, not to ask for your help. We saw you and we recognized the quetzal. And what we see, Titlacauan sees."

"What is this 'quetzal'? I don't know anything about this power or why you call me that. Jacob said the tattoo of Quetzalcoatl on my back was the source of the power. What did he mean?"

Phoebe shuddered and drooped against the table. For a moment Rafe thought she'd passed out.

"Phoebe?" He moved toward her in concern, putting a hand on her shoulder.

"He's gone." She braced her head in her hands and groaned. "And he left me with a residual migraine."

"Can I get you anything?"

"A cup of lavender chamomile would be awesome." She massaged her temples. "And maybe tell Ernesto to shove it."

Rafe couldn't help but smile. She couldn't be too bad off if she was cursing shades. "You got it. Tea's in the pantry?"

The rain had stopped at some point during Ernesto's visit. As Rafe stood and glanced out the window behind Phoebe at the spectacular sunset, his smile died on his lips. In the shadows across the dirt road leading to the house, a coyote stared in at him, eyes glittering as they met his without hesitation. Before the coyote loped away into the brush, he could swear it opened its mouth, tongue lolling to one side, and grinned.

Chapter 11

After Phoebe was situated with her cup of tea, Rafe made
an excuse about having things to do and took his leave.
The coyote had disappeared into the brush, but its presence, following the appearance of the owl and combined
with Jacob's claims about the Diamante legacy and this
"quetzal" power, was too troubling to ignore.

He'd taken the Escalade when he'd left the house to
make sure the reporters wouldn't spot him on his way out.
Coming back was another story. News vans were parked
on either side of the gate at Stone Canyon, and stopping
to punch in his code would put him in plain view of their
camera crews. He kept driving, heading north toward the
pine forests and stunning heights that hid the exclusive
enclave where his father's estate nestled. It was time Rafe
got some answers.

They hadn't spoken directly since the death of his father's business partner over a year ago. Rafael Sr. hadn't
cared for what Rafe had said about Ford Langley after the
funeral. Rafe had waited to say it until Langley was in the
ground. As far as he was concerned, he'd exercised con-
siderable restraint.

He drove up the curving red-dirt drive over rain-deepened tire-tread ruts. Someone had come this way not long before him. No other car occupied the circular loop before the house, so whoever it was had already gone. Rafe had always thought this place should be a boutique hotel. It had rooms enough to be at least a bustling bed-and-breakfast, and everything was so overly designed it was hard to imagine the architect hadn't intended for it to be on constant display.

He rang the bell, an oddly uncomfortable thing to do at the door of the home one had once lived in, but he and his father weren't exactly on "dropping by" terms.

Instead of the housekeeper, Rafael himself opened the door. Rafe hadn't quite been prepared.

"Rafa." His father hated the Anglicized "Rafe" he preferred. "What are you doing here?"

"Nice to see you, too, Dad."

Rafael's eyes were drawn to Rafe's bare feet. "Why are you wandering around like a vagabond?"

"They took my only pair of shoes from me in jail."

"Very funny." Rafael didn't crack a smile. "Well, don't just stand there. Come inside."

Rafe wiped his feet on the monogrammed coir mat and stepped into the foyer. The stunning fountain in the atrium with its glass walls and open ceiling, like an impluvium from an ancient Roman villa, never failed to bring him up short. Rainwater bubbled up against the stepping stones.

Ice tinkled in the highball Rafael jiggled in his hand. "Glenlivet and ginger. You want one?"

Rafe nodded and followed him to the bar in the family room that had never lived up to its name. Without speaking, Rafael plunked two ice cubes into a glass from the icemaker under the bar—heaven forbid anyone should have to bring an ice bucket from the kitchen—and poured the Scotch, with just a splash of ginger ale. Rafe accepted it and sipped the drink, savoring the woody bite, still standing while his father sat heavily in one of the lounge chairs and stared up at him.

"I trust Hamilton is handling things to your satisfaction."

"Oh, he's a peach." Rafe took another sip, letting the heat of the alcohol warm his tongue. "I'm surprised you didn't just pay off the chief of police or a judge or something."

His father's dark bushy eyebrows narrowed steeply, a stark contrast to hair that was more salt than pepper these days. Rafe supposed he might have added a few of the white strands himself.

"You think a murder charge is amusing, Rafa? Do you have any idea what you're putting me through? I'm probably going to lose my state senate seat—and my bid for the US senate."

"Yeah, that would be terrible. Much worse than life in prison or death by lethal injection. I can see how upsetting this must be for you."

Rafael's empty highball clanged against the glass end table as he set it down. "Everything's about you, isn't it? Anything that takes attention away from you is inconsequential."

How did he always manage to make Rafe feel like a spoiled teenager thinking only of himself, even when it came to something unequivocally about him? "This actually *is* about me. I'm the one facing the charges. You should be damn glad it's not happening to you."

"Charges Carter Hamilton is going to get dismissed. You'll have your fifteen minutes in the limelight, do a few interviews—maybe even self publish some damn crap about your harrowing brush with the law—and then go back to your rough life as a bon vivant with no responsibilities."

"Bon vivant?" Rafe laughed out loud. "I'm out there at the job sites managing the workers who actually *do* the jobs for you, five days a week. When do you even set foot in the field anymore?"

His father took his glass to the bar and filled it once more, not bothering with the soda. "That's your problem, Rafa. You think all there is to running a successful business is standing around looking pretty."

"Making sure the jobs are done to specs and deadlines are met is a far cry from standing around looking pretty."

Rafael ignored him. "This business is about the negotiations and the deals, the networking that translates into contracts won and money in the bank. The business *I* operate and you benefit from. I should have had two sons to carry on my legacy, to care about what I've built. But you couldn't even keep an eye on Gabrielito."

Rafe clenched his jaw, resisting the urge to point out that he hadn't even been living here at the time. It was his father who ought to have been looking out for Gabriel, but he'd been too busy with his political career.

"And now everything I've worked for, everything I've built, will be irrevocably tarnished. All because you couldn't just fuck the help like everybody else."

Rafe nearly choked on the sip of Scotch he'd taken while waiting out his father's rant. "What the *fuck* are you talking about?"

"Hamilton's been keeping me apprised—"

"Oh, keeping *you* apprised. I thought he was the Covent's bright young star."

"Don't you dare interrupt me. He says this 'psychic' you were seeing was really a call girl. I don't believe for a minute you killed that woman. But when this hits the papers and gets splashed all over every cable channel, that's the one thing people are going to focus on: state senator's son caught with a dead prostitute—and lying to the cops about what he was doing there." He picked up his drink again and finished it in one swallow. "You're a Diamante, goddammit. There's no reason to be paying for it. I've never paid for sex in my life."

Rafe clutched the highball to keep from hurling it at him. "So you believe that part without question. That I'm so completely incapable of having a real relationship with a woman that I'm trolling sex websites for low-rent prostitutes. And that I'm just stupid enough to lie about it during a murder investigation."

His father's eyes met his, their expression stony. "Your word doesn't mean much to me, Rafa. I don't know you anymore—why you do the things you do or what makes you say the things you say. Maybe you're pathological. But you've lost my trust."

Rafe set his glass on the bar. "That's what you've decided. Because you want to believe I'm a liar. Because you'd rather believe in the man who slept with your wife behind your back for twenty years than believe your own son."

Rafael's chest rose and fell with deep, rapid breaths, his face almost purple with fury. "Get the hell out of my house."

It wasn't until Rafe was halfway down the highway that he remembered why he'd gone there in the first place. He'd blown any chance of finding out what his father knew about the family legacy.

His eyes were heavy as he drove the back way toward home and he had to shake his head to clear it more than once. Driving over the dark hills was hypnotic. No news vans waited for him at the more private rear gate at Stone Canyon and Rafe headed in, grateful for the reprieve. He couldn't put them off for long, but at least he could have some peace tonight. He fixed himself another Scotch—hold the ginger ale—and proceeded to pass out on the couch.

* * *

His phone woke him in the morning out of a deep, le-
thargic sleep. Somehow, the ringtone sounded ominous.

Rafe fumbled the device out of his pocket and put it to
his ear, eyes still closed. "This is Rafe."

"Rafael Diamante Junior?" The voice was clinically
professional and hesitant at the same time.

"Yes?"

"I'm calling from the Verde Valley Medical Center,
Sedona Campus. Your father was admitted early this morn-
ing, suffering from chest pains and shortness of breath.
We think you'll want to get here right away."

Rafe ignored the reporters who'd apparently camped
there all night as he blazed through the gates and drove for
the hospital. He should have seen this coming, the way his
father was worked up when he left. He should have kept
his mouth shut. What did any of that matter now? It was
all in the past, where Rafe should have left it.

When he arrived at the cardiac wing, the faces of the
staff told him he was too late. But they weren't going to
be the ones to tell him. Hospital protocol, he supposed. A
solemn "the doctor will be right out to speak with you"
was the most he would get. As he waited, Carter Hamilton
stepped out of the elevator looking unusually harried, tie
loose and jacket wrinkled over his arm, with a large coffee in his hand.

He stopped short as he saw Rafe. "Thank goodness
you're here. I've been calling you all morning."

Rafe glanced down at the phone he was still holding. He
hadn't even noticed the missed calls, but there they were.
"I must have been sleeping pretty hard. They called you?"
Maybe they'd found Hamilton's card in his father's wallet.

"No, I brought him in. I had a meeting with him this

morning, and when I got to the house, he was in bad shape. I called an ambulance and rode in with him."

Rafe opened his mouth but the doctor approached before he even knew what he'd meant to say.

The look on the man's face confirmed his fear. "Mr. Diamante?"

"Yes. How's my father? Can I see him?"

The doctor took off his wire frames and rubbed the lenses against his lab coat, perhaps making it easier to say what he had to say without being able to focus on Rafe's face. "Your father was in cardiac arrest when he arrived at the hospital. We were able to revive him briefly, but he never regained consciousness. I'm sorry."

Rafe nodded stupidly.

Hamilton put a hand on his shoulder. "I'm sure they did everything they could."

The doctor put his glasses back on. "There was some irregularity I wanted to discuss with you."

The lawyer gave Rafe's shoulder a squeeze. "I'll be in the waiting area if you need me."

Rafe felt like he was moving in slow motion, out of sync with the people around him. "What sort of irregularity?"

"Your father's symptoms indicate that he may have been suffering from ingestion of batrachotoxin. We believe it's what caused his heart to stop."

"Batrachotoxin?"

"It's a neurotoxin produced by the Dendrobates species. A species of Central American poison dart frog, to be exact." The doctor held his gaze. "To be perfectly blunt, we believe your father was poisoned."

Chapter 12

Puddleglum's bowl hadn't been touched since yesterday afternoon. Phoebe frowned as she scanned the backyard for any sign of the cat. She'd called him repeatedly, but he hadn't appeared. It wasn't like him to forgo both dinner and breakfast.

Listening to the morning news as she finished getting ready, she paused with her toothbrush halfway to her mouth, arrested by the name the hostess had mentioned. Phoebe peered down the hallway at the television screen. Rafe walked with his head lowered, wearing dark glasses, as Carter Hamilton led him out of a hospital entrance.

A reporter in front of the hospital faced the camera. "More trouble follows Sedona businessman Rafe Diamante this morning as questions arise about the sudden death of his father earlier today. A source at Verde Valley Medical Center in Sedona, who spoke with me a few moments ago, says Rafael Diamante Senior was—get this—*poisoned* by this adorable tree frog." An image of a slippery, bright red frog perched on a tropical leaf appeared on the screen. "This cute little guy, known as the strawberry poison dart frog, produces a neurotoxin once used by Aztec warriors to ambush their enemies."

Phoebe nearly swallowed her toothpaste.

"Diamante Junior hasn't been charged with the crime, but it doesn't look good for him. By his own admission, Diamante and his father argued late last night."

After spitting out the toothpaste and rinsing, Phoebe grabbed her phone and tried to reach Rafe, but the call went straight to voice mail. She'd have to try to him later. If she didn't leave now, she'd be late for her court date.

After a last glance around the yard to call for Puddleglum, she headed out. The cat would probably be taking ownership of her papasan chair by the time she came home.

The bottle of Scotch his father had been drinking had tested positive for batrachotoxin. Hamilton gave Rafe the news when he stopped by to deliver a strongbox full of papers from his trunk—the contents of a safe-deposit box Rafael and Hamilton had planned to go over at their meeting.

Rafe shifted the box to one side, hooked under his arm. "But I drank some of that Scotch."

"How much?"

"An ounce—maybe two."

"The poison was in pretty low concentration, but your dad drank a significant amount. Probably started long before you got there last night and continued afterward. He finished off the bottle." Hamilton studied him. "Did you feel at all ill?"

Rafe nodded, recalling how hard it been to stay awake on the drive back. "Kind of woozy. I was surprised such a small amount of alcohol had hit me so hard."

"And then you slept through my calls in the morning." Hamilton rubbed at his blond stubble. He looked like a hipster Ken doll. "Just like what you described at Barbara Fisher's place."

The connection was too obvious to ignore. "You think whoever killed Fisher poisoned my father."

Hamilton shrugged. "Makes sense. Seems like too much of a coincidence otherwise."

"But why? My father didn't have anything to do with the shades I was communicating with."

"As far as you know." That was a sobering thought. "I had the opportunity to talk with the DA Off the record, they don't have enough evidence to charge you, but they aren't ready to write you off, either. In light of the Fisher murder, and the circumstances, you're the unofficial prime suspect."

Rafe sighed. "I suppose I should have seen that coming."

"I wouldn't fret about it too much. They're going to have a hard time coming up with anything to tie you to it since there's no way you could have tampered with the Scotch when he'd been drinking it before you got there."

Rafe went through the box after Hamilton had gone. He set a pile of paperwork for the business aside after finding a series of Covent journals, going back decades, buried underneath. Holed up inside, away from the media encampment at the gate, Rafe spent the afternoon poring over them. Rafael Sr. had never specifically mentioned the quetzal but "the family legacy" featured prominently in the journals, mostly in the context of the importance of its continuance within the Covent.

"The Diamantes," his father had written, "have passed this torch from generation to generation, have bequeathed this responsibility to our offspring as the legacy of our Aztec ancestors, scions of the divine blood." The claims of Aztec blood were nothing new, but it was the first time he'd heard mention of divine origins.

The Covent kept a compendium of pagan archetypes among its library. Maybe he'd find something there. Rafe logged on to the Covent's network—at least they hadn't revoked his access—and pulled up the compendium. There it was: *quetzal*.

Rafe read aloud. "'An embodied avatar of Quetzalcoatl. Believed to be a conduit for the god's energy, the quetzal may have the ability to transform into nagual form while possessed by the power of Quetzalcoatl. Mesoamerican dragon archetype.'"

In archetypal terms, the dragon and the serpent were synonymous as images of primal, seductive power that appeared across cultures. The quetzal, then, was primal power embodied in human form, with the attributes of the god.

If it were those attributes the necromancer sought to acquire—wisdom, knowledge, fertility—Rafe still had no clear picture of what he wanted them for. Quetzalcoatl was also associated with wind and light, and, in some myths, the creation of the current world of man through the mixing of the god's own blood with the bones of the dead in Mictlan. Whatever the necromancer was after, Rafe couldn't see how the power of the "quetzal" was uniquely desirable.

The case Phoebe had been assigned today turned out to be far more complicated than a simple possession charge. Her client was a sex worker who claimed to have been hired by the cop who'd arrested her—after having sex with her first, and, in lieu of paying her with money as agreed, giving her the meth he'd then charged her with possessing. Throw in a little police brutality that had left her with a badly bruised face and a broken clavicle, and the fact that the young woman was four months pregnant, and both the state and Phoebe had a giant mess on their hands.

The upside was finally having a case she was confident she could win in court—if the prosecutor let it go that far. Public sentiment would be in her favor, and there were witnesses who could corroborate the woman's story if Phoebe could get them to testify. There were a lot of "ifs" in this scenario.

But the bail hearing and subsequent consultation with the client took most of the day and Phoebe had nearly forgotten what Rafe had been dealing with—until Monique, her client, mentioned Barbara Fisher.

Phoebe played back the video of the session on her tablet as she drove home.

"Maybe I should just plead guilty and get it over with," Monique had said for the dozenth time, followed by Phoebe's audible sigh.

"What you should be doing is countersuing. You have an excellent case."

"I don't want to end up like Barbie."

"Who's Barbie?"

"Barbie Fisher. The one that senator's son killed."

Phoebe's stunned pause was notable. "Barbara Fisher? Why would you end up like her?"

"We got our clients from the same place. Bunch of power-tripping dicks like that Diamante. They act like they're respectable. Make it seem safer meeting up with them than taking a risk on letting some random psycho into your house. They are the psychos."

Phoebe couldn't help glancing at the video while she waited at a stoplight, watching Monique press her fingers gingerly to the side of her swollen eye.

"I thought Barbara Fisher was a medium. A psychic." She'd tried to say it as matter-of-factly as possible.

Monique laughed and then winced. "Yeah, and I'm a physical therapist."

* * *

What waited for her at home, however, knocked Monique and the disturbing revelation about Barbara Fisher right out of Phoebe's head. As she stepped out of the Jeep in the carport, a low growl made the hair stand on the back of her neck. A pair of eyes glowed at her from under the gardening shelf. It took a moment to realize both the growl and the eyes were Puddleglum's.

A quick squeeze of the LED flashlight on her keychain confirmed it was Puddleglum and not some feral cat. "Glum, sweetie, what are you doing under there? What's the matter?" Phoebe crouched in front of the shelf, surprised when Puddleglum hissed at her. Before she could shine the flashlight on him again, a sound behind her made her whirl around. Puddleglum growled again, and when Phoebe pointed the weak beam of light into the darkness, it became obvious why. A large male coyote stood staring at her, unblinking and undaunted by her presence.

Phoebe clapped her hands at it. "Yah! Go on! Get out of here!" The coyote was unfazed until she chucked a gardening trowel in its direction. The animal trotted away into the darkness without any sense of fear or urgency.

Puddleglum was still growling, but he didn't hiss this time as she reached under the shelf to pull him out. Only then did she realize why he'd been hiding and why she hadn't seen him since last night. Dried blood matted his fur on one hind leg. The coyote must have been waiting him out after trying to nab him.

That settled it. The cat door was going. Puddleglum wasn't going to like it, but his nomadic hunter days were over. Two of Puddleglum's least favorite things followed: being put into his carrier and a drive to the vet.

While she waited for Puddleglum to get stitched up at the veterinary ER, Phoebe's phone rang. Rafe's name appeared on the display. God, she'd almost forgotten how the day had started.

"Rafe, hey. Are you okay? I saw the news."

"Yeah. I just saw that you called. It's been a… It's been weird. And shitty."

"I'm so sorry, Rafe."

"We weren't close." Rafe sighed. "I don't know why I felt like I had to say that. I don't really know how to do any of this."

"Of course not. No one does." When her parents were killed in a car accident, it felt like she'd missed a class somewhere, something she ought to have learned somehow about how to behave in the face of unexpected loss.

The veterinary assistant came out with an unhappy but groggy Puddleglum in his carrier. "Puddleglum's all ready to go home."

"Thanks." She stood and took the carrier, shifting the phone to her other ear. "Sorry. I'm at the vet. Just taking Puddleglum home."

"Anything wrong? It's kind of late for the vet's office, isn't it?"

"He got in a fight with a coyote. Can you hang on a sec?" Phoebe set down the carrier and took out her credit card to pay Puddleglum's bill. "Sorry. Juggling cats and money."

"Did you say coyote?" Rafe's voice was sharp.

"Yeah. I guess I'm going to have to keep Glum inside from now on. The rotten thing was still hanging around waiting for the cat when I got home, just staring me down. They've gotten really bold. Guess it's our fault for encroaching on their territory."

"Phoebe… I don't think you should go home."

"What?" She paused with the pen on the credit card receipt.

"Bring Puddleglum over to my place. I'll text you the directions."

"Your place? Rafe, it's just a coyote. I can handle it."

"It's not just a coyote. It's nagual."

"It's what?"

"The necromancer."

Chapter 13

At the gate to Stone Canyon, Phoebe punched in the guest code Rafe had texted her, while Puddleglum made impressively demonic noises beside her, doing his best to terrify the car and carrier into setting him free. The vet had given the cat methadone to calm him down for the stitches, but he seemed to be pretty much over his buzz. The stops on the way to pick up cat supplies—and some dinner at Dairy Queen after Rafe had mentioned he'd already eaten—hadn't helped matters much.

She had to admit as she wound through the hills that the view up here was spectacular, though she couldn't help thinking Rafe was overreacting about the coyote. Sightings of the animals in urban areas had been on the rise in recent years. And Sedona wasn't exactly an urban hub.

The house itself was stunning. Phoebe felt thoroughly out of place in her bargain-store smock shirt and leggings and her scuffed sandals as she carried Puddleglum up the artfully placed stone walk. Desert landscaping meant to make it seem as though it wasn't landscaped at all—it just happened to be a botanical-garden-worthy desert paradise completely by accident—complemented the adobe construction.

Rafe waited for her in the mosaic stone entryway—stone seemed to be a theme here in Stone Canyon. Imagine that. As usual, he managed to wear his casual clothes almost as immaculately as his lawn wore its landscaping, the dark olive T-shirt hugging his muscular frame just enough to invite thoughts of spreading her hands over it, and the khaki pants wrinkled in all the right places. The bare feet on the clay tile brought the whole unbearable, effortlessly sensual, look together.

"I heard you coming." He cast a wry glance at the cat carrier as he took it from her and headed inside. "We can set him up in the great room for the night."

Phoebe scanned the spacious room with its cream sheepskin rugs and French doors on both sides. Damn. Even rich people's living rooms were "great."

"I'll get him settled." Rafe took the pet supplies out of her hand. "You go eat…" he glanced at the Dairy Queen bag "…whatever that is."

"It's a burger and fries. I'm not eating ice cream for dinner."

Rafe grinned. "Not judging."

While Rafe took Puddleglum to a corner of the room by one of the floor-to-ceiling windows behind an Aztec-carved wooden screen, Phoebe sat on the couch and wolfed down her meal.

Both cat and host were relaxing in a pile of cushions by the time she'd finished, and Rafe had turned the top of Puddleglum's carrier into a makeshift privacy hood for the cat box, while the bottom held food and water dishes in a separate station.

"Wow." Phoebe stared at the scene as she came around the screen. "This is nicer than my place."

Rafe laughed as he stroked the cat. "It's a good spot to curl up in with a book during a thunderstorm."

Dear God. He liked cats and he curled up with books during thunderstorms. This man was not human.

Phoebe knelt in front of the cushions. "So you think the necromancer, this Tezcatlipoca guy, sent the coyote to attack Glum?"

"No, I think he sent the coyote to warn you away from me. Or he *is* the coyote. I believe it's his nagual, his protector animal."

"And you think he can transform into it? He's a shape-shifter?"

"I don't know what to think." Rafe frowned as he avoided the stitches on Puddleglum's thigh. "That's the mythology. Which until a few days ago I would have said was just that. Mythology. Symbolism and nothing more. But it's too much of a coincidence. That owl in your yard— it's a symbol for Mictlantecuhtli—and now the coyote. I saw it yesterday watching us from across the road. I should have said something then but I didn't want to alarm you needlessly." Rafe pinched the bridge of his nose. "God, was that yesterday? I need a drink."

Two gin and tonics later, Phoebe and Rafe had taken over the pile of cushions, while Puddleglum stalked off to curl up under the coffee table.

Rafe stared into his glass at the melting ice as he held it up to the light. "The last thing I said to my father was a dig about my mother cheating on him."

"Beats 'I wish you were dead.'"

Rafe's eyes fixed on her as if he thought she was mocking him.

"That's what I said to my parents," Phoebe clarified. "Not directly to them. But after they dropped me off at boarding school. I said it while glaring at the door as they drove away. They were killed in a seven-car pile-up on I-17 half an hour later."

"Wow." Rafe lowered his glass. "How old were you?"

"Fifteen. They thought I needed spiritual guidance I wasn't getting at home to cure me of my delusions about talking to dead people."

"Seems like an understandable response from a fifteen-year-old. You couldn't have known what would happen."

"Sure, and I get that intellectually, but it's still something I have to live with, remembering how much I was hating them at the moment they died, and that they certainly knew it." Phoebe took a sip of her drink. "That's just how it is. We can't predict when someone's going to die, and as much as we'd like to, it isn't reasonable to expect to be able to go through life never being pissed at the people we care about in case it might be the last time we see them. I have to believe my parents understood that, too. I've communicated with a lot of shades over the years, and no one has ever been on the other side wondering if the loved ones they left behind actually hated them. It's always the ones left behind who are afraid the people they've lost believed that."

While Phoebe spoke, Rafe had mixed himself another drink, mostly gin, and he downed half of it. "He may not have died thinking I hated him, but I'm fairly certain my father died hating me."

Lounging beside him, Phoebe put a hand on his knee. "I'm sure that's not true."

"I insisted on tarnishing the memory of the people who meant the most to him. I took away all his good memories." Rafe finished his drink and set the glass on the floor, slipping his fingers between Phoebe's where they rested on his knee. "And I'd do it again. Not to hurt him, but because it was the truth. I was tired of having to protect other people's lies at the expense of myself." He glanced at Phoebe, obviously more than a little buzzed. "We owe ourselves that, don't we? The right to speak the truth?"

Phoebe squeezed his hand. "Yeah, we do." His eyes were intense and full of turmoil. And, damn, was he beautiful. There was a possibility she might be a little buzzed, too.

Unexpectedly, Rafe rolled onto his side on the cushions and brought his other hand to the side of Phoebe's head. "*Yeah*, we do," he repeated emphatically, and his lips met hers.

Phoebe closed her eyes and slid her hands over the ripple of muscles at his sides as Rafe dug his fingers into her hair, freeing it from its habitual ponytail. She moaned into him, surrendering to the exploration of his tongue and his hands. His touch was less demanding, less possessing, than it had been under Jacob's influence, but the sensual, tentative caresses were more arousing in a way, as she could sense his desire to experience every inch of her with a kind of newness and wonder that had been lacking in Jacob's aggressive presumption of her reciprocation.

Not that she wasn't wholeheartedly reciprocating now. Her hands slipped under his shirt to stroke his skin, and the warmth of his flesh beneath her fingers tingled into nerves far removed from her hands. When she reached the tiny peaks of his nipples with her thumbs, he arched against her touch with a groan of appreciation, the vibration of sound in her mouth sending blood rushing to her clit.

She pulled the shirt over Rafe's head, separating their mouths, and then placed hers against one of the dark nipples. Rafe swore softly, sexily, arms braced beside her as he paused for a moment at the sensation before he began working through the buttons at the front of her shirt. Leaning back, he pulled her into his lap, freeing the hooks of her bra to let it fall away and expose her breasts. Drawing her close once more with his hands at the sides of her head, he rocked his hips against hers as he kissed her more forcefully, her breasts brushing his chest, and his erection teasing against the damp heat between her thighs beneath the fabric of the leggings.

Dizzy with need for him, Phoebe undid the button at his waist and unzipped his pants, drawing her nails over the bulge beneath the tight underwear before tearing her mouth away from his to scramble back and dip down to taste him, freed from the elastic band. A musky bead of liquid dripped against her tongue.

Rafe rose onto his knees to give her room, clutching her upper arms with a groan as she swallowed him, and then tensed after a moment and drew back, pulling her off.

Phoebe blinked up at him. "What's wrong?"

"Nothing." He shook his head, though his expression seemed to say otherwise. "Nothing at all. God, that felt good, but I think we're both a little drunk. I don't want to take advantage of you."

"You are *not* taking advantage of me. Not even a little." Phoebe tried to reach for him once more, but Rafe held her away. He kissed her again, as if to reassure her, but his hands dropped away from her to put himself back together and zip up before he broke contact with her mouth.

"Maybe we should slow down a little." He drew her to the cushions and wrapped his broad arms around her.

He wanted to cuddle? She rested her head on his chest, heat rising in her cheeks. Was she that out of practice that she'd done it badly? Her head was swimming. Maybe Rafe was right and she really had drunk too much. He was certainly the first guy she'd been with to care about that. Just her luck—she'd met one of the rare *actually* nice guys. She hoped.

In the back of her mind, she heard Monique's voice. *Bunch of power-tripping dicks like that Diamante. They act like they're respectable.*

Rafe kissed her hair. "S'nice having you here."

Phoebe sighed and closed her eyes. As much as she hated to admit it, this hadn't been a great idea, anyway. He'd just lost his father and was drowning his grief in drink and desire. He'd probably regret it in the morning.

But in the pale, otherworldly light of false dawn, Phoebe woke to much more emphatic kisses against her throat. Rafe kissed his way downward, lavishing attention on both breasts in turn until Phoebe's moans had become desperate pleas for more, before continuing along her stomach to her navel. She gasped as he pulled down her leggings and panties with his teeth and spread her open with a generous lap of his tongue while he slid the fabric over her thighs to trap her ankles.

Propped on her elbows, she watched the dark head dip down, buried in her lap, before the intense sensations of his expert oral dexterity made it too hard to focus. She arched back, whimpering moans rising in pitch and tempo, and at last crescendoing into full-throated cries.

But Rafe was just getting started. Phoebe reached for him as he peeled the leggings off her feet, but he pinned her wrists and descended on her once more. He teased her with his tongue, pulling away repeatedly until Phoebe was thrashing and moaning with delightful frustration.

He brought his sticky mouth up to hers and Phoebe moaned at the taste of her own pleasure. "Please," she whimpered when he let up and appeared to be heading back to torment her once more.

Rafe paused, hovering over her. "Please what?" His voice was deep and husky with desire.

"I want to feel you inside me."

His dark eyes glittered in the dim light of the paling sky. "You want me to fuck you." The blunt, unvarnished sexuality of the word, and the low growl of the hard consonants in his throat, made the blood rush into all the right places.

"*Fuck*, yes," she breathed. "*Please.*"

Rafe pushed himself to standing and Phoebe watched him strip off his pants and underwear, revealing an unabashed and generous erection. He stroked himself as he looked down at her, seeming to ponder something before dropping onto his knees between her thighs and taking a foil packet from his pocket as she hooked her legs around him. The lubed condom escaped the foil when he opened it and Phoebe caught it.

Rafe groaned as she rolled it over his cock in one swift motion, for a brief instant exhibiting none of the stoic yet delicious control with which he'd been approaching this encounter. The little shudder along his spine made her want to feel him lose control. Inside her.

She came up onto her knees and straddled his thighs, and Rafe clutched her by the hair at her nape as she lowered herself onto him. She'd been expecting a bit of discomfort with his size after being out of the game so long, but he'd gotten her so wet that her body eagerly took him in deep, his cock filling her like he was made for her. His fist tightened in her hair and Phoebe relinquished control, hanging loose in his grip as he began to thrust into her vigorously. In this position, the curve of his cock hit that sweet spot inside her just right, and Phoebe rocketed into another climax, sure she was making enough noise this time to wake the dead, but not caring. No one had ever gotten her this hot before or fit her so perfectly.

Tipping her onto her back while she was still shuddering, Rafe dropped his weight onto her, arms wrapped tightly around her body, eager, growling vocalizations accompanying his motions while she wrapped her legs around his pumping hips and hung on for the ride.

Her whole body was tingling with aftershocks when

Rafe made a sudden, frustrated growl against her throat and pushed himself up with his fists balled into the cushions, drawing a moan of protest from her as they separated.

"I can't do this," he growled. "I've changed my mind. Fuck off."

Phoebe gaped at him as her legs dropped away from his hips. "What?"

"No, no. Not you. Oh, gods, not *you*." Rafe's midnight eyes went wide with mortification and he scrambled back. "Phoebe, no, sorry, I— *Fuck*."

That tingling, expectant energy traveling over her— that hadn't been aftershocks. "What the—? Are you kidding me? *Jacob?*" Phoebe leaped to her feet, not caring that she was naked. "Did you *conjure* him?" His hesitation was answer enough. She grabbed her underwear and leggings and yanked them on. "You're unbelievable. Is this how you get your kicks? Was this your plan from the start? A little metaphysical gangbang with the stupid evocator?"

"*No*. Phoebe, wait." He reached out for her but Phoebe sidestepped him, grabbing her shirt from the cushions. Her bra was somehow across the tile on the other side of him. She put on the shirt without it and jerked the buttons into the holes while she looked around for her sandals. She must have left them by the couch.

Rafe was zipping up his pants when she came back with the sandals tucked under one arm and Puddleglum under the other. "Phoebe, please listen to me."

She should have paid attention to Monique's warning. "I'm starting to get why no one ever sleeps with you more than once. You don't have intimacy issues. You have asshole issues. You sick freak." Her reach for the cat carrier to try to put it back together alerted Puddleglum to his imminent confinement and Phoebe lost the battle to hold on to either. "Dammit, Puddleglum!" He was off like a flash and the doors to the foyer were open.

"Phoebe, let me explain."

"Go fuck yourself, Diamante. Puddleglum!" She ran barefoot into the foyer, but there was no telling where the cat had gone. Or how huge this house was. Phoebe blinked back tears, feeling like Kim Novak in *Bell, Book and Candle* looking for Pyewacket and realizing from her tears that she'd fallen in love with Jimmy Stewart and given up her power. God, Phoebe was an idiot.

"I'll bring him to you," said Rafe quietly behind her. "You can go if you want."

Phoebe whirled on him. So now the creep was dismissing her. At least he wasn't planning on tying her up in his basement. "You can have your lawyer bring him to me. I don't want to see you again."

Rafe buried his hands in his pockets. "Fair enough."

Phoebe put on the sandals, lifting each foot behind her and slipping on the sandal from the back to keep Rafe in full view. Who knew what he was capable of? He'd probably murdered Barbara Fisher. "If you do anything to my cat, I swear, I will hunt you down." She brushed past him and went out and slammed the door before he could respond.

Chapter 14

What had possessed him to do something so stupid? After vomiting up the bitter juniper-berry taste of gin, Rafe slumped onto his ass on the bathroom floor and laughed at the ironic idiocy of the question then fought the urge to cry. His hair still smelled like Phoebe.

She'd never forgive him for this. All he seemed to be able to do lately was let down the people he cared about. Gabriel, Matthew, his father—and now Phoebe.

He hadn't had a chance to tell her he hadn't let Jacob in. He'd woken up to find her sleeping beside him, dark hair damp against her temple and smelling like the desert dawn itself, and the idea that ought to have been a fleeting fantasy had taken hold of him.

After trying in vain to go back to sleep, he'd crept away to his altar to utter the invocation and make the bargain with the shade. It had seemed like the perfect solution. Though it was a problem he'd never have had if he hadn't suggested she stay here last night. And now she was heading straight back to her house, unprotected from Tezcatlipoca's nagual. He might as well have not warned her at all.

But what he'd experienced this morning—besides the best sex he'd ever had in his life—might have changed everything. As he'd joined with Phoebe, he'd felt the ink moving again on his back—and then he'd felt...something else. Something inside him waking. Something powerful and strong. If Tezcatlipoca could project or appear as nagual, Rafe had felt at that moment he could simply *become* nagual. He'd felt a sensation like wings rising from his shoulders, independent of the ink, driven skyward by the sheer delight of being so close to Phoebe. He'd almost been surprised when she hadn't remarked on them, certain they must be visible.

If he could reach that state again, he thought he might even be able to fly.

All of which meant he was very likely losing his mind.

Behind him in the mirror, Puddleglum slunk past the bathroom door on his suspicious inspection of the house. Rafe managed to grab him and get him into the carrier with a minimum of bloodletting. Hamilton agreed without question when Rafe called to request the pick-up and delivery of the animal.

"Your father's estate is paying me well," Hamilton assured him when Rafe tried to offer a lame explanation. "If it needs doing and if whatever happened doesn't impact the case in any way, I'm happy to help out, and it's none of my business. Besides, given the news that just broke, I don't think you should be going for a drive anytime soon."

Rafe's muscles tensed as he asked the question he already knew the answer to. "What news?"

"A source at the police department leaked the information about Barbara Fisher's sideline business. And your alleged involvement as a client."

Phoebe stared at the far wall of the shower while the hot water beat down on her. To say she felt violated was an understatement. And yet, how close had she come—twice—to letting Jacob use Rafe for her own pleasure? But she'd stopped him before it had gone that far. And she sure as hell hadn't conjured Jacob up to take advantage of Rafe.

What she couldn't understand was why he'd done it. Despite her initial reaction, she couldn't believe he'd been playing her this whole time like some kind of psycho. Phoebe leaned her head against the tile, not sure what to believe, the sweet ache between her thighs making it difficult to accept the apparent reality behind the mind-blowing sex she'd just had.

Phoebe sighed. She couldn't stay in here forever. She turned off the shower and dried off. Pulling on her bathrobe as she stepped out of the bathroom, Phoebe nearly jumped out of her skin. A shadow had fallen over the narrow window beside the front door. The knock that followed was jarring, even though the shadow had prepared her for it. Rafe's warnings, and the morning's unexpected turn, had left her completely on edge, like she'd guzzled an entire pot of black tea. It wasn't as if a magical coyote was going to knock before it came to rip out her throat.

Phoebe tied her bathrobe tighter as she reached the door. "Who's there?"

"It's Carter Hanson Hamilton."

"Carter?" Phoebe opened the door, relieved to see him holding up Puddleglum in his carrier—glaring out at her as if he'd been much misused and had given up wailing about it. She hadn't really expected Rafe to send the lawyer over with the cat, and certainly not so quickly.

"Puddleglum." She unlocked the screen door and let Carter in to take the carrier from him. "I was afraid he'd be lost in that great big house. Thank you so much for bringing him by." Since she'd already locked up the cat door in the kitchen, she set the carrier in the entryway and released him. Offended, Puddleglum made a low dash for her bedroom.

Phoebe gave Carter a grateful smile as she straightened. "Would you like something to drink? I've got lemonade and sparkling water."

Carter shrugged amiably. "I just wanted to see your little friend home safely, but now that you've said it, lemonade sounds really good."

Phoebe went to the kitchen to get him a glass. "I suppose Rafe told you how the cat ended up there." She tried to keep the heat out of her face.

Carter followed her through the sunken living room, pausing on the other side of the breakfast bar. "He mentioned something about the emergency vet being closer to his place and the late hour. I was happy to help him out, considering how difficult it's going to be for him to deal with the public right now."

Phoebe brought him the lemonade. "Because of his father, you mean."

"That." Carter took a sip with an appreciative nod. "And the bombshell that hit the news stations this morning."

"What bombshell?"

"As his lawyer, I can't comment on the story, of course, but since it's all over the news, I suppose there's no harm in my telling you what's been reported. The police department has an anonymous source claiming Barbara Fisher's business with Rafael was of a more personal nature than just a psychic reading."

"Personal?" Phoebe's inner I-told-you-so cuckoo was going off like crazy.

"Ms. Fisher's main business was apparently soliciting." Carter drank the rest of his lemonade. "The media loves a sex scandal. So much more interesting than a mere murder." He handed back the empty glass, his expression thoughtful as he studied her. "The vet wasn't anywhere close to Rafael's place, was it?"

Phoebe sighed. "Not exactly, no."

"It's none of my business, so feel free to tell me to take a hike, but completely aside from any of these rumors or the case—I'd be careful around Rafael."

Phoebe tried not to stiffen visibly. "What do you mean?"

"I only know him through his father and the Covent, though from what I've seen, he's a thoughtful practitioner and a trustworthy man. I'd stake my reputation on his innocence with regard to the charges against him. But Rafael has some mental health issues I'm not sure you're aware of." Carter brushed a hand through his hair in a sign of discomfort with the topic. "I wouldn't presume to give him an armchair diagnosis. I'm not an expert. But his father spoke to me about Rafael's history at some length. He's exhibited signs of paranoia and delusions since he was a boy. There's a history of mental illness on his mother's side."

"I see." The same had been said of her throughout her childhood, culminating in the "exile" to the parochial boarding school.

"I hope you don't think I've been out of line." Carter smiled apologetically. "Maybe I have. It's really none of my business. I'm just looking out for you. And him. I suppose I feel a bit protective of Rafael."

Phoebe couldn't help but smile at the sincerity in his expression. "Don't worry about it. I appreciate you letting me know. And bringing Puddleglum home."

She contemplated Carter's words after he'd gone, toying with the idea of calling Ione to find out what she knew about Rafe. That, of course, would be inviting a lecture. The fact that she was almost willing to endure Ione's criticism meant Rafe had really gotten under her skin. Of course he had. He'd been inside her. Cobwebs and all.

The phone rang while she pondered the idea, jangling Phoebe's already raw nerves. Terrific. Having the stupid idea had conjured Ione herself. Phoebe chewed her bottom lip. She didn't want to deal with her older sister right now, but she couldn't avoid talking to Ione forever.

"Ione."

A brief, stunned silence followed. "Phoebe... I didn't expect you to pick up. Have you seen the news this morning?"

She kept her voice neutral. "About Diamante's relationship with Barbara Fisher? Yeah, I heard."

"No, not..." Ione wasn't usually at a loss for words. "Turn on the TV. Channel 3. Now."

Irritated at her tone, Phoebe picked up the remote and punched the button. "Okay. It's on. What's so—?" The phone slipped out of her hand and Phoebe's mouth dropped open. Her picture was on the screen next to a suited talking head. She turned up the sound.

"...identified the mystery woman seen leaving Diamante's house early this morning. Carlisle is an assistant public defender for Yavapai County, who sources say was initially part of the Sedona business owner's defense team."

Frame-in-frame footage rolled of Phoebe doing the walk of shame to her car before the studio camera panned to a smirking female co-anchor. "Looks like she's switched to a little one-on-one consultation, Bob. A user on Reddit shared this even more revealing video. We can only show you a partial image."

Phoebe's stomach sank as a shaky zoom-lens image showed her through Rafe's window. Fuzzy pixelation covered most of her torso—and Rafe's head.

"Phoebe?" Ione's anxious voice carried from the couch cushion where the phone had slid. Phoebe scrambled for it as she muted the television. "Are you there?"

"Yeah, I'm here."

"You're not a public figure. They can't show that."

Phoebe wouldn't have expected those to be the first words out of Ione's mouth.

"Rafe is a public figure. He's a murder suspect and the son of a state senator."

"Doesn't matter. The shot outside the house is one thing, but the other video is a clear violation of privacy. They had to be on private property with special surveillance equipment to get it. I'm texting Carter Hamilton your number. He's representing Rafe. He'll get this yanked, at least from the legitimate news sources."

"I sort of expected a big 'I told you so' from you."

"Well, I did tell you so, but you're an adult. You can sleep with whomever you want. Doesn't mean you deserve to have film of it broadcast around the globe."

"Thanks. I think."

"And, frankly, after seeing that clip, I'm actually a little jealous, even if he is a bit of a hot mess. But I'm sorry it's blown up in your face."

Phoebe laughed. She couldn't remember the last time that had happened in conversation with Ione. "Don't be too jealous. It's never happening again. He's even more of a hot mess than you know."

"Sorry, Phoebes. But you're okay?"

"I think so. As okay as I can be. For now."

Phoebe cringed as the censored video showed on the screen once more. Her phone beeped, announcing another call. It was bound to be a busy day.

"That's Theia calling. I'd better take it. But...thanks, Ione." She clicked over to the incoming call, accepting Theia's FaceTime request. "Theia."

"Wow, honey. When you clear out the cobwebs, you do not mess around."

"Yeah, I figured why not go big?"

Theia's twin, Rhea, darted into the frame in front of her. "*How* big?"

Phoebe shook her head. "God, you're the worst."

"Somebody has to keep your ego in check now that you're famous."

Phoebe snorted. "I think the media's got that job covered."

Rhea's expression turned serious. "You know if you need moral support, we're there."

"Summer session finals just finished," Theia added from behind her.

"So we're just hanging out in Flag Town."

"We can be there in an hour."

Phoebe was starting to lose track of who was who. "Don't jump in the car just yet. I think I can handle it. And Ione just offered me moral support, actually."

Rhea's blond, scruffy pixie cut popped back into the frame. "I thought you two weren't speaking."

"Yeah, so did I. Weird, huh? Anyway, it's going to be crazy here so there's no point in coming down. But don't worry about me. I'll be okay."

As soon as she'd disconnected, the phone rang again. Phoebe's stomach knotted. *Rafe.* She let it ring twice, finger hovering over the ignore button, then answered, after all.

"Phoebe." His voice was thick with relief. "Thank you for answering."

"Yeah, well, it's kind of my thing today."

"I am so sorry about all this. Hamilton's issuing a cease and desist on the video."

"Too bad he can't issue one for my brain."

"Phoebe... I know you probably don't want to hear this—"

"Not really."

"—but I need to talk about what happened this morning."

Her jaw clenched together like a vise but she let him continue.

"First I need to explain something. I lied to you before."

There was a surprise. "When I said I'd been with a lot of women and couldn't handle the intimacy...that wasn't strictly true. I've only been with a few women. Very few." Phoebe found that hard to believe. "And last night, with you, things were moving fast."

"So you panicked and called in a pinch hitter."

"*No.* I mean...not exactly. Shit, don't hang up. This is coming out all wrong. What I'm trying to say is that I didn't want to disappoint you, and I was very much afraid that I would. Not because of any failing in you, but because of me."

Now he was trying "it's not you, it's me"? "Rafe, let's just forget this ever happened. Obviously the media isn't going to let us forget it anytime soon, but we don't need to talk about it—and we don't need to talk, period. I don't know what your problem is—"

"I'm impotent."

The rest of Phoebe's sentence was strangled in her throat on an incoherent guttural noise. She stared at the phone, speechless. Now he was just yanking her chain. He certainly hadn't had a problem while she was sucking his cock.

"Arousal isn't an issue." He'd anticipated her train of thought. "It's the follow-through. And last night, with you... you have no idea how badly I wanted to be able to follow through. You looked so confused and disappointed when I stopped you. I just—a really stupid idea occurred to me and I acted on it without thinking. I knew Jacob could follow through. It's not a physical condition—it's psychological. He was able to override everything when he took control before. So I thought if I let him—God, this sounds even worse out loud. I conjured him and made a deal with him, that he could step in and take over when he was drawn by your...peak. But when I felt him trying to step in, I didn't want it that way. I didn't want him in between us. That's why I stopped." He went silent, having apparently said his piece.

Phoebe tucked her feet under her on the couch, trying to process this.

A full minute must have passed before Rafe spoke again. "Are you still there?"

"Yes. Sorry. I'm… I don't know what to say."

"That's okay. That's the usual response." Rafe laughed nervously. "I mean, not to *this*. I've never done anything like this before. But to my problem. It's uncomfortable. Anyway, I'm not expecting you to forgive me for how I handled it, and I'm not excusing myself. I just wanted you to know that I didn't go through with it, and that it wasn't intentionally malicious. Just…really goddamn stupid. And I also thought it would be fair to warn you about my problem since the topic is likely to come up in light of the video. Journalists dig up everything."

"Right."

"Okay." Rafe expelled a long breath. "So that's all I wanted to say. Thanks for hearing me out."

"Rafe."

"Yeah."

"Thank you for explaining."

"Yeah."

Phoebe bit her lip, conflicted about whether to ask the question at the forefront of her mind. "There's one thing I need to know."

Rafe let out another long, slow breath. "Yeah."

"This morning… He wasn't part of it? At all?" Her skin flushed with heat at the memory of how he'd touched her. "That was all you?"

A long pause followed before he answered. "Everything I've got, love."

Chapter 15

Rafe sat with his head between his knees after he hung up the phone. What had prompted him to add "love" to that sentence? He'd just told her one of the worst things he ever wanted to have to admit to anyone, especially a woman. Instead of that skin-crawling feeling of revulsion he usually got once someone knew his secret, he wished she were here with him. Which was bad news. Needing anyone was bad news. But falling for a woman whose trust he'd violated in a way there was no coming back from wasn't just bad news. It was completely fucked up.

Unfortunately he had more urgent problems to deal with right now. Hamilton had convinced him it was time to make a public statement. He'd called a press conference for this afternoon in front of the courthouse, and Rafe had to present the right image. For a start, he needed a shower and a shave, and Hamilton was on his way over to coach him and pick out his suit. He just hoped to hell Hamilton knew what he was doing.

Having a suit picked out for him rankled. When Hamilton arrived and rummaged through Rafe's closet, he told the lawyer so in no uncertain terms.

"If you don't mind my saying, Rafael, your judgment

hasn't been the best lately." Hamilton handed him a stuffy, funereal, double-breasted number. "You need to present an image of a grieving son and an embattled, ordinary upstanding citizen. Neither of which you demonstrated with your activities early this morning." It was like his father was still alive.

"I'm aware of the myriad ways in which my judgment this morning was poor. You have no idea."

The look Hamilton gave him was part sympathy, part reproach. "I see you've drawn the curtains on the front windows. That's a good start."

Rafe stepped into the adjacent bathroom to change while they continued talking. "I wasn't expecting anyone to be skulking outside with an extreme telephoto lens. How did they even get inside the gate?"

"I'm guessing someone bribed one of your fine, upstanding neighbors for their code. Luckily, Arizona intrusion tort law is in your favor. The takedown orders for the video apply to the regular news outlets as well as the Reddits and YouTubes, regardless of jurisdiction of the website." Hamilton nodded his approval as Rafe stepped out in the charcoal-gray worsted, and handed him a darker gray tie. "That's exactly the right look. I don't suppose you'd consider trimming the hair?"

Rafe slipped the tie under his collar. "I would not."

"Might have to change your mind on that when this goes to trial. But for today, just slick it back. No tail. That says Colombian drug lord or telenovela star. Neither of which will do you any favors today."

Rafe lifted an eyebrow and grabbed a hair tie from the bureau. "You say 'telenovela' like it's a bad thing."

Carter had texted Phoebe a warning about the press conference. It was like watching video of a train wreck she'd already been in, but she couldn't look away.

She barely recognized Rafe when he stepped up to the podium in a suit that seemed more like something Carter would wear. Yet even in his un-Rafe-like costume, he was intimidatingly stunning. Despite the way things had gone this morning, she couldn't stop thinking about how he'd tasted and smelled, and the warm texture of his skin—and his tongue against the warmth of hers. Follow-through or no follow-through, the sex had been insanely hot. And then there were his parting words on the phone.

Standing in front of him to the left, Carter leaned in to the cluster of mikes on the podium. "My client, Rafael Diamante Junior, and I appreciate you all coming out today to hear his statement on the recent allegations made against him in the press, and on the death of his father, State Senator Rafael Diamante Senior, a longtime beloved member of this community.

"We request you hold any questions until after Mr. Diamante reads from his prepared statement, at which time you may direct them to me. Thank you." He stepped aside and nodded to Rafe, who took a sheet of paper from his pocket and unfolded it on the podium. As he stood staring at it for several seconds without speaking, the crowd went silent enough to hear the repeated whir and click of cameras and camera phones from all directions.

"As you know, my father passed away yesterday at Verde Valley Medical Center." The tempo of the whirs and clicks increased. "Many of you have sent your kind condolences, which I deeply appreciate. This loss could not have come at a more difficult time in my life, when the support of family is so important and its absence so keenly felt. While I'm confident the truth will support my innocence of the charges against me in the death of Barbara Fisher, I would like to address the allegations appearing in the press today with regard to the nature of my business relationship with Ms. Fisher."

Rafe took a breath, looking strained, and Carter whispered something to him before he went on.

"At no time during my dealings with Ms. Fisher was I aware of her secondary business as a private escort. I hired Ms. Fisher for her advertised services as a psychic medium, consulting with her regarding a spiritual matter. Those were the services she provided, and nothing more. I would ask that you respect my privacy during this emotionally difficult time as I cope with both the strain of defending myself against these false charges and the devastating loss of my only remaining family. Thank you."

The silence exploded into a brief cacophony as reporters clamored to get their questions in first, but Carter calmly defused it. "We'll only be answering a few questions since time is limited. Please don't waste it." He nodded to a woman holding her mike in his face.

Despite the mike trained on Carter, the reporter faced Rafe. "Mr. Diamante, was Phoebe Carlisle helping you grieve or consulting with you on a spiritual matter?" She grinned as the crowd erupted into laughter.

Carter was unfazed. "Mr. Diamante will not be answering any questions of a personal nature. Thank you." He nodded to the next reporter.

"Has your client been implicated in the poisoning death of Rafael Diamante Senior?"

"No, he has not. The investigation into the possibly tainted alcohol Senator Diamante ingested is still ongoing, so I can't comment as to the specifics, but my client is not a person of interest in that investigation at this time." Carter pointed to another reporter. "Yes?"

"How do you respond to the allegations that the website hosting Barbara Fisher's adult entertainment web page shows your client accessing it on multiple occasions prior to her murder?"

To Rafe's credit, he showed no outward response to the question.

"I can't comment on any specific allegations pursuant to the case against my client, but Mr. Diamante stands by his claim that he had no knowledge of Ms. Fisher's alleged illegal activities and maintains his innocence of all charges against him in this case."

Several reporters tried for a follow-up question, but one voice rose above the rest. "Mr. Diamante, county records show you were under the care of various mental health professionals from the ages of twelve to seventeen. Can you respond to reports you were being treated for a behavioral disorder?"

Rafe's expression hardened but he kept silent.

Carter leaned toward the mikes. "My client will not be answering any questions of a personal nature."

The man persisted. "I have sources who say your treatment stemmed from ongoing childhood trauma. Was there trouble at home, Mr. Diamante? Did your father abuse you?"

Rafe's face went red with anger. Before Carter could stop him, he stepped forward and grabbed the mike out of the reporter's hand. "That is absolutely false. Who told you that? My father never laid a hand on me in his life."

"Rafael." Carter stepped between them as Rafe pushed the mike back at the reporter. "Thank you, ladies and gentlemen. There will be no more questions."

Phoebe turned off the television, not wanting to hear the commentary that followed—or to see the footage of her sex tape being trotted out again. God. She had a sex tape.

Carter's warning about Rafe's mental health issues took on more significance in light of the reporter's ambush questions. How much of what Rafe had said on the phone this morning could she even believe? She knew nothing about him, really. Not the real Rafe.

The air began to shimmer with the migraine-like aura that presaged the presence of the dead. She was mentally exhausted, but she'd committed to seeing this thing through.

The hesitant approach and the sudden jolting as if she'd come to the end of a people mover without warning had all the earmarks of the shade who'd come to her on the morning Barbara died, but she could tell now it wasn't Barbara. This was the shade who'd tried to speak to her outside the temple, the one who'd led her there.

"I'm not supposed to be here. I only have a moment. I can't get close to him."

"Close to whom? To Rafe?"

"He's not what you think. None of this is what you think."

"Tell me, then. Tell me who you are." The shade stopped communicating abruptly, as if a steel door had slammed down between them. "Matthew?" Phoebe doubled over as something struck her psychic center like a fist plunged through her body, dragging the shade with it. But another was taking its place before she could pause for breath.

"So you're the evocator." The soft Southern accent was as breathless as Phoebe felt.

"Barbara?"

"Geez, you're good. See, I thought I was for real, but it turns out I was a joke. You're the real deal." The shade's energy was jumpy and scattered, as if she were looking over her shoulder on the metaphysical plane, ready to leap out at any moment.

"You're safe here. You can talk to me."

A high-pitched, frightened laugh came out of Phoebe's mouth. "Safe? You have no idea. You saw what they did to Monique, and that was nothing."

The mental leaps were as dizzying as the little physical ones. "To Monique? You mean her client? The cop that beat her up?"

"Wasn't the cop. I mean, he let him in, so maybe it was him, too. But they pay extra for the ride-along."

"Who does?" Phoebe clutched her head as Barbara pulled away sharply and snapped back without stepping out.

"He'll know I was here. I just wanted to warn you." Tears started to flow from Phoebe's eyes, a peculiar sensation when they weren't her own. "You know, you think at least when you're dead, you won't have to worry about working or getting out of the business. It's not fair. But Monique didn't deserve to be dragged into this. You should have left it alone. Maybe it'll stop with her. But just, *please*, let it be, Phoebe Carlisle. You don't understand what you've stumbled into, and we don't need you making it worse."

Phoebe clutched her head as the shade left her. Barbara Fisher was like the worst amusement-park ride ever. Except Phoebe had been the ride. *The ride.* Was that what Barbara had meant by a ride-along? Phoebe had been thinking in terms of a ride in a cop car. But what if she'd meant the shades were the ride-alongs? But who was going along for the ride? The client or the escort?

As Phoebe's equilibrium reset, Barbara's cryptic warning about Monique began to worry her. Monique's deposition in the county's case against her was tomorrow. What if whoever was behind Barbara's murder intended to intimidate Monique into keeping her mouth shut about the truth of what was going on?

She tried Monique's number but got her voice mail after several rings. Maybe Monique was busy with a client and had the ringer off. As Phoebe started to click the screen off, a text message appeared—from Rafe. How's Puddleglum? I forgot to ask.

He's fine, thanks, Phoebe wrote. Sulking about his cat

door being closed, but otherwise okay. She sent the message then typed another. Saw the press conference. How are you?

A pause followed but the message app indicated he was typing. Phoebe was expecting a long reply, but what eventually came was Wrecked.

I'm sorry, she replied. It looked pretty brutal.

Anyone bothering you? A slight pause. Besides me.

Phoebe smiled as she typed back, You're not bothering me. And no. No fallout yet. Just my sisters wanting to know how— She jerked her hand back from the keypad, realizing she'd been about to tell him they'd teased her about how big Rafe's cock was. *So* not appropriate. But the partial sentence had accidentally sent.

To know how…? he texted back after a moment.

Phoebe reddened, glad he couldn't see her face. How I'm doing.

And how are you doing?

She considered the answer. Better than I was this morning.

Yeah?

Yeah. She added a smiley as an afterthought then wondered if that was too much.

Rafe didn't text again. Apparently, it was.

Phoebe's message floated on the screen of his phone like a smiley-shaped life raft. She couldn't have any idea how much that little emoticon meant to him right now. His world was falling apart.

The reporter who'd raised the specter of Rafe's counseling sessions from middle school and high school had put a crack in the dam that held back Rafe's darkest secrets. If records of those private sessions had somehow been made public, the details of what he'd discussed with his counselors soon would be, too. Maybe it was a good thing his father was gone. Because this would have killed him.

Hamilton assured Rafe he was "on it." He'd have an injunction in place by this afternoon to prevent the release of any more privileged information. But, like prehistoric life in *Jurassic Park*, information would find a way.

Unless Rafe did something to put a stop to it himself.

He prepared his altar for a spell to confound, but in the smoke rising from the burning parchment on which he'd written the words, the shape of a coyote seemed to dance—two embers leaping up like glowing eyes and another below them like a laughing tongue—before dissipating with the rest of the ash.

Chapter 16

The following afternoon, there was still no sign of Monique. Phoebe waited downstairs by the entrance to the courthouse as long as she could. She'd warned her client this wasn't optional.

As she gave up and headed inside, a commotion broke out at the security check behind her.

"Ms. Carlisle!"

Stupidly, she turned, and a camera crew began rolling from outside the barrier while smartphones went up all over the place.

"Are you involved in building the defense for your lover, Rafe Diamante?"

Phoebe headed up the stairs, doing her best to ignore the clamoring calls behind her. Hopefully she'd be inside a courtroom before they got through security.

"Do you have anything to say about the death of Monique Hernandez?"

Phoebe stopped short. That couldn't be what she'd heard.

The reporter had managed to clear security and he bounded up the stairs behind her to push his mike in front of her. "I understand you were representing Hernandez in the DA's case against her for possession, solicitation and assault of an officer of the law. Is there a connection between her death and that of fellow call girl Barbara Fisher?"

Phoebe tried to go around him but the traffic on the stairs was at a standstill with people stopping to stare at her and others coming out of the nearby courtrooms to see what was going on. "I'm unaware of the reports of my client's death and I have no comment at this time."

"So she was your client."

Phoebe sighed. "Yes. I'm her court-appointed public defender."

Other reporters who'd made their way in while the first waylaid her were starting to surround her.

"Ms. Carlisle, are you and Rafe Diamante romantically involved or was yesterday morning's house call a one-time thing?"

"Has your boyfriend been named as a suspect in your client's death?"

"Do you work for the same escort service as Fisher and Hernandez?"

A voice carried from the crowd below. "Looked like he was down there a long time. How's his technique?" Laughter followed and Phoebe closed her eyes, trying to take calming breaths.

"Ms. Carlisle won't be answering any more questions." Carter Hamilton's calm, authoritative voice was a welcome relief. "You can all clear out of here or be brought up on charges of contempt from every judge in this courthouse whose sessions you're disrupting right now."

Phoebe opened her eyes as he descended the steps toward her, expertly weaving through the gawkers, and took her by the arm to lead her through the upper corridor into an empty conference room.

He closed the door as she sank into the nearest chair. "Are you all right?"

"Just a little stunned. I was waiting for my client—she was going to be deposed—one of the reporters asked if I had a comment on her death and I just froze." She started to get up. "I should go check to be sure it's true."

"If your client is Monique Hernandez, it's true. I was watching the television in the jury assembly room while waiting for my appointment when they interrupted *Judge Judy* with a special report."

"Murdered?"

"The police haven't released a statement on the cause of death. Just says she was found unresponsive in her apartment."

Barbara Fisher's aimless rambling about Monique came back to her. *Maybe it'll stop with her.* What if her seemingly disjointed words hadn't been aimless? What if Barbara had been warning her Monique was next?

Carter was watching her with a worried look.

"Thanks for rescuing me. I guess I'm going to have to be better prepared for this sort of thing from now on." Phoebe bit her lip, trying to keep from blushing. "Rafe says you got the, um, video taken down, too. I can't thank you enough."

"My pleasure." Carter glanced at his feet with a slight smile that said he'd obviously seen the extended version but had the good grace not to bring it up. "It'll blow over before too long. Every couple of days something new becomes the internet frenzy. Fortunately for you, but not so fortunately for Rafael, I think the serious media players are now more interested in his distant past than in yesterday morning."

Phoebe shook her head. "How did someone get their hands on his juvenile mental health records?"

"I imagine the same way someone got into his gated

community to take that footage. There's always someone willing to bend the law for the right compensation." Carter put his hand into his pocket to silence his phone as it buzzed. "You're going to need some help getting out of here. Feel like getting something to eat?"

"Don't you have an appointment?"

"It looks like the other party's going to be tied up in court for the rest of the day. I was actually heading out after getting a text from him when I saw you."

Phoebe smiled. "Well, in that case, I'd love an escort. But I think we'd draw attention if we tried to eat anywhere together."

"Anywhere public, sure. I was thinking of my hotel suite." Carter smiled. "Strictly a business lunch, of course. Or dinner. I suppose it's getting a little late for lunch."

Dinner en suite didn't sound exactly like strictly business, but it was difficult to take Carter Hamilton as anything but sincere. He had an almost anachronistic gentlemanliness about him.

Phoebe shrugged. "Why not?"

He also had a way of projecting an air people respected, which was useful in getting out to his car without being surrounded by the press again. Reporters still tried to get his and Phoebe's attention, but they stayed back at a respectable distance and took "no comment" for an answer.

"I'll have someone from the hotel bring your car by while we're eating so you can slip out and head home without a fuss whenever you like."

Phoebe nodded and handed over her keys to let him make the arrangements. It was kind of nice to have someone who wanted to do everything for her. He even opened the car door.

Dinner was served on Carter's balcony. The afternoon rain had hit on the drive over, but the balcony was perfectly protected and provided a lovely view of the storm against the ridge of red rocks.

Carter kicked off his shoes while they relaxed inside afterward. "So would it be rude of me to ask you about your ability with the shades? I must admit to being terribly curious."

"Not at all." Phoebe slipped off her own shoes and tucked her feet under her legs. "What do you want to know?"

"Have you always had the ability? Or is it something you sought out?"

"Always." She nodded, taking a sip of her amaro. "My parents thought they were imaginary friends when I was little. I just thought everyone had them."

"So they just came to you? Any shade that happened to be near?"

"No, it was mostly limited to the dead who were similar in age to me. Kids that had drowned or died in accidents. A lot of times they didn't know they were dead or didn't understand what it meant. I was the first person they could find who actually talked to them, so they'd be pretty relieved to have someone listen."

Carter tilted his glass in the light of the fire, admiring the color of the liqueur. "But you don't just listen. I mean, step-ins take over the body, don't they? Speaking through you, taking independent action with your physical frame. That's why the standard doctrine of the Covent is that they're too dangerous. Have you never encountered a shade who wouldn't honor your desires? I mean, has a shade ever taken even temporary control of you?"

"There have been one or two who were extremely strong-willed." She wasn't about to mention her recent experiences—certainly not what had happened with Rafe. "But I can generally reason with them. You just have to be firm about your own intent. They can pick up on an uncon-

scious willingness to do something you might not otherwise do—kind of like alcohol lowering one's inhibitions."
She laughed as she set down her empty glass. "Moderation
is the key, as in so many things in life."

Carter filled her glass again from the crystal decanter.
"Even moderation should only be done in moderation."
He winked and held the drink out to her.

She eyed it dubiously. They'd had spicy lillet as aperi-
tifs before the meal, as well as white wine with dinner. "I
still have to drive home tonight. This might not be much
for someone else, but I'm kind of a lightweight."

"You're welcome to stay here." Carter's expression remained neutral, not revealing whether this was an invitation to something more or just a polite offer to ease her
mind. "There are two beds. No pressure." He set the glass
on the table. "I'll leave it up to your judgment."

Phoebe was starting to feel a little foolish about her hesitation. She laughed at herself and took the drink. "I think
I'm a little rusty at socialization. Sorry if I'm being weird."

"Not at all. It's refreshing." Carter's smile put her at
ease. "And if you're at all uncomfortable with the idea of
staying here, I'd be happy to pay for a cab to get you home.
You can pick up your car tomorrow."

She really was being silly. "Thanks. I appreciate it."
Phoebe smiled and drank the amaro. "And I *am* enjoying
this. I've never had an amaro before."

Carter smiled. "I'm a big fan of taking advantage of
whatever amenities a place has to offer."

"Makes sense to me." The room seemed to sway away
from her a little as she set the glass aside.

He reached for her with concern. "Are you okay?"

"I think that may have been one too many, after all."

"Why don't you lie down on the couch for a bit? You
can take a little nap and then decide if you're up to the

drive home or a cab later." Carter eased her back against the throw pillows propped in front of the arm of the couch.

Phoebe started to tell him she was fine but the pull of the horizontal seemed to override her planned response. "Maybe just for a minute." She closed her eyes, sinking into the comfortable loft of the pillows. Soft, warm fabric drifted over her as Carter covered her with a blanket. "Sorry to be such…lame company."

A moment of disorientation struck when she opened her eyes, unable to remember where she'd gone to sleep. The room didn't look familiar and she couldn't place what time it was. Phoebe sat up in the unfamiliar bed, groggy and nursing a throbbing headache.

"Ah, you've joined the land of the living."

She turned to find Carter Hamilton seated at a desk with a laptop. This was a hotel room. Carter's hotel room.

"How long was I out?" The sound of her own voice in her head made her cringe.

"About fifteen hours."

"*What?* What time is it?"

"A little after one."

Phoebe threw off the covers and realized she was in her bra and underwear.

"Before you ask, you undressed yourself. My chivalrous instinct was to let you continue to sleep in your clothes, but you insisted they'd get wrinkled." Carter smiled. "You were pretty out of it. I had to prod you off the couch around midnight and lead you in here so you wouldn't get a stiff neck."

She'd never gotten so drunk that she'd blacked out before. "I don't know what to say. I'm really embarrassed."

"Don't be. You obviously needed the sleep." He rose and closed his laptop with a nod toward the closet. "I hung up your clothes in there."

Phoebe discovered the clothes weren't just hanging up—they'd been laundered and pressed. Talk about service. She stepped into the bathroom after she'd slipped on the blouse and skirt, taking a few minutes to smooth down her hair with some water and splash some on her face. Her eyes were puffy and red and she looked like she'd been wrestling alligators all night, but she was as decent as she was going to get.

Her phone lay on the table next to the bed. Phoebe clicked the button to see if she'd missed any calls, but it didn't respond. She couldn't remember the last time she'd charged it.

When Phoebe came out, footage of a sheet-draped body being wheeled out of a house appeared on the muted television, a picture of a smiling Monique in the corner of the frame.

Carter nodded at the screen. "They're ruling it a suicide. Looks like she overdosed. Apparently she posted on her Facebook account shortly before she took the pills that there was only 'one way out of this mess' and apologized to her friends and family for disappointing them."

It seemed like a reasonable conclusion. If one didn't consider Barbara's warning.

A car she didn't recognize was parked in her drive when she arrived home. Phoebe parked behind it and got out warily, expecting to be waylaid by reporters or cameras, but there was no sign of anyone hanging around. When she headed up the walk, however, her front door opened. Phoebe's adrenaline spiked until she saw it was Rafe.

Anger replaced the rush of fear. "What the hell are you doing in my house?"

"I've been trying to reach you since yesterday afternoon, but your phone rolls straight to voice mail."

"So you thought you should just break and enter since I wasn't returning your calls?"

"I thought something had happened to you. I came by to check on you—no easy feat sneaking out of Stone Canyon unnoticed, by the way, so you're welcome—and when I saw Puddleglum meowing inside with an empty dish, I climbed in the kitchen window, expecting to find you dead on the floor somewhere."

"Oh, damn. Puddleglum." Phoebe hurried inside past him to find Puddleglum curled up in the papasan chair having a bath and looking quite pleased with himself. And extremely disdainful of her.

"I fed him," said Rafe as he closed the door. "I'm not completely bereft of good judgment."

Phoebe's brow flicked upward at his choice of words. "Thanks for looking out for him. And me."

"So, what happened? I saw footage from the courthouse yesterday on the news. Where have you been?"

"Carter got me out of there and I had dinner at his hotel. I had a little too much to drink so I ended up staying the night." She blushed as she realized how that sounded. "I mean, I was in no condition to drive. I passed out on the couch." Was it her imagination or had Rafe's jaw tightened at the idea of her spending the night with Carter? "Anyway, I guess my phone died."

"Oh." Rafe seemed to realize his posture was contentious and he relaxed his stance with a glance around the room. "Seems like I may have overreacted. I just thought... what with the nagual and the aggressive reporters, I imagined the worst."

Despite the fact that he'd gone a little off the rails, his concern was touching. Extra points for his concern for Puddleglum.

Rafe threaded his fingers through the hair at his crown. "Sorry to hear about your client. I saw on the news this morning it was a suicide. As horrible as that is, after learning about her connection with Barbara Fisher, I was relieved to hear it wasn't murder."

"I'm not so sure it wasn't." Phoebe hadn't meant to tell him about her step-in experience with Barbara, but after everything that had happened, she found herself wanting to tell someone. Maybe if she left out the shade's identity… "I had a visit from a shade yesterday."

Rafe's ears went a little pink. "One of our…friends?"

"No, it was someone who knew Monique Hernandez. The shade said something that made me think Monique may have been manipulated by a step-in into taking her own life. She referred to something called 'ride-alongs.'"

"Ride-alongs?"

"Monique was caught up in some kind of prostitution ring that included cops and government officials. And it sounded like there were step-ins involved."

"Involved?" Rafe frowned. "As in…stepping into the prostitutes?"

"Or the clients. It wasn't clear. The shade was pretty agitated. But I got the impression there was no getting out of the arrangement for the girls—not even through death."

Rafe looked ill. "You mean someone's compelling shades to…?"

"Keep working." Phoebe shuddered. "Yeah. I know. Do you think it could all be part of the same thing? Could the necromancer be behind the ride-alongs?"

"He'd almost have to be, wouldn't he? Unless there's a rash of unaffiliated magical practitioners taking advantage of the dead in Sedona." Rafe rubbed at his stubble. "If Barbara was involved in it, she might have even been working for him. Connecting me with the shades could have been a setup from the start."

"Except Ernesto said they'd come to warn you. That Barbara was a weak evocator."

"He could have been lying." Rafe sighed. "Well, this all gives me food for thought. I've been reading through some journals my father kept, trying to find out about this 'quetzal' power the shades keep mentioning. I haven't come across anything concrete, but there's definitely some family legacy involving the Aztec pantheon. If I could figure out how all this fits together, maybe I'd be able to come up with a motive for the necromancer's actions. And then I'd be one step closer to figuring out who he is and putting a stop to it."

Phoebe nodded, though putting a stop to the necromancer's enterprise was starting to seem like an extremely ambitious goal. Her head began to throb again. From Rafe's reaction, it must have been obvious in her expression.

"I should get going before the reporters catch on to my ruse." He pulled a cable company cap out of his back pocket and put it on, tugging his ponytail through the loop at the back. Rafe stepped into the entryway and turned toward the door. "Sorry about the misunderstanding. And the breaking and entering." He gave her a contrite grin. "Charge your phone."

Phoebe smiled. "Yeah, I'll do that." She walked him to the door, conscious of the unspoken awkwardness still between them surrounding his transgression with Jacob and the admission he'd made to her afterward. "Rafe."

He paused on the gravel walkway and looked back. There was something absurdly endearing about that cap.

"I can't tell you for certain how I would have reacted if you'd been honest with me the other night, and I guess we'll never know." She leaned against the door frame, holding the screen door closed to make sure Puddleglum didn't try to make a dash for it. "But I can tell you—knowing what I know now—it wouldn't be a deal-breaker for me."

Rafe's forehead wrinkled, maybe from squinting at the sunlight hitting him directly as the shadows from the house began to narrow on the path, or maybe because he couldn't make out what Phoebe was trying to say.

She stood on one foot, scratching the back of her calf with the toe of her sandal. "I mean, it *isn't* a deal-breaker. In case you were wondering."

His eyes widened, despite the glare of the sun. "Oh." Rafe gave her a tentative smile. "Well, that's…definitely more food for thought."

"Any other undisclosed involvement with shades, on the other hand, is a definite deal-breaker." She wanted to make sure he knew he wasn't off the hook.

The smile faded and he nodded soberly. "Right. You have my word."

"Okay. Well…just wanted to put that out there. Talk to you later." Phoebe closed the door and leaned back against it, her face flushing with heat as she realized she'd essentially just propositioned Rafe Diamante. On the other hand, he hadn't seemed to mind.

Chapter 17

When Phoebe's phone had charged up enough to restart, she found three messages from Rafe, along with half a dozen texts expressing increasing concern. She smiled as she read through them. It was kind of nice to have someone worry about her. The Public Defender's Office had also left an urgent message asking her to call in. Her head was still fuzzy, but she had the sinking feeling she'd missed a consultation with a client or a meeting with a prosecutor. Or worse, a court date.

She called and got Sylvia, the receptionist. "Hey, Syl. It's Phoebe Carlisle. I got a message—"

"Hang on." That didn't bode well. Sylvia was normally a sweetheart. The hold music came on for a minute before Sylvia clicked back onto the line. "Mr. Arbogast wants to speak with you. I'll connect you." The hangover headache started to throb.

"Ms. Carlisle." That *really* did not bode well. They were usually on a first-name basis.

Phoebe decided to pretend she didn't notice. "Hi, Bob. My phone's been on the fritz and I just got it charged up. Anything wrong?"

"I would have preferred to talk about this in person, but that's actually the heart of the matter."

Phoebe swallowed. "The heart of what matter?"

"You've become a distraction at the courthouse. I'm not making any judgments about your personal life, but when it begins to affect this office, that's a problem."

"I understand things have been awkward." Phoebe rolled her eyes at the understatement. "I can't apologize enough. But I can promise you I'm taking every precaution to make sure I don't find myself in a position for the media to take further advantage. I think if we just give it a few days—"

"There have also been some questions about potential conflicts of interest."

Phoebe's stomach did a nauseating flip.

"I'm sure you're right and this will blow over, but in light of the allegations, I'm afraid I'm going to have to reassign your outstanding cases until further notice." Arbogast sighed. "You're a good attorney, Phoebe. I'd hate to see something like this damage your career. But I'm obligated to act in the best interests of the Public Defender's Office and in our clients' best interests."

Tears were prickling behind her eyes and Phoebe shook them away in irritation. He'd taken her under his wing when she'd first started, and she felt like she was disappointing her own father. "I understand."

"I hope so, Ms. Carlisle." Things had gotten formal again. "I really hope you can resolve your…publicity issues."

She sank into the couch as she tossed the phone back onto the table to finish charging. Fabulous. Because who needed to pay a mortgage or eat? Maybe it was time to hang out her shingle as a medium. There was an opening in Sedona, after all.

Phoebe sighed. She was still wearing yesterday's clothes, and the weather had been sticky lately, not to mention she'd been nervous-sweating when the cameras had converged on her at the courthouse. She headed for the shower, undressing as she went, but paused before the mirror as she slipped off her bra. There was a reddish mark on her right breast that almost looked like a hickey. Her skin went clammy and she was shaking as she finished undressing. There was nothing else, no bruises, no reason to think anything sinister about the mark. She'd probably caught her skin in the strap of the bra at some point and just hadn't noticed because her senses had been dulled with drink.

But she couldn't shake the feeling that something else had happened last night. Surely, Carter would have said something if things had gotten physical between them. Could she have had that much to drink that she wouldn't remember?

She huddled under the shower with the temperature almost scalding. She'd had an experience in college with a friend—or someone she'd thought was a friend—slipping something into her drink at a party. Her roommate had walked in on Phoebe's "friend" undressing her while she lay unconscious on her bunk and had booted his ass from the dormitory permanently. Phoebe had been lucky nothing worse had happened, but the feeling of violation had stuck with her for a long time afterward. She was feeling that now.

She had no real proof anything had happened, only the gut feeling. And whatever might have happened, she was sure she hadn't been raped—at least not in the textbook definition of the term. But she had a growing conviction Carter Hamilton had lured her to his hotel with less than altruistic motives and had either gotten her drunk on purpose or given her something in her drink to knock her out.

And she was certain now she hadn't undressed herself and crawled into bed on her own.

No amount of scalding water was going to make that feeling go away.

She considered as she dressed whether she ought to confront Carter, but she knew how that would go. Her college "friend" had denied everything when she'd confronted him, even to her roommate's face, despite the fact that the roommate had caught him in the act. Men like that were pathological, able to convince themselves they had a right to women's bodies, especially women they deemed "stupid enough" to lower their inhibitions in their presence—stupid enough to trust them, in other words—and those they felt owed them something by virtue of having gone on a date with them, or having gone to their room, home…or hotel.

After realizing she'd been staring at nothing for several minutes, seated on the edge of her bed, Phoebe picked up her phone, fully charged now, and thought about calling one of the twins. But it wasn't fair to dump something like this on them. It would only make them worry when there was nothing they could do about it.

But she could talk to Rafe.

His last message was still open in the app, his concern for her evident. But Carter was his lawyer. And from everything she'd heard, he was an excellent one. Phoebe couldn't risk damaging that relationship when Rafe's life might hang in the balance. She clicked the messaging app shut.

Rafe had a nagging feeling Phoebe wasn't telling him the whole truth about spending the night at Hamilton's hotel, but he hadn't expected the visceral reaction the suspicion prompted. His heart thudded in his chest like he was in a physical fight, his gut tightening and his fists clenching.

It even seemed to set the tattoo off. He hadn't felt the ink moving for the past day or two, but it was undulating through his skin right now. Rafe had the distinct impression the serpent itself—or dragon, as the compendium called it—was riled with jealousy. On the other hand, it was entirely possible Rafe was losing his mind. The fact that he was beginning to think of his own tattoo as a separate entity wasn't exactly a healthy sign.

But he also couldn't stop thinking about the necromancer's nagual outside Phoebe's house. She wasn't safe. He knew that with certainty. And it was because of him. So he was going to have to do something about it.

Mindful of the intrusion of the coyote's image into his last spell-casting, Rafe was careful not to mention Tezcatlipoca this time. He invoked Quetzalcoatl and immediately felt the power of the quetzal moving through his ink. Using a figure of Xochiquetzal, goddess of female sexuality, as his centerpiece on the altar to represent Phoebe, he cast a spell of protection around her.

"Surround her, O Quetzalcoatl, O Ehecatl, with your enveloping wind, keeping all harm from her." As he spoke the name of the wind-god aspect of Quetzalcoatl, the wind outside picked up once again, rattling the French doors that opened onto the garden. Whether this was resistance from the necromancer or just a coincidence, he doubled his efforts, adding a symbolic blood sacrifice as he had the time the tattoo first became activated.

His spine began to tingle as he squeezed the blood into the censer, the prickling sensation spreading outward to his shoulders as if Quetzalcoatl were spreading his wings. With a sudden bang, the garden doors flew open, the brisk monsoon wind whipping through the room and making the candles on the altar sputter. It lifted Rafe's hair—he always wore it down for ritual—and then an odd sensation followed in the tattooed skin on his back, as if the wind were drawing the ink out of him. The sky lit up with a multi-branched fork of lightning. With the nearly simultaneous thunderclap, Rafe hit the floor, dazed, as though the current had traveled through the ground into the room and he'd conducted it out.

The sound of beating wings overhead made him roll swiftly onto his back and he watched in disbelief as a massive crow flew out of his room and into the storm. As soon as the crow took flight, he knew what it was and what had happened. Rafe got up and went to the mirror, turning to look over his shoulder. The tattoo was gone.

In his mind's eye, a sort of picture-in-picture display of the crow's-eye view was visible as it flew south—not constant, as if he were flying himself, but as if the nagual were periodically checking in with him, keeping him apprised of what it saw. Because there was only one explanation for what was happening here—Rafe had released his own nagual.

While a refreshing wind flowed through his room and against his bare skin, Rafe sat on the bed and watched the crow arrive at Phoebe's house, seeing through its eyes as the crow alighted on the palo verde tree in the yard. Phoebe crossed in front of the window wearing a short, silk kimono, her bare legs reminding him of how they'd felt wrapped around his hips.

Before he could let that train of thought get out of hand, one eye of the nagual focused on the road as movement caught it. Just a slight flutter of what could have been only the buffalo grass, but which Rafe—or the nagual—instinctively knew was Coyote hiding within it. "Crow" imparted this to Rafe through a kind of instant telepathic understanding, as though both naguals were the avatars of legend.

Coyote saw Crow, the yellow eyes revealing naked animosity instead of the amusement Coyote had viewed Rafe with during his recent encounters. Crow's presence meant Rafe's quetzal was awake and aware, and Coyote wasn't pleased.

Coyote paced along the perimeter of Phoebe's property. Perhaps that was also part of his displeasure. It seemed Rafe's protection spell was working and Coyote couldn't cross the imaginary boundary Rafe had envisioned around Phoebe's house.

Crow fluffed its feathers as the clouds broke overhead and rain began to fall, its other eye trained on Phoebe. The water obscured her somewhat through the pane, like a watercolor filter in a photo-editing program. Her hair was tied up in that bouncy ponytail again, fresh from the shower, and Rafe could imagine the smell of her shampoo and body wash. He was, as his mother would have put it, thoroughly smitten. But the thought of his mother depressed him and he wished he hadn't gone there.

His mother's infidelity was inextricably linked with Rafe's trust issues. Not simply because she'd been unfaithful to his father, but because of whom she'd been unfaithful with. The usual rage accompanied this line of thinking. How could she have not known what kind of a piece-of-shit, dirt-bag loser Ford was? And that putting her son in close proximity with him just to facilitate her own affair would damage Rafe irrevocably? How could she not have seen?

The flood of angry emotion and adrenaline had drawn his consciousness away from Crow and he could no longer see Phoebe. Rafe leaped from the bed and paced, as Coyote had, fists clenched at his sides. He came up short before the mirror and it took everything in him not to smash his fist into the glass. Irrational bursts of anger, his school therapist had told him all those years ago, were hallmarks of PTSD.

Rafe had been getting in trouble at school for starting fights. Teachers, and his father, thought it was because of his mother's recent death—the overdose of her bipolar meds ruled accidental because no one wanted to damage Rafael Diamante Sr.'s reputation. And there was certainly that in it—anger at his mother for dying. And for screwing around on his dad. But the school-assigned therapist had managed to discern that Rafe's anger had a deeper, more personal, source.

The candles on his altar went out in a gust of wind and Rafe shook himself. He'd left Phoebe vulnerable. The circle he'd cast hadn't been properly opened. He closed his eyes and tried to reconnect with the nagual. The images from it were hazy and jumbled. Someone was yelling. *Phoebe.*

With a kind of heavy, mental thud, Rafe was back, viewing the world through Crow's eyes. Coyote was attacking him and Crow screeched as the other nagual whipped him about by the left wing, going in for the kill at his throat.

The yelling he'd heard turned into screaming and Phoebe ran at them through the rain, wielding a broom. "Let go of him, you bastard! Get the hell off my lawn!" She swung and hit Coyote in the rump and Coyote let go of Crow and turned and snarled at her.

Rafe's consciousness began to overwhelm the primal instincts of the crow—or to merge with them, perhaps— and he lunged at the coyote. Only crows didn't lunge, exactly. The crow flapped its wings, screeching furiously, and then Rafe was stumbling on his two feet in the mud, an odd, howling yell coming out of his mouth as he went for the coyote, instinct telling him to tear it apart.

"Oh, my God." Phoebe gaped at him and Rafe real-

ized he was naked—and human—and standing in Phoebe's yard threatening a coyote. The animal bolted into the
darkness and Rafe slipped and landed on his ass.

Chapter 18

There were worse things Phoebe could think of to find in her front yard than a stark-naked Rafe Diamante. Though how the hell he'd gotten there she couldn't begin to understand.

As she'd helped him up and into the house, he'd given her some excuse about the necromancer casting illusions that was obviously nonsense. One minute, the coyote had been attacking a defenseless bird. The next, Rafe had been barreling across her yard in its place, naked and howling like an Aztec warrior. That had been no illusion.

He was in her shower now, washing off the mud, while Phoebe tried to find him something to wear. Spare men's clothing wasn't exactly a thing she kept around. When he came out of the bathroom wrapped in a towel, she handed him a pair of roomy stretch-cotton pajama bottoms and an extra-large T-shirt she sometimes wore to sleep in. He looked askance at the pink-and-white-striped bottoms.

"Sorry." Phoebe shrugged. "That's the only thing I've got that might fit you."

"Well, this should be interesting."

Phoebe couldn't suppress a little smirk when he'd dressed

and emerged from the bathroom. The pajama bottoms came midway down his shins and hugged his body snugly, leaving nothing to the imagination, and the faded red T-shirt stretched across his abs left the little trail of hair below his navel visible.

Rafe rolled his eyes. "I look like the gay Hulk."

"Now why hasn't anybody done that?" Phoebe grinned. "That would be an awesome idea for a comic."

"But would it be gay Bruce Banner or would straight Bruce Banner just suddenly hulk out in style?"

"Tough call. Except he'd be wearing the pants beforehand, of course. The real question is would his skin be green or something more fabulous?" She folded her arms across her damp bathrobe and flicked her eyebrows. "So. Would you like to tell me what's really going on?"

Rafe sighed. "I was working a protection spell for you because I was worried about the necromancer's nagual— with good reason, as it turns out—and I…seem to have activated my own."

"Your own…what?"

"Nagual. The crow—it emerged from the ink and separated from me. The tattoo was gone." He turned and tugged up the back of his borrowed shirt, revealing the colorful serpent. "It's back now, I assume."

Phoebe nodded. "Right where it's supposed to be. But why a crow? Why not the feathered serpent?"

"Maybe because its intent was to go unnoticed? A flying, feathered snake would definitely draw attention." Rafe let the shirt slide back down over the smooth, strong muscles of his back. "I don't really know why a crow, except they're sometimes associated with Quetzalcoatl. Maybe I chose it unconsciously."

"To do what?"

That telltale pink appeared at the tips of his ears. "To watch over you, I guess. I didn't expect that to happen literally, but it turned out I could see through the crow's eyes, like a sort of running background image in my head." He nodded toward the living room window. "You should close those curtains, by the way. Maybe all your curtains."

With a frown, Phoebe stepped into the living room and drew the drapes, reaching up on tiptoe to pull them tight at the top. When she turned around, Rafe's Hulk pants were noticeably tighter at the crotch.

She cast her eyes deliberately toward the bulge and back to his face. "Well, thank you very much. It's nice to be appreciated."

Rafe glanced down with his hands on his hips. "Jesus. Sorry. Your robe is all damp and clingy, and when you were up on your toes—" He swallowed. "I should probably go."

Phoebe couldn't help but burst out laughing. "What, are you going to walk all the way to Stone Canyon like that?"

Rafe grinned. "I'm pretty sure it won't be like *this*—" he copied her downward eye graze "—for more than the first mile. Two miles, tops."

"Wow, two miles? I'm impressed. You did seem to have some serious stamina the other night." Phoebe gave him a sideways look. "It does beg a certain question in my mind, but I'm not sure if it's rude to ask."

Rafe lifted an eyebrow. "Ask away."

"In the relationships you've had before…" Phoebe bit her lip. "It was actually a problem for these women…that you…had such staying power?"

To her relief, Rafe laughed good-naturedly. "As much as I'd like to claim superhuman powers in that department, I have to attribute a fair amount of my "staying power" that night to just how much I'm attracted to you. Which is a significant amount, as I think is pretty obvious by now." His grin broadened. "But the experiences I've had with other women were, to put it mildly, extremely frustrating. For both of us."

Phoebe wanted to kick herself. Of course they were. "I'm sorry. That was insensitive of me, just thinking in terms of my own pleasure."

Rafe cocked his head, reminding her of the crow. "Are you? I mean—thinking of it?"

She laughed, brushing her hands up her forearms into her sleeves. "Uh, yeah. Definitely thinking of it. Really kind of hard to think of anything else at the moment."

Rafe's smile was still quizzical. "When you said my problem wasn't a deal-breaker, I kind of thought you meant…sometime in the future, maybe. If I were to somehow manage to redeem myself."

Phoebe smiled. "I think materializing in my yard to save me from an evil coyote spirit ranks right up there in the redeeming-yourself department. And the gay Hulk pants really clinch the deal." Rafe laughed again, but he still had the uncertain look on his face. "Anyway, I don't mean to put pressure on you. I'm just trying to subtly, maybe not so subtly, suggest you stay here tonight. We can just talk. Maybe watch *The Hulk*." She winked and his smile broadened.

"That would be nice." Rafe folded his arms, leaning against the support beam between the hallway and the living room. After a brief moment his arms unfolded once more and he straightened. "Wait. Are you saying you own a copy of *The Hulk*?"

Phoebe laughed. "Yes."

"As in *The Incredible Hulk* with Edward Norton? Or the Eric Bana version?"

"Both, actually. I have all the Avengers movies. I also have the complete Bill Bixby series."

"Oh, my God. I might have to marry you, Phoebe Carlisle." It was clearly a joke, but her heart did a little flip-flop just the same. She gave him a wry smile. "Let's just start with dinner and a movie and see where it goes from there."

True to her word, after ordering a pizza, Phoebe broke out *The Incredible Hulk*. Rafe had never spent such a relaxed evening with a woman before. Every date he'd ever been on had been fraught with tension. Knowing the evening would inevitably end in awkwardness if he didn't make a move, or disappointment and frustration if he did, made it hard to just be himself with a woman.

With Phoebe, the awkwardness was already out of the way. And instead of setting up in the living room, she'd grabbed the pizza and the movie and headed straight to the bedroom to watch and eat from bed. No transition from one room to the other necessary to signal something was expected to happen. They were just two friends hanging out. If something happened, great. But if it didn't, he felt completely at ease that she'd be fine with it.

Before the movie was halfway through, however, it was obvious Option A was in play. Still wearing the silky robe, Phoebe had snuggled up against him with Rafe spooned around her—while Puddleglum surreptitiously made off with her pizza crust—and Rafe had become unbearably distracted by the scent of her hair.

He leaned in close to breathe it in and placed his lips against the side of her neck.

"Hey. Blonsky's about to turn into the Abomination and go on a rampage." The shiver as she moved her head to the side gave the lie to her casual tone.

"Spoiler alert," he murmured, kissing lower on her neck. "Hulk defeats him. Almost kills him. Betty stops him. And finds him better pants than the ones you gave me."

Phoebe chuckled as he moved down the slope of her neck. "Well, damn. I guess we can just turn it off then."

"Guess we can," Rafe agreed, reaching around her for the remote and taking matters into his own hands.

Tossing the remote aside, he slid her robe from one shoulder, his cock growing hard as the tip of her breast was exposed. He tilted her head back against his shoulder and leaned over her to taste it, and Phoebe moaned appreciatively.

While he sucked the hard nipple into his mouth, Phoebe loosened her robe at her thighs and teased herself open with her fingertips. If not for his problem, Rafe might have come right then. It was incredibly hot watching her fingers dip between the blush of her sex—shaved since last time, he noticed, though she'd left a neatly trimmed bush above—and disappear inside her, reemerging glistening and sticky before they dipped again.

Phoebe reclined against him. "Can I ask you another personal question?"

Rafe pulled his mouth away from her breast with a slick pop, cupping the breast in his hand and strafing the damp nipple with his thumb. "You can ask. But you may not get an answer. I'm kinda preoccupied."

Phoebe rubbed a wet finger against her clit, eliciting an involuntary groan from him. "Can you…follow through… manually?" Ah, the million-dollar question.

Rafe slid his hand over hers to intertwine their fingers so he could feel exactly how she liked to stroke herself. "When I'm alone, sure. Unfortunately it's not a magic fix for the problem of finishing something I've started with someone else."

"No, of course not." Phoebe guided his middle finger with hers into the slick heat inside her for a moment with a sweet little noise of pleasure before pulling him out. Rafe loosened the tie on the Hulk pants with his other hand to give himself some air. "I was just thinking maybe we could both take care of ourselves. Together. But I'm okay with whatever you want to do. Or not do. Seriously. No pressure."

Rafe paused in drawing his damp finger over her thigh. "Together? You mean…like next to each other? At the same time?"

She tilted her head back and glanced up at him with a soft, self-conscious laugh. "Is that a stupid idea? Should I just shut up?"

He couldn't help but turn her head toward him for a smothering kiss before answering. "Not a stupid idea at all. You're amazing."

Phoebe laughed again with the same soft, sexy self-deprecation. "Or maybe I'm just horny. But I think it would be fun." She turned around and came up onto her knees, straddling his thighs—which were broad enough with his legs stretched on the bed that her own thighs were generously spread, giving him a fantastic view. And that one exposed breast was almost hotter than if she were naked. "Like this? Will this work?"

Rafe released himself from the Hulk pants with a groan, stroking almost unconsciously as he looked up at her. "God, yes." He wasn't even concentrating on his own stimulation as he watched her spread herself open, two fingers slowly penetrating. She pinched her nipple with her other hand, rocking into her strokes and making whimpering noises as her eyes closed.

He stroked himself with vigor as he watched Phoebe gyrate into her hand, pumping faster, the slick sound of her fingers and the breathless rhythm of her little moans making him harder. She seemed to be balanced so precariously as her excitement built that he reached out with his free hand and cupped her ass to steady her, letting his fingertips curl into the cleft.

That seemed to push her over the edge. Phoebe let out an almost-surprised little cry as she clenched her knees against his thighs, followed by a rapid succession of little gasps in a rising pitch, her fingers deeply buried, until at last she let out something between a sigh and a wail and let her weight sink back into his hand.

She opened her eyes, bright with pleasure, and Rafe's unconscious, rapid stroking became incredibly conscious. The usual anxious feeling seized his gut and he moved his hand away, rubbing the back of it across the sweat at his forehead in a nervous gesture.

Phoebe sat back on her heels as he let go of her. "Oh, God. I'm sorry, Rafe."

"Don't be sorry. That was incredibly hot."

"But I shouldn't have pressured you."

"You didn't pressure me." Rafe tried to put himself back together nonchalantly. "It was a great idea. It's just…not going to work out."

Phoebe pulled her robe up over her shoulder and swung one leg off his lap, leaning on her hip beside him. "Us, you mean?"

"Well, *this*, anyway." Rafe made a vague gesture at the still uncomfortably prominent bulge in the pink-striped pants. "This" usually meant "us" eventually. And judging by the other night, *this* was something Phoebe particularly enjoyed. And who didn't? Except him.

Phoebe studied him. Probably trying to figure out how broken he was. Wondering if he was a fixer-upper. "I don't mind watching movies." She gave him a saucy smirk. "Even if you spoil them from time to time."

Rafe laughed. "I did pretty much start it, didn't I? I seem to get a little out of control around you, Phoebe Carlisle. I'm the one who should apologize."

Phoebe rolled her eyes and curled up next to him again, grabbing his arm to wrap it around her as she tucked herself under it. "Hey, I asked you to stay the night, and kept walking around in my tiny robe when I could have gotten dressed." She grinned as his mouth dropped open in mock surprise. "Let's both not be sorry. Like I said, it's not a deal-breaker."

He drew her close, amazed she wasn't sending him packing.

Phoebe played with the hair on his arm. "Is there…anything you need me to do? Anything you need to go…do?"

Rafe chuckled. "No, I'm good. Falling asleep with you is all I need right now."

She glanced up again, searching his eyes. "You sure? Don't feel like you have to be stoic about it."

"I'm sure." Rafe smiled and held up his hand in the three-fingered Boy Scout salute. "Scout's honor." He kissed her before she could protest further.

As Phoebe closed her eyes and snuggled against him, Puddleglum hopped onto the bed and wedged himself between their legs.

Rafe grinned at the domestic picture, the grin widening at the sight of Phoebe's robe slipping open again to bare her breast. Domestic with a touch of soft porn. But the grin faded as he noticed something on the pale swell above her nipple. She had a love bite. And Rafe sure as hell hadn't given it to her.

Chapter 19

Rafe was distant in the morning, as if he'd lain awake thinking better of the previous evening. Phoebe offered to drive him home but Rafe, already up and showered before she'd woken, had called Carter Hamilton to get the spare keys from his father's place so he could get back into the house.

"We could just meet him there." She didn't particularly want Carter anywhere near her house after whatever had happened at his hotel. Not that she wanted to see him at all, but a minute or two through a car window would be better than here.

Rafe stood leaning back against the breakfast bar with his arms folded. "I need to talk to him, anyway, about my father's funeral arrangements."

A twinge of guilt twisted in her side. With everything that had happened, she'd forgotten he was dealing with the loss of his father.

"Besides, I have a feeling he knows his way around your neighborhood pretty well by now."

It took her a moment to process the last part. What was

that supposed to mean? Phoebe opened her mouth to ask but Carter's horn sounded on the drive.

Rafe pushed himself away from the bar. "Don't forget to keep your curtains closed and your doors locked. I did a little protection spell work around the perimeter this morning to keep the necromancer out, but I'm not sure it'll hold against nosy reporters." He moved toward the door but turned back as if trying to decide on the right protocol for almost-sex on an almost-date. "Thanks for putting up with me last night." He leaned down and gave her a chaste kiss. "Sorry if it was a little disappointing."

"It was *not* disappointing. I like having you here. And I like sleeping with you. Just sleeping. It's nice. Anything else is just a bonus."

A half smile formed on his lips as if it had surprised him. "Well, anyway…thanks." He turned to go and Phoebe followed him to the door.

"Rafe." She latched the screen after he stepped out, studying his face through the mesh as he turned back. "Is something wrong?"

The corner of his mouth twitched, but not with a smile. "Why would anything be wrong?"

"I don't know. I feel like I've done something to upset you. I thought we were good last night when we went to sleep."

This time he did smile, though it seemed forced. "You didn't do anything wrong. It's just…me. Figuring out some things."

Carter gave Phoebe a friendly wave from the car as Rafe climbed into it. Not wanting to alert Rafe that anything was weird between her and his lawyer, she returned the greeting before stepping back and closing the door on a full-body shudder of revulsion.

* * *

"Nice pants." Hamilton gave him a sideways smirk as he backed down the drive. "When you said you'd lost your keys, I didn't realize you'd also lost the pants they were in."

"They're in Phoebe's laundry." Let him think whatever he wanted to about that.

Hamilton eyed him sidelong as he turned onto the street. "I'm not sure it's wise to be continuing a physical relationship with Phoebe Carlisle after the publicity you've already gotten. Despite its irrelevance to the law, you're being tried in the court of public opinion, and your actions are giving the impression of a man who isn't terribly concerned about the dead body he was recently found with. Or the death of his father."

Rafe suppressed a snarl. "Why don't you let me worry about my public image?"

"Part of my job, Rafael, is managing your public image. You're paying me quite a bit for my advice, so I suggest you take it. And you might want to give a thought to Ms. Carlisle's public image while you're at it."

He couldn't help the sharp laugh that escaped him. "Right. Like you were doing when you drove her from the courthouse straight to your hotel room."

Hamilton was quiet for a moment, concentrating on the road until he came to a red light. "So Phoebe told you about what happened."

"She didn't elaborate. But she didn't have to. It was fairly obvious."

Hamilton sighed. "Not that I have to explain myself to you—any more than Phoebe does—but I offered her a ride because the encounter at the courthouse had shaken her up and the reporters were mobbing her. They would have followed her home, so I offered to let her hide out in my suite for the afternoon and have a bite to eat. I didn't expect her to spend the night, but things happen. In retrospect, I should have insisted she take a cab home after she had a little too much to drink with dinner, but she's a very attractive, persuasive woman. As you've no doubt noticed."

Rafe's fingers dug into the fabric of the seat as he tried to ignore the impulse to punch his lawyer in his smug face.

"At any rate, I, at least, made an effort to be discreet. You, on the other hand, seem bent on drawing attention to both yourself and Phoebe." Hamilton threw a sideways glance at the pajama pants. "As your lawyer, I'm asking you to think about what effect that may have on your reputation. And if not yours, then at least hers."

"I think Phoebe has demonstrated she's perfectly capable of handling her own reputation."

"Then I take it she didn't mention her involvement with you has cost her her job."

Rafe turned to look him in the eye. "What?"

"She's been suspended from the Public Defender's Office while they investigate any possible conflicts of interest or misconduct."

"You're shitting me."

Hamilton smiled his best lawyerly smile. "I assure you, Rafael, I would never 'shit' you."

When Phoebe didn't hear from Rafe over the weekend, she tried not to let it get to her. He had a lot on his plate, to say the least. But there was one thing she could take off it. Or try to, anyway. Unfortunately she'd have to ask Ione for help, because waiting around for one of the shades to make another visit on their own was too unpredictable, and potentially doing a shade-summoning spell wrong wasn't a risk she wanted to take.

It also wasn't the kind of thing she could just call up Ione and ask for, like Mom's recipe for lasagna. Phoebe would have to see her in person. Which meant, of all things, a visit to the Chapel of the Holy Cross.

Phoebe hadn't been near a church in years, but Ione insisted on going to the Taizé prayer service every Monday evening at five—meditative prayer in chanting and song. She always arrived half an hour early to sit and pray by herself, as if she could somehow be absolved of practicing witchcraft by being devout enough. It was absurd. Phoebe had long ago accepted that the church didn't want her. She no longer belonged. And she hadn't missed it. But Ione couldn't let go of who she once was—who she thought she still ought to be. Maybe because she'd been closer to their parents, it was harder to walk away from the church they'd raised her in before her "sinful nature" had become apparent.

Phoebe might have avoided the whole chapel scene by calling Ione and asking her to meet, but it wasn't a conversation she wanted to have over the phone. Ione would manage to talk her out of it, or refuse to help and cut off the conversation, like she always did. She couldn't afford to play Ione's control games right now.

At least the drive up Chapel Road was worth taking regardless of the destination. And the chapel itself was stunning, built into the hillside of the red rock formations, with the center post of a great cross that formed the frame of the building and divided the towering windows tucked between two buttes. Phoebe had never been a spiritual person, even when she'd believed, but it was hard not to feel a little tingle of something unexplainable in the face of the natural and architectural beauty.

As she drove up the winding hill to the parking lot, Phoebe wondered if she should have called, after all. Ione wasn't going to appreciate the interruption of her weekly absolution ritual, particularly to discuss not just spell work inside the church, but the kind of spell work Ione would never approve of. But by the time she'd parked and started the trek up the hill, it was too late to come up with a better plan.

She found Ione sitting in the back row of pews, just where she'd left her the last time she'd been to services at the parish church—right after their parents' funeral. Ione had been forced to interrupt her freshman year at Berkeley to come home and become legal guardian to her sisters. She'd taken Phoebe out of private school—with their parents gone, there hadn't been money—but she'd tried to insist Phoebe return to church as if nothing had changed. As if Phoebe hadn't been essentially excommunicated for communing with spirits by the time she was thirteen. She was an abomination. And Ione never hesitated to make it clear she thought so, too—on both a spiritual and spiritualist level.

Phoebe had never attended the Taizé prayer service, though she'd been to the chapel before when services weren't being held. And what the chapel had in abundance was peaceful quiet—and shades. She had to be careful not to let any get too close. They didn't generally come here looking for someone like her to communicate through— she supposed they were attracted by the same things the living came for—but if they recognized her as an open portal, some might be tempted to make contact, and she couldn't afford to indulge any step-ins within a church.

Head bowed and eyes closed, Ione didn't look up when Phoebe sat beside her on the rustic bench. But after a moment, sensing Phoebe watching her, she raised her head.

Her eyes widened. "Phoebe? What are you doing here? Is something wrong?"

Phoebe had to work not to laugh. It was a fair question. "No, not wrong, exactly. I just need to ask you for a favor, and it isn't something I wanted to ask over the phone."

Ione stiffened. "Okay. What do you need?"

Phoebe kept her voice low. "I need the summoning spell. The one the Covent uses to call shades before they give them the bum's rush." Maybe she could have worded that a little more nicely. Maybe she didn't care.

Ione's gaze darted around the peaceful chapel. "Are you out of your mind? You came here to ask me for that? I had no idea you hated me this much."

"Jesus, Ione." When the poor choice of exclamation made Ione cringe, Phoebe lowered her voice even more. "Don't be melodramatic. I don't hate you. I didn't come here to ruin anything for you. I just need your help, and I knew if I asked you on the phone you'd put me off."

"So you ambushed me here—at my place of worship."

"It's not an ambush." Maybe it was kind of an ambush. Phoebe chewed on her bottom lip. "Okay, maybe this wasn't such a good idea. Can we talk outside at least?"

"We don't have anything to talk about, Phoebe. You've made it perfectly clear you have no respect for my beliefs—in God or anything else. And you have the audacity to come here to demand my help in doing something that goes against both."

"It's your spell," Phoebe hissed under her breath. "How does it go against your beliefs? I'm not asking you to participate in a step-in. I just need you to help me reach a shade so I can help Rafe. You're the one who told me to help him, or had you forgotten?"

"I told you to work with him, for his own sake, because he was obviously going to do it anyway. Just like you do." Ione scowled, managing to look uncannily like their mother. "And he knows how to do what you're asking, so why are you asking me?"

"He has a lot to deal with right now. I thought if I could make some progress on this particular problem on my own, it would give him a chance to focus on…other things."

"What other things? You?"

Phoebe resisted the urge to smack her. "No, not me. But thank you for thinking I'm that shallow." She ignored the little voice in the back of her head trying to point out it would certainly be a side bonus. "His father's estate, for one. The reporters hounding him, for another. It was a media circus without me, but I haven't helped any."

Ione's look softened. "I heard about what happened at the courthouse." She glanced at the front of the chapel then back toward the doors before straightening with a sigh. "We only have a few minutes before the service. Let's go outside and I'll walk you through it."

Phoebe hadn't expected such swift capitulation. She followed Ione out to a secluded spot on the edge of the paved drive. "Not that I don't appreciate this, but why the sudden change of heart?"

Ione pursed her lips. "It's not a change of heart. You've violated my sacred space in the most unconscionable way. I'm only giving you what you've asked for because I know you're going to go ahead and try the summoning anyway, and I don't want to read about you online tomorrow as the killer's next victim. The spell I'm going to give you includes a binding element to prevent the shade from controlling you. If you're going to allow the step-in—which I have no doubt you are, despite any warnings I could give you to the contrary—this will keep it separate from you, only able to communicate through you and nothing more."

She sat on a section of the stone bench forming a little wall along the perimeter of the mesa and Phoebe sat beside her. "I'll give you the spell on one condition."

"Which is?"

"You join me for the service afterward. And sit through the whole thing. It's only half an hour." Phoebe could see Ione wasn't about to compromise. She'd compromised her own beliefs enough, in her estimation, and it was Phoebe's turn.

"I'm not going to sing."

"Fair enough." Ione proceeded to walk her through the

summoning spell—with a side of binding—and with the help of a few notes on her phone, Phoebe committed it to memory before they headed back inside the chapel.

The service turned out to be rather lovely. Even if the ideas behind the songs no longer held meaning for her, Phoebe could appreciate the beauty of them. She could see why Ione was drawn to it, even if she couldn't understand her sister's need to belong to something that condemned her. The chanting even seemed to calm the shades Phoebe sensed. A few had tried to get her attention when she'd returned inside, but as the service began, they seemed to collectively settle, perhaps finding others to step into who weren't aware of their presence—the way most step-ins actually occurred—in order to participate in the spiritual connection of song.

But Phoebe had apparently let down her guard too much in taking in the experience. As the last piece of music began, she felt a familiar, insistent tugging inside her head.

She tried to grit her teeth to keep the shade out, but found herself joining in on the last line of the chant, louder than necessary. Ione gave her a curious glance, a tentative smile on her face until the shade burst out laughing—through Phoebe's mouth. *Lila.*

"Gotta run." Phoebe jumped up as the service ended. "Thanks." Ione's favorite stony look was back. Too bad. She was the one who'd insisted Phoebe stay.

The rain broke as Phoebe headed down the snaking drive to the Wrangler, and she made a dash for it, soaked to the skin already by the time she hopped inside.

Her hair dripped water into her eyes as she gripped the steering wheel. "Lila. I know you're still there."

"Funny." The deep, smoky voice came from her mouth. "You didn't notice the last time I was here."

The flesh on Phoebe's arms tightened with goose bumps

that had nothing to do with Lila's presence or the rain. "What are you talking about?"

"Went for a little ride-along. Since you've been fooling around with my Jacob, it seemed only fair." Phoebe's heart began to pound and Lila noticed. Just as Lila would have experienced any physical sensation in Phoebe's body—if she were along for the ride. "You don't like not knowing what happened, do you? But you know something happened."

A surge of anger overtook the spike of anxiety. "What did you do?"

"I could tell you. But I won't. You'll find out soon enough. Barbara tried to warn you to stay out of things that don't concern you. But you keep sticking your nose in it. And your little ride? It's nothing to what we've been put through, those of us on this side. But you just keep making it worse."

"How? What have I done to you?"

"You give him exactly what he wants."

"Jacob?"

Lila laughed riotously—one of the more unnerving sensations when allowing a step-in. "Jacob does what he chooses to do. Though why he'd choose to do it with you— he must simply be desperate or bored. No. It's what you're doing to the quetzal. Tezcatlipoca's power grows as the quetzal awakens. And with every touch, you awaken it. The quetzal has slept a very long time. You know the saying, 'let sleeping dogs lie.' So leave the damned dog alone."

Phoebe began to cry, but they weren't her tears. "Lila, I can help you. Despite the way you feel about me, I want to help you. If you'd just let me—"

"Stop helping!" The crying turned into sobbing, and Phoebe wept into her hands, feeling Lila's hopelessness and fear. "Leave us alone. Just go away. I don't want to do anything worse to you, but he can make me. Why would you want that? Just go!"

With that, Lila was gone, leaving Phoebe with the miserable emotion she'd stirred up as if it were her own, along with the terrible feeling in her gut about the "ride-along" Lila had alluded to. Whatever had happened with Carter, she was certain now it was part of this. Part of what Monique had been telling her before she'd been murdered. The client list Monique had talked about—the "respectable, power-tripping dicks"—Carter had to be one of them. Maybe he'd even purchased the ride-along.

Phoebe stopped crying, no longer feeling Lila's residual emotion. Now she just felt sick.

Chapter 20

Summoning Lila with Ione's spell would be a waste of magic, and Ernesto seemed so frightened for his family Phoebe doubted he'd ever betray Tezcatlipoca. Jacob was the only reasonable option. He did as he chose, as Lila had said. Perhaps he was more willing to cross the necromancer.

Trying to ignore the unsettling feeling Lila's words had given her, she set up the altar the way Rafe had taught her, using the bureau in her bedroom on Ione's advice instead of the coffee table. An altar, Ione had explained, should be something more intimate, with meaning to the witch. Of course, Phoebe was no witch, but she saw the logic behind it. It stood to reason there would be more power behind the spell if the individual's energy was stronger, and one's energy, Phoebe knew from dealing with shades, was strongest in one's own domain.

She debated undressing, knowing Jacob would make a thing of it, and decided on the bra-and-underwear approach.

Lighting the candles and the incense, Phoebe called the corners and gave the invocation. Instead of the Aztec deities Rafe had called upon, she used the generic "god and goddess" on Ione's recommendation.

Her stomach clenched when she called Jacob to her. After her last encounter with him, and after what Lila had revealed, there was no telling how he'd respond. She almost forgot the binding element of the spell, quickly adding it as she felt Jacob's energy coalescing.

"Well, that's not very nice." Jacob's lower, sensuous register came from her mouth. "Ask a man to enter you and then tell him he can't move." Disconcertingly, her own eyes looked back at her from the mirror above the bureau with obvious desire.

"Hello, Jacob."

"Lovely to be inside you, though I would have preferred it the conventional way."

Phoebe snorted. "I'll bet."

"To what do I owe the honor?"

"I don't suppose you'd just tell me the name of the one who calls himself Tezcatlipoca."

"And what would you give me in return, lovely Phoebe?"

Phoebe smiled wryly at her face in the mirror. "I can only imagine one thing you want. Can't really give you that on my own."

"You could lift the binding spell and let me touch you."

"Touch me?" Her reflection's cheeks reddened in the mirror. "You mean let you masturbate."

Phoebe's expression changed to a shudder of distaste from Jacob. "What a terrible word. Please. I mean let me pleasure you. It would be a unique experience for me to feel it from your perspective."

"Yeah, how about *no*, Casper."

Her reflection's eyebrow lifted nonchalantly—a gesture she'd never been able to master herself. "Just as well. I can't tell you the name."

"He's bound you from telling me?"

"No." Jacob smiled. "I just don't know it." And yet he'd tried to get her to give him sexy time on the pretext that he did. Nice.

Phoebe tried another tack. "Does Lila know it?"

Her expression didn't change. "I believe she does, yes."

"And you know what she does for him. What she did to me."

Jacob turned her mouth downward. "She serves Titlacauan against her will. We're all influenced by him in one way or another."

"But you less than the others."

"I stay because of her. I won't abandon her to the necromancer. I abandoned her in life, years ago, allowing money and power to come between us, and died before I could tell her I regretted it. I've stayed by her ever since."

"Would Lila tell you the name if you asked her?"

Jacob smiled sadly. "How can I ask her? We're kept apart. The only time I've been able to speak with her in almost thirty years was through you. The first time she occupied another mortal frame, I stepped into one myself, trying to connect with her, but she was bound by Tezcatlipoca's terms." Phoebe's reflection in the mirror was as downcast as she'd ever seen it. "It was worse than being apart from her to have her so close and yet realize she was acting as his puppet, not my Lila."

Phoebe sighed. Any hope she'd had of somehow cracking this thing on her own was quickly evaporating. It was all much more complicated than she'd understood. But Carter, and Monique's cop, and whoever else was patronizing the sex workers who were participating in ride-alongs had to lead to something.

"What do you know about ride-alongs?"

Jacob's look through her eyes was guarded. "I know what they are."

"Have you participated in them?"

"You're asking if I've ever stepped into someone in order to give them a sexual experience they couldn't otherwise have on their own?" Her mouth turned up in a sly grin at his direction. "I think you know the answer to that question."

Her head throbbed with the sustained hosting of the shade, making it hard for her to concentrate and maintain her hold on the separation of identities. Phoebe gritted her teeth and pressed her fingers to her temples. She had to know.

"But have you done it for the necromancer—for anyone who's paid for the experience? Have you done it with Rafe?"

Jacob hesitated longer than was comfortable before answering. "Never against another's will."

Perhaps it was the method with which she'd summoned Jacob to step in—it was, after all, a question of consent—but Phoebe couldn't hold on to him any longer. Limbs shaking uncontrollably, she collapsed onto the bed and let his shade slip away. He hadn't given her a direct answer. Whether it was just Jacob being Jacob or whether his prevarication meant something more troubling, she couldn't be sure.

She realized she'd dozed off when the insistent ringing of her doorbell—someone was pressing it compulsively in rapid succession—woke her. Phoebe wiped the saliva off the corner of her mouth where she'd drooled onto the bedspread and grabbed her robe from the back of the door.

"Coming," she called as she hurried down the hall. "Hang on."

She yanked the door open, ready to yell at whatever idiotic delivery person was violating her doorbell, only to find Theia and Rhea grinning at her.

"Surprise!"

"It's us!"

Phoebe couldn't help but break into a grin herself as she unlocked the screen door to let them in. "Yeah, I can see it's you." They enveloped her in a dual side hug like only the twins could. "What are you guys doing here?"

"Just felt like you needed some company."

"What are you doing half naked?" Rhea pulled back to look her in the eye. "Is that *totally fucking hot guy* here?" Her voice started out soft and got deliberately loud as she projected down the hallway toward Phoebe's room.

Phoebe pinched her. "Brat. No, he's not here. That was a one-time thing."

Theia shared a look with Rhea. "Uh-huh." She glanced back at Phoebe, staring her down in the unnerving way she had when she wanted to get something out of her.

"Okay," Phoebe admitted. "There was another sort-of thing. It didn't end well. And I think I may have gotten myself into something… I can't even explain. I'm actually really freaked out." She threw a look at Rhea, who'd crouched to give Puddleglum a vigorous chin scritch as he came out to greet the company. "So please don't make any more jokes about him."

Rhea straightened, rubbing her tattooed arms. "A no-joke-zone Phoebe. You are freaked out."

Theia, who'd been holding one arm behind her back, produced a six-pack of IPA. "Do you want to talk about it?"

Phoebe smiled and took the beers. "I can't. It has to do with a case. Client confidentiality." It was sort of true.

"You're working on Rafe Diamante's case?"

"No, another case. Or I was working on it, until my client became the second victim of Barbara Fisher's killer."

"Oh, my God," they said together.

"Plus, I got suspended from the PD's office for being a giant slut." She grinned to make light of the situation, but they weren't buying it.

"I can't believe that. I mean, you're obviously a giant slut." There was no way Rhea would have been able to pass that one up. Phoebe had handed it to her, really. "But they're punishing you for being one? That's a bit Nathaniel Hawthorne."

Phoebe shrugged. "I'm sure it'll blow over." She headed into the kitchen as Puddleglum began to complain of his imminent starvation. "Have you guys eaten? Should we get a pizza?"

The doorbell rang again before the words were out of her mouth.

Theia grinned and pulled out her wallet as she went to answer it. "We figured you'd say that, so we called ahead."

"I told her to wait." Rhea shrugged. "I mean, what if we hit traffic or something?"

Theia came back with an extra-large pizza box. "Doubting Thomasina."

"God, that smells good." Phoebe's stomach announced its agreement while she finished feeding Puddleglum. She grabbed some plates and a bottle opener to bring to the living room where Rhea and Theia were already seated around the coffee table digging into the pizza.

"Any more weird omens?" Rhea never let a mouth full of food stop her from talking.

Phoebe pretended to be concerned with her own chewing while she decided how much to tell them. "There's been a coyote hanging around. He went for Glum—hence the fashionably shaved hip. And he can't go outside anymore, so be careful with the doors."

"Aw, poor Glum." Rhea frowned. "I was about to ask about that, but then you were all 'slutty PD' and I got distracted."

"Coyote." Theia swallowed her bite. "Like the Trickster." That was certainly one word for him. "Usually they're a good omen, a sign not to take ourselves so seriously. But a coyote attacking Puddleglum—that doesn't sound so good. You sure it didn't have rabies?"

"It doesn't act rabid, just sort of stalkerish, but thanks to Rhea pestering me, Glum's vaccinations are up to date."

"So you've seen it more than once." Theia popped open an IPA.

Phoebe nodded around a bite of pizza. "Three times. Or twice that I saw it. Rafe saw it once before. Right after we saw the owl, actually."

Theia took another slice. "You didn't mention it then."

"No, because he hadn't mentioned it to me. He only remembered seeing it hanging around the property when I told him what happened to Glum. That's how I ended up at his place. He thinks the coyote is a nagual—a sort of Aztec totem of the necromancer who's responsible for the murders—and he didn't think it was safe for me to stay here."

Rhea set down her slice and wiped her hands on her pants. "I don't like the sound of that. Necromancers and evil coyote totems? Maybe Rafe's right. You could stay with Ione for a while."

Phoebe laughed. "Yeah, that's hilarious, Rhe."

"You said you'd started talking to her again."

"And then I totally pissed her off by crashing her Taizé service at Holy Cross for a summoning spell. She made me stay for the service—and I had a visitor."

"Get *out*," they said in unison.

"That's what *I* said." Phoebe took a bite of her pizza.

Theia shook her head. "Sweetie, you lead the most interesting life."

"I think I'd settle for a whole lot of dull at this point."

"I think that would be Ione's realm." Rhea gave her a wicked grin. "By the way, I call—"

"Guest bed." Theia was smug. "Called. Too late."

Rhea tossed an olive at her. "If I have to sleep on the couch, I get Puddleglum."

Phoebe shrugged. "Good luck with that. He thinks the guest bed is his."

After finishing off the IPA while commiserating about their collectively spectacular bad dating karma, they retired for the night.

The baying of coyotes woke Phoebe from a fitful sleep a few hours later. It sounded like there were several of them, calling back and forth to each other. She went to the living room to look out the window and found Rhea already peering through the curtains.

"Can that necromancer duplicate himself with several of those coyote avatar things?"

"I don't think so." Phoebe joined her and saw two pairs of glowing eyes crossing paths along the edge of the property.

"That's three I've seen on this side of the house."

"At least two more out back." Theia shuffled into the living room in her stocking feet, her dark bob of hair tousled.

"They don't seem to be coming any closer." Rhea leaned against the windowsill of the large picture window. "They just keep circling the edge of the drive."

Phoebe yawned, nodding. "Rafe laid a protection spell when he left Saturday morning."

Rhea turned around. "Saturday morning, huh?"

"We're not going to joke about it, remember?"

"Yeah, but I can still leer, can't I?"

"Just leer quietly to yourself." Phoebe watched as the pack of coyotes trotted restlessly. Her vision had adjusted enough that they were monochromatic dog shapes instead of just glowing eyes. The baying seemed to be getting louder.

"I don't think they like whatever magic Rafe used to

keep them out." Theia shivered, despite the temperature. "That big one keeps coming around to the front and snarling when he can't get any closer."

"I'm pretty sure that's the one I saw before, the one that attacked Glum." Maybe he was the necromancer's nagual and the others were just local coyotes drawn by his call. But they seemed to be moving with purpose, following his lead as the alpha. Could the necromancer compel shades to step into animals? She'd never heard of shades occupying non-human hosts before, but the coyotes had a familiar air to them now. There seemed to be three besides the alpha. Jacob, Lila and Ernesto? But Theia had said there were two in back, as well.

Phoebe glanced over her shoulder at the kitchen windows, though she couldn't see out at this distance. Maybe Barbara and Monique had been roped into this, too.

A little electrified frisson of recognition danced along her skin. "I think they're shades."

Rhea glanced at her. "Shades? Inhabiting coyotes?"

"The necromancer seems to be able to manipulate them in ways I've never heard of before. But the hair on my arms is standing on end, like there are shades near, even though none are trying to step in. And it's the right number for some of the shades I've been dealing with. If you add my dead client."

"Ugh." Theia backed away from the window. "I don't like this. Maybe we should call Di."

Phoebe folded her arms. "Absolutely not. We're grownups. I think we can handle a small pack of coyotes outside a locked house without running to Ione."

"But if the spell doesn't hold, there's no telling what they might do. Ione might be able to help us strengthen it."

"I said no."

"Then we need to do something ourselves." Rhea shared

a look with her twin. "Maybe it's time." But Theia shook her head.

Phoebe glanced from one to the other. "Time for what?"

Theia answered after a moment of hesitation. "There's a theory I've been working on. Rhe and I have been researching our family history."

"On Dad's side," Rhea added. "Specifically, Greek history."

"I'm not sure what you're getting at."

Rhea dropped into the papasan and drew her feet up to sit cross-legged. "Our names—you know they come from a specific set of goddesses."

"The first daughters of Uranus and Gaia." Theia pulled up the matching ottoman and straddled it. "The Titanides."

Phoebe kept one eye on the window, not entirely listening. "Yeah, so?"

"So," said Theia, "we've always thought maybe our... affinity for the esoteric had something to do with our ancestry. Like maybe early Greek ancestry."

"But it doesn't," said Rhea. "At least, not the way we thought."

"What do you mean?"

"We signed up for that ancestor website and looked back as far as we could. The Greek bloodline is pretty watered-down. But the other side, the Carlisles—they have an interesting history with the Covent."

Phoebe turned away from the window. "Interesting how?"

"They were one of the founding families, like the Diamantes. Only...we kind of got thrown out several generations back."

"Thrown out?"

"The Covent was originally founded as a heretical off-shoot of the Catholic church. Turns out our great-great-great-something-or-other grandfather married someone even the Covent considered worthy of burning at the stake. She was reputed to have…"

Theia paused and Rhea finished the sentence. "Demon blood."

They'd gotten Phoebe's full attention. "She had what, now?"

"Specifically, the blood of Lilith."

Lilith. Where had Phoebe heard someone mention her recently? "As in the supposed first wife of Adam, Lilith?"

"That would be the one, yeah."

"But here's the kicker," said Rhea. That wasn't the kicker? "Mom's ancestry traced back to the same woman."

"And apparently the Lilith blood only manifests in female children." Theia became more excited as she spoke. "Meaning there must be a recessive 'Lilith blood' allele and we got two copies—one from Dad's side, one from Mom's—which gave us the 'Lilith blood' phenotype." Theia seemed to realize she'd gone into biology-geek mode and she grinned and threw her arms out in a gesture encompassing the three of them. "So I guess you'd say we're super demon-y. Ta-da!"

Phoebe laughed out loud. They were putting her on, and she'd fallen for it. Why they'd chosen right now, she had no idea. Maybe they'd thought taking her mind off the situation would help. "Good one. You guys almost had me."

Rhea folded her arms. "We're not kidding."

Stress and lack of sleep were starting to make her cranky. "Look, I don't have the patience for this right now. I thought you two were going to come up with something helpful, and you're inventing fantasies about being the descendants of a Sumerian demoness."

Theia was subdued. "Akkadian, actually."

"That's in dispute." Rhea's stance was still sullen. "She may be Babylonian or Assyrian. But Lilith's origins can be considered both demonic and divine, depending on your perspective."

Phoebe sighed. "I don't care if she's an Icelandic warrior princess. Just tell me why the heck you two are going on about her while possessed coyotes are circling my damn house."

"If our gifts are attributable to Lilith," said Theia patiently, "and the gene is only present in female offspring, then maybe the magic is also exponential, and together, our gifts would be amplified." She shared a look with her twin. "We just want to test our theory. It's a full moon out there, which is supposed to enhance magical energy, and even the coyotes seem to be drawing some power from it. If those five coyotes are being controlled by shades, with our added energy…"

Rhea finished for her. "You should be able to vanquish them."

Phoebe's fists clenched involuntarily at her sides. "You did *not* just say that."

"We don't mean force them to cross over. We're not advocating that."

"Then what are you advocating?"

"More like an exorcism. Just…" Rhea made a shoving gesture with her hands. "Give them a push to make them step out of the coyotes they've stepped into."

She'd certainly told shades to get out before, but usually only from herself, which she had the obvious right to do. This seemed too much like what Ione and the Covent engaged in. Or even the necromancer himself. Then again, she *had* commanded Jacob to leave Rafe. But Jacob had been inhabiting him without permission. And coyotes couldn't exactly grant permission. At least, she didn't think so.

"How do I know I wouldn't be hurting them somehow?"

Rhea grinned. "See? I knew she'd come around."

"Don't third-person me. And I didn't say I'd do it. I'm not sure I *can* do it. I'm just wondering if it's something I *should* do. Consent is paramount in working with shades. Just like the living. That's why what the Covent does is so unconscionable."

"Do you think they're consenting to doing the necromancer's bidding?"

A particularly unnerving bay punctuated Theia's sentence—a mournful, hopeless howl that made her think of Lila and her unfulfilled need for Jacob. What the necromancer was making the shades do—all of it, but especially the ride-alongs—definitely wasn't consensual. They did his bidding, by all accounts, because they had no choice. The very thing the Covent warned against—manipulation by a dark practitioner.

Phoebe unclenched her fists. "No. And I did promise to help Rafe stop him." She sighed resolutely. "So how do you propose we do this 'amplification'?"

The two of them were wearing grins like it was Christmas Eve. They'd obviously been planning this for a while.

Rhea jumped up and took Theia's hand, holding her other out to Phoebe. "I think we need to form a physical connection first."

Phoebe couldn't help laughing as she clasped Rhea's hand and completed the circuit. They'd joked about being the Charmed Ones for years, complete with their own Phoebe. "I am *not* chanting 'the power of three will set us free.'"

"Don't worry." Theia squeezed her hand. "No chanting. You just do your thing and try to consciously draw power from us."

Phoebe didn't really have a "thing," but she figured a little invocation of the cardinal directions along with Ione's spell to call shades would be as good a start as any.

She named the five, hoping she was right and not calling shades she had no business calling. As she sensed the shades being drawn to her, she concentrated on Theia and Rhea on either side of her. There *was* a sort of current flowing from them into her, reminiscent of shade energy.

Through the window, the coyotes were running back and forth on the property line in agitation. The alpha wasn't visible.

Phoebe addressed them. "Jacob, Lila, Ernesto, Barbara and Monique—if you're the shades inhabiting the physical form of these coyotes, it's time for you to go. Let go of them. Let them be. Get out." Her arms shook, making it an effort to hold on to her sisters' hands.

"Phoebe? Are you okay?" She wasn't sure which one of them had spoken. The coyotes were vocalizing in frantic yips and yowls, scrabbling at the ground, running in circles. Phoebe couldn't answer.

Electric current seemed to rush through the twins into Phoebe, and then up and out, like a reverse lightning strike. Her sisters both shrieked at the same time and let go of her hands, wringing theirs, just as the clamor from the coyotes outside ceased and turned into whimpering as they scampered off into the darkness. All but one, who'd made it to the bushes on the other side of the drive before the alpha leaped from its cover and took the fleeing coyote by the throat, shaking it and snapping the animal's neck.

The nagual bared its teeth at Phoebe through the window, its eyes glowing with menace, before it, too, disappeared into the night. Whatever had been keeping Phoebe upright until that moment vanished and she dropped to the floor in a heap.

Chapter 21

The twins knelt over her, shaking her by the shoulders and calling her name.

"Shit, Rhe. What did we do?" Theia's voice was high and thin.

"Stop it." Phoebe realized her eyes were closed and opened them. Both of her sisters were pale and wide-eyed.

"Oh, my God, Phoebe."

"Are you okay?"

"I think so." She lifted her head as Rhea slipped a pillow under it. "Just a little dazed."

Theia tried to hide tears of relief. "I thought we'd really done it when you started jabbering in all those voices at once."

"When I what?" Phoebe sat up, ignoring the throbbing in the back of her skull that advised against it.

"It was absolutely creepy." Rhea shuddered. "Horror-movie bad. I thought we'd have to call an exorcist."

"I don't remember that at all."

The three of them jumped at the sound of loud banging on the front door. Phoebe's stomach dropped. Had the necromancer ditched the nagual just to come straight out and kill them?

"Phoebe, open the door! Can you hear me? Phoebe!"

Her muscles unclenched with relief. "It's Rafe." She fumbled to her feet, waving her sisters away as she stepped up to open the door.

Rafe, dressed in baby-blue pajama pants and loafers, stared at her with sleep-mussed hair. And, damn, if he didn't somehow manage to make that look sexy.

"Rafe? What are you doing here?"

"I felt...something." He blinked with confusion as the twins stepped up on either side of her. Rhea didn't even try to pretend she wasn't checking him out.

"My sisters, Theia and Rhea. Guys, this is Rafael Diamante." Phoebe opened the screen door. "You might as well come in, and do it quick before Puddleglum—" She grabbed the little bugger as he dashed between her legs and swept him up.

"*Damn.* I mean, how do you do?" Rhea held out her hand and Rafe shook it, bemused, as he stepped inside.

Theia's greeting was more subdued, with a nod and a little, "Hey."

"Sorry." Rafe rubbed his forehead. "I didn't mean to intrude on your family gathering. I just—can we talk in private?"

Phoebe threw her sisters a look that promised trouble if they gave her any grief right now. "Could you guys make us all some coffee? I don't think anybody's going back to sleep at this point."

Theia headed for the kitchen. "Sure thing."

Rhea stayed in the hallway a moment longer as Phoebe waved Rafe ahead of her to her room. Before Phoebe closed the bedroom door, Rhea coughed into her hand and the cough sounded suspiciously like "hottie."

Phoebe rolled her eyes and sat on the bed while Rafe remained standing. "You said you felt something?"

"My tattoo. It was writhing over my back like it was

trying to get out of my skin. Woke me up. I don't know how, but I knew it was something to do with you. That the nagual was here." Rafe raked his fingers through his hair. "I saw a dead coyote on your driveway with its throat torn out. You didn't actually—that's not the nagual?"

"No." Phoebe rubbed her arms, goose-pimpling with cold in the aftermath of what must have been a group step-in, however brief. "The nagual killed it. He showed up here with a pack of them, howling and circling the place. I took a chance the pack was being controlled by shades and cast them out."

Rafe's face registered pure shock. "You crossed them?"

"No. God, no. I would never do that. I just told them to get out and leave the coyotes alone. It seems to have worked. And it seems to have really pissed off the necromancer."

"Wow." Rafe regarded her with surprise. "I didn't know you could do that."

"Neither did I. My sisters suggested we combine our energy—they have this theory we have some kind of…" Phoebe paused, not sure she wanted to go into the whole "demon blood" thing. "We're descended from some sort of divine bloodline—and somehow that seems to have amplified my ability. But your spell held. So thanks for that."

Rafe's eyebrow lifted but he didn't ask for clarification. "I think that must be what I felt. The necromancer was using everything he had to try to cross the barrier I'd put up."

Things still felt awkward between them. Phoebe wanted to ask what was bothering him, but she was also acutely aware of what Jacob had said to her—and not said to her—right before he'd stepped out of her earlier this evening.

What she ended up saying sounded combative. "Why didn't you call?"

He blinked, as though it hadn't occurred to him, and his

ears went pink. "I... I don't know. I was functioning on instinct, I guess, following my blood—or the ink. They're starting to seem like one and the same. Something activated my magic and I just went with it. Jumped in the car."

"No reporters at the gate?"

"Not this time. I don't think the story they're hoping for is good enough for them to sleep in their vans." He smiled, but it was strained. "Anyway, it looks like you and your sisters have everything under control."

"You don't have to go." Phoebe gave him an encouraging smile, trying to dispel whatever weirdness had come between them—probably it was just because *she* was acting odd. "I like having you here."

Rafe's posture was tense. "I don't think that's a good idea."

"We don't need to do anything."

"Yeah, I guess you've been fully taken care of in that department." The sudden hostility radiating from him took her aback.

"I beg your pardon?"

"Look, it's none of my business what you do or whom you do it with. I just sort of thought something was happening between us, and I feel pretty stupid after opening up to you about my problem. But you're an adult, I'm an adult. Whatever. Let's just focus on stopping the necromancer and forget about the rest of it."

"Rafe, I don't know what you're talking about. I'm not doing anything with anyone."

"Funny. That's not what he said."

Phoebe's stomach tightened. "What *who* said?"

Rafe's eyes flashed dangerously. "Carter. Hanson. *Hamilton.*" He bit out each word through clenched teeth. "My goddamn lawyer. Guess a little suspension from the PD's office for misconduct doesn't faze you. That Girl Scout act you put on is something else, Phoebe Carlisle."

Before Phoebe could recover from the surprise of the accusation, Rafe yanked open the door and swept down the hall. She stood and watched him slam the screen door behind him without saying anything to stop him.

Theia peered around the kitchen corner. "What happened?"

"Rafe Diamante happened." Phoebe came down the hall and took the coffee mug Theia held out. "And he's an asshole." Her eyes were prickling with the threat of tears she had no intention of indulging in front of her little sisters. If she started talking about what Rafe thought, she'd have to explain about Carter, and she knew if she tried to dance around what had happened—or what she feared had happened—they'd be onto her in an instant.

Theia gave her a side hug as she drank the coffee. Phoebe wasn't even sure what time it was. This whole night had been surreal.

"Sorry, Phoebes." Rhea emerged from the kitchen with her own mug. "Mostly because *damn*." She shook her head. "I don't know which part to perv over—those abs, the awesome tattoo or that ass."

Phoebe smiled in spite of herself. "I can always count on you to put things into perspective, Rhe." She warmed her hands on the mug and sighed. "It is a pretty spectacular ass."

"Well, look at it this way. You got to see it walking away. Just hold on to that image. And get a good vibrator."

"Ha." Phoebe swallowed a sip of her coffee. "Might as well."

Rhea took her phone from her pocket. "In fact, I'm going to…" Her voice trailed off and her expression turned grim, but before Phoebe could ask what was wrong, both Phoebe's and Theia's phones chirped with a notification.

As she went to her room to get hers, the twins spoke simultaneously from the kitchen.

"Holy shit."

"Phoebe, don't."

She'd received a text from a number she didn't recognize. "What do you mean, don—?" The last letter was strangled in her throat as an image appeared. Phoebe felt the blood drain from her face. It was a picture of her—topless and on her knees, smiling up at a man she'd never seen before, with an expression that didn't belong to her—in Carter's hotel room.

Rafe drove through the dark, trying once again to get Phoebe out of his head—not to mention the tiny pink tank top she'd been wearing without a bra. Something kept drawing him back to her. He was like an addict. Or a lunatic. He knew he had no business being this affected by what she did—being eaten up with jealousy over the thought of her with Hamilton. She wasn't his girlfriend. She hadn't made him any promises. And he'd put her off repeatedly—not to mention the stupid stunt with the shade. She had every right to go elsewhere.

But did it have to be *Carter fucking Hamilton*? The slick, flawless, golden-haired-frat-boy persona stuck in Rafe's craw. Spending most of the day with him going over funeral arrangements had only fueled Rafe's simmering resentment. Hamilton had been perfectly pleasant and helpful and hadn't brought Phoebe up again. And Rafe had fantasized all day about knocking him on his ass and pummeling his fancy face for touching her.

He considered that she might have been so drunk she didn't remember. Hamilton had said she'd overindulged. Maybe the look of sheer baffled outrage she'd given Rafe had been genuine. But the fact remained that of all the people she could have chosen, drunk or not, she'd screwed his pretty-boy lawyer.

Rafe's phone chimed and he flicked to the screen while

he sat at a red light. The image took several seconds to load and the light turned green just as Phoebe's face came into view—and Phoebe's naked torso—and—

"What the *fuck*?"

Theia and Rhea sat beside Phoebe on the couch, trying to calm her down. She'd alternated between hysterical tears and incoherent rage, too freaked out to explain that, consciously, it wasn't even her. She could barely even comprehend the fact that Carter had paid for a ride-along shade to animate her unconscious body. And for what? Blackmail? Just because he got off on it? But that there had been other men involved... She had no idea how many, or who. Or what she'd done.

Phoebe clutched the edges of the couch cushion, certain she was going to be sick.

"Honey, don't worry." Rhea rubbed her back. "The video blew over—or it will soon. This will blow over, too. In a couple of weeks, nobody will care who you boinked. They won't even remember your name."

Phoebe let out a choked laugh at the word "boinked" and the laugh turned into a half sob. "But I didn't. You don't understand." No matter how painful it was, she had to tell them. "It was a shade."

They shared a look across her. "You let a shade...?" Theia left the sentence unfinished.

"I didn't *let* the shade do anything. I had dinner with Rafe's lawyer the other night—he got me out of a jam at the courthouse—and apparently..." Phoebe had to pause and swallow hard. "Apparently he roofied me. One of the shades I've been dealing with told me yesterday she stepped into me while I was unconscious in his hotel room."

"Oh, Phoebes."

Rhea jumped up from the couch and began to pace.

"Goddammit. Who is this guy? Rafe's *lawyer*? I mean, isn't he in Ione's coven?"

Phoebe nodded, twisting her shirt in her hands. "From the Phoenix chapter."

"Have you told her?"

"No, I haven't told her." Phoebe looked up. "And you're not going to tell her, either. Do you hear me?"

"Phoebe—"

"I can't prove anything, I can't *do* anything, and I sure as hell can't afford to get involved in an anti-defamation lawsuit with a lawyer of his caliber. Because I can tell you right now, that's exactly what would happen if I accused him."

Theia tucked her short bob behind one ear. "But Phoebe, if there's a predator in the Covent, other women have to be warned. Ione needs to know."

Phoebe's stomach churned. She knew Theia was right. "I have to find out who's involved first. The case I couldn't tell you about—this is part of it." She told them about Monique's experience with the effectively un-prosecutable clients, and what Barbara Fisher had told her about the continued coercion of the sex workers' shades.

Theia shuddered. "That's like…afterlife sex slavery."

Rhea's response, as usual, was more action-oriented. "We need to find this necromancer and mess him up."

"That's what Rafe and I have been trying to do. Find him, anyway. And stop him, somehow." Except she was no longer sure she could trust Rafe. But Phoebe wasn't going into that with them. She'd already shared more than enough. "Carter Hamilton is the only living connection I have to this group right now." Phoebe smoothed the shirt she'd wrinkled with her twisting as she began thinking aloud. "I don't know if he knows who's behind it, or if Rafe has told him anything about our work with the shades. But sending this picture—it's obviously a threat. And drugging me and conjuring Lila's shade was all part of the threat."

"That's why we got the message, too. We helped you break the necromancer's hold on the shades tonight and he's pissed off." Theia glanced at her phone. "It was addressed specifically to us. It may not have gone any further—yet."

Rhea stopped pacing. "I'll check to see if it's been posted anywhere. Where's your laptop?"

"In my room. How are you going to search for it?"

Rhea headed to the bedroom. "Revenge porn sites. Reddit forums. The usual suspects."

Theia looked thoughtful. "Phoebe, I think there's one strong possibility you should consider."

"Which is?"

"That this pig Carter Hamilton *is* the necromancer."

The thought had crossed her mind.

Chapter 22

Rafe had to pull off the road into a grocery store parking lot to avoid wrecking the car. The text message was from an unidentified number. Who the hell would have sent this? It certainly wasn't Phoebe, unless she was a total mental case. And the man in the picture wasn't Hamilton, at least. Then again, he wasn't sure if this wasn't worse than seeing her with Hamilton. And whoever took it, there had obviously been more than two people involved in this intimate little encounter. Had Hamilton himself taken the picture and sent it to him? Just to get under his skin? But that would mean there'd been some kind of orgy at Hamilton's hotel the other night, and it just didn't make any sense.

His phone chimed again and Rafe stiffened. He thought about turning the phone off—or throwing it out the window and smashing it—but when it sounded again with a reminder notification, he opened the text, breathing a sigh of relief that at least there was no picture attached this time.

It was from Hamilton. Received a disturbing text a few minutes ago. Wondering if you had anything to do with it.

So it wasn't him. What was going on?

I received one, as well, he typed back. More tabloid harassment, I guess.

A moment later Hamilton called him. Rafe pressed the speaker button.

"Rafael. Thank you for answering. I know this is awkward, but I think we need to figure out the significance of this little stunt. I don't think a tabloid would bother sending personal messages. Is Phoebe in some kind of situation I'm not aware of? I know the Public Defender's Office isn't the most lucrative position. Women of Phoebe's means don't have that many options."

"Of Phoebe's means?"

"Struggling financially, with no spouse or family to fall back on." He paused. "Like Barbara Fisher."

Rafe felt his teeth grinding together. "You think Phoebe is moonlighting as a prostitute."

"It's not unheard of. And I'm not judging. But if she's somehow involved with these people—the people who killed Ms. Fisher—well, it looks like they're letting us know."

Rafe was having a hard time believing this. But then, he'd had a hard time believing Phoebe would sleep with Hamilton. And mostly because of ego. He'd imagined her attraction to him was something unique and special, that Rafe alone got her fired up…the way she got. But why shouldn't she choose to sleep with Hamilton? He was a prominent attorney with connections. He could help Phoebe move on to bigger and better things than the Yavapai County Public Defender's Office. Though that was a rather crass way of looking at things that maybe said more about Rafe than it did about Phoebe.

"Are you still there, Rafael?"

"Yes, I'm here."

"I think this is a warning we'd probably better take heed of. It doesn't look like this picture has been released to the public. Not so far, anyway. But if a revelation about your involvement with yet another working girl were to come out…well, we can kiss a fair trial in Yavapai County—or anywhere in Arizona—goodbye."

"So exactly how am I supposed to 'take heed'? What's the warning? All I'm seeing is a big, giant sign that says 'You're screwed—and here's a nice visual to go with it.'"

Hamilton sighed. "I think the best thing either of us can do right now is keep our distance from Ms. Carlisle and concentrate on building your defense. And laying your father to rest."

Rafe glanced at the clock on the dash. The funeral was in four hours. "Yeah. Guess I'd better start picking out a suit. And I think I can handle this one on my own, thanks."

He arrived home as the stars over Stone Canyon were being swallowed up into the pale prelude to sunrise. The last funeral he'd attended had been Ford's—just weeks after his brother's—when Rafe had given his father the double whammy of maligning the memory of his long-time business partner and friend while they were both still grieving Gabriel. There hadn't been any reason to tell him; Rafe had to acknowledge that now. He'd only done it to make himself feel better and less like there was some-thing wrong with him—something that had made Ford do what he'd done.

The picture of Phoebe had triggered everything Rafe had been trying to forget. A picture like that had once ap-peared in his locker at school. Rafe had gotten drunk for the first time at sleep-away soccer camp when he was only twelve. Ford, his coach, had been "cool" like that, treating him, Rafe thought, like a real man. His father had let him drink a small glass of wine once or twice at big holiday dinners, but that was a gesture to a boy. Ford had cracked open a couple of beers in his cabin to celebrate their victory on the field earlier that day and told Rafe to drink up. He'd earned it.

Trying to show Ford he could handle it, Rafe had drunk not one but three beers, and gotten violently ill. Ford had held up Rafe's drooping head as Rafe heaved into the toilet, and then led him to his bunk and held him, stroking the sweaty hair out of his eyes while the bed spun. Rafe—or Rafa, as he'd been known then—had looked up to Ford, a father figure who paid attention to him and praised him when he'd done something well. Rafael Sr. was too busy running for office to notice Rafe. Or to notice what was going on between his best friend and his wife right under his nose.

Rafe supposed it wasn't surprising his father hadn't noticed when his friend had switched his attentions to his son. That night in the cabin, Rafe had been confused by Ford's affection. Kisses of comfort on his forehead had become less comforting kisses on his mouth. Rafe was so out of it, he couldn't push Ford away or tell him to stop. His eyes wouldn't stay open.

The hangover the next morning had made him forget all about Ford's odd behavior the night before. He'd gone home from camp early with the "flu." But when he'd returned to school the following week, he'd found an envelope in his locker with his name on it. He thought maybe someone had left him a get-well card. When he opened it, Rafe had felt the ground drop out from under him as if he were hanging from the edge of a cliff over a chasm with no bottom. It was a photo of Rafe lying on Ford's bunk with his pants around his knees. Ford had been in the picture, too, but not his face.

On the back of the picture was a penciled note: "If you tell anyone, there will be copies of this in every locker in the gym." Rafe had been too young and naïve to realize Ford would never have let that picture get out. Even without his face, it would have been fairly easy to guess who it was. But Rafe had believed the threat—and subsequent threats—enough to be too afraid to try to put a stop to what was happening to him. Part of him believed, as Ford constantly implied, that what was happening was Rafe's fault. Something about him had stirred Ford's inappropriate desire. He'd even felt sorry for the man, unable to help himself because of whatever was wrong with Rafe.

But the rage and acting out at school that had landed him in counseling had started almost immediately after that.

Rhea confirmed there was no sign of the picture online so far. "Don't Google yourself, though. Just...don't do it."

She had no intention of Googling herself. But what to do now, she wasn't sure. She couldn't expect Rafe's help in figuring out what she was tangled up in. She couldn't cast doubt on the attorney building his defense—or ignore that small bit of uncertainty about his involvement with the group responsible for the shades' exploitation, even peripherally. Maybe he'd been telling the truth—or maybe his bargain with Jacob that night hadn't really been the first time he'd done it.

Then Carter had come on the scene, hired by Rafe's own father, and endorsed by the Covent. It was too great a coincidence that Carter just happened to be involved in, as Theia had put it, the afterlife sex slavery trade. He either worked for the necromancer or he *was* the necromancer. And he'd set Phoebe up to let her know he could destroy her. Which meant Phoebe had been getting close to something. Barbara and Lila had said as much. He was warning her to back off. Which was exactly what she was *not* going to do.

Rhea and Theia raided her pantry as breakfast making

ensued in the kitchen. The sun was coming up. Seemed like a reasonable action to take.

Phoebe leaned against the countertop of the breakfast bar. "Rhe, how would I go about placing an adult personal ad?"

Rhea poised with her fork in mid-whisk in a fluffy bowl of raw eggs. "Um...okay. One—why do you immediately think I'd know? And, two—why on earth would you want to? Mr. Awesome Ass not doing it for you?"

Phoebe sighed. "Okay. One—I'm not actually looking for a date, I want to lure someone out who might be involved in this thing. See if I can find an actual living, breathing, human being who can give me some information about it. And, two—Mr. Awesome Ass basically just called me a sloppy whore and walked out. Or did you miss that part?"

"Honey, if he thinks you're a *sloppy* whore, you're doing it wrong."

Phoebe lunged over the counter and grabbed for her, missing Rhea's shirt by an inch. Instead she stuck her finger in the batter and flicked some at her little sister.

"Hey!" Theia whisked the bowl out of her reach. "No food fights with my unborn waffles. You do *not* want to mess with the hungry Theia Bear." She'd earned the nickname when they were kids because of her prominent stomach growling whenever she even came close to missing a meal. Her stomach gave an impressive demonstration of it now.

Rhea went back to beating eggs. "I *might* know of some websites you can check out. But I only learned about them from Googling your name." She grinned and stuck out her tongue.

Despite her tendency to give Phoebe an unwarranted amount of little-sisterly shit just because it amused her,

Rhea came through after they'd eaten their fill of waffles and scrambled eggs. Instead of placing an ad, they decided Phoebe should answer one—with a fake male profile.

Within an hour she had a "date" with an escort, a sort of pre-screening coffee date, presumably to make sure the client was someone the escort was willing to enter-tain and that he was real and not a cop. Phoebe's invented persona was also a lawyer—she figured she'd need to fit the profile—and she'd dropped hints about having known Monique, expressing her regrets and disappointment that a date she'd arranged with Monique a few days ago was no longer possible. She'd wanted Monique's "special skills." After running through the script on a few chats, she'd landed the coffee date with "Kimber."

They agreed to meet that afternoon at a little garden café in Tlaquepaque, a trendy arts-and-crafts shopping center styled after a Mexican village, just a mile or so from Phoebe's neck of the woods across Oak Creek. Since Phoebe's persona—Rob—had claimed to be a weekend visitor from Phoenix, trendy was the just the thing.

She spotted Kimber in a shady corner under the syca-mores as soon as she arrived. The bright pink sundress Kimber had promised to wear was the only one in the café.

Phoebe walked up to the table and held out her hand. "Hi, Kimber. Rob couldn't make it. I'm Phoebe."

The fresh-faced, college-aged blonde frowned and started to gather her purse without taking Phoebe's hand. "I think you have the wrong person."

Phoebe sat before Kimber could tell her to get lost. "Sorry for the games. I'm not a cop or anything. I'm a friend of Monique's."

"Seriously," Kimber insisted. "You're mistaking me for someone else. If you don't stop bothering me, I'm going to call the manager."

"Could you just hear me out for a minute? I wasn't lying when I said I was a lawyer. I was Monique's lawyer, and I'm just trying to get some justice for her. She didn't deserve what happened to her." Phoebe looked up at the waitress approaching them and raised her voice. "Just a latte for me, thanks."

Kimber stared at her as the waitress walked away. "You're the one from the video."

Phoebe tried to control the blush so she wouldn't match Kimber's dress. "Yeah. That's me."

Kimber eyed her with new appreciation. "How'd you manage to bag the mythical beast?"

"I beg your pardon?"

"Diamante. He's notorious for turning women down. Everyone thought he was gay."

Phoebe tried not to smile at the thought of being the only woman who'd ever gotten close to Rafe Diamante. She had to remind herself he might be further involved than he claimed. "Nope. Not gay."

"So, what do you want with me? I don't know anything about what Monique was into."

Phoebe flicked her brows upward. "That's not what you said when we talked online. You said you could hook me up with something 'extra special,' just like Monique."

Kimber sipped her iced tea. "You don't want to mess with these people."

"Unfortunately they're already messing with me." Phoebe's latte arrived and she busied herself blowing on the foam to cool it while waiting for the waitress to move out of earshot.

Her "date" studied her. "You don't look like any lawyer I've ever met."

"Yeah, I get that a lot. I think it's the bangs."

Kimber laughed, the obvious tension she'd been holding in her body since Phoebe's arrival easing somewhat. "Well, anyway, I still don't know how I can help you."

"I suppose it's too much to hope you'd be able to hook me up with the Heidi Fleiss of Sedona."

"Heidi who?"

"Someone in charge of the client list."

The stiffness in Kimber's body language was back. "I wouldn't know."

Phoebe decided to take a different tack. "Did you know Barbara Fisher? Barbie?"

Kimber's expression was guarded. "Maybe."

"Do you know whether she ever saw Rafe Diamante professionally, like they're saying?"

"Why don't you ask him?"

"I have." Phoebe sipped her latte, licking foam off her upper lip. "I'm just trying to get some independent verification. It's a lawyer thing."

Kimber was silent a moment, drinking her iced tea, and Phoebe thought she wasn't going to answer until she spoke quietly while leaning over her drink, still holding the straw to her mouth. "Like I said, he's considered very elusive. I've known a few girls who tried to hook up with him at country club parties and political social events. None of them were professional. Unless you count constantly being on the lookout for a wealthy boyfriend as a profession."

She took a sip of her tea. "They all said he was nice. A little too nice. Never made a move on any of them or took them up on any offers. Not even a blowjob. That's why we figured he wasn't playing for our team. I don't know anything about who Barbie was seeing professionally, but I think it would have been news to a lot of people if Rafe Diamante were dating a woman. In any sense of the word." Kimber looked up. "Which is why your video was such a runaway hit."

Phoebe couldn't help blushing this time. "I really wish

it hadn't been. We had no idea anyone could get close enough to see us, let alone film us through the window."

Kimber smiled. "Well, anyway, congrats. You've made a lot of women jealous."

"Wasn't really my plan." Phoebe concentrated on her coffee until the heat in her cheeks went down. "What about Rafe's lawyer, Carter Hamilton? I know he's from out of town, but has he been around the scene before? Know anyone who's dated him?"

Kimber sat back in her chair and raised her hand to catch the waitress's attention. "I think we're done here."

Kimber's reaction meant Carter wasn't just some client. His was definitely a name that inspired fear. It was as much of an answer to her unasked question as Phoebe was likely to get.

"Can I ask you one more thing?"

Kimber shrugged, digging through her purse for her wallet.

"Who conjures the ride-alongs? How is that done?"

Kimber put her money on the tray as the waitress set it on the table. "Keep the change." She rose and gave Phoebe a chilling look. "You've gotten the wrong idea about me. I don't know anything about 'ride-alongs.' All I know is certain men will pay a lot of money for a custom experience. Pretending to be the ex who jilted them, for instance, in a punishment fantasy. It's all negotiated in advance. For the right price, I've agreed to let a client get a little rough— dress up like the woman he wants to get back at, let him call me by her name and tell me I've got it coming—but it's all fantasy. Everyone's consenting in the transaction. But, for some guys, that isn't enough. They want something one step up from the fantasy. They don't want a substitute, if you see what I'm saying."

The sick feeling in Phoebe's stomach said she probably did.

Kimber leaned in, hands braced against the table. "You couldn't pay me enough to participate in something like that. I wouldn't do it. I doubt there's a girl alive who would."

Chapter 23

Kimber's words haunted Phoebe as she left Tlaquepaque and headed for the grocery store. *Not a girl alive.* But dead ones—shades who could be compelled to step into an unsuspecting object of the revenge fantasy the way Lila had stepped into Phoebe in Carter's hotel room after she'd been drugged? That's what the ride-alongs were doing.

She'd promised her sisters she'd let them know she was okay as soon as the meeting ended. As she navigated the roundabout of the Y intersection of Highways 179 and 89A, she voice-dialed Theia.

"Hey, Phoebes. How'd it go?"

"About as well as we expected. She didn't give me any real information about who's behind it, but she freaked when I brought up Carter's name and ended the conversation."

"Well, we already knew he was bad news. Slimeball."

"Yeah. And it sounds like they use these ride-alongs for the same kind of thing he did to me. Creeps pay to use step-ins for revenge."

"Gross."

"I think you guys are right. I have to tell Ione about

Carter. I just wish we had some real evidence, some way to stop what he's doing." Even as she said it, she knew what was needed. Magic that could bind the necromancer from controlling the shades—the magic of the Covent. But that meant putting the shades in the Covent's crosshairs. There was no way the Covent would agree to help bind the necromancer without insisting on controlling the shades, as well—and banishing them from the mortal plane.

The sky grew darker as she headed west. Another afternoon storm was rolling in.

"I'm stopping at the grocery store to stock up before you guys eat me out of house and home."

"What house and home?" Rhea had taken the phone from Theia. "You've got a box of stale cereal, a quarter cup of milk, some dried beans and an egg."

"Yeah, I wonder who ate an entire carton of eggs just this morning?"

"She's blaming us for the eggs, Theia."

Theia's voice came from the background. "Ingrate! I made you waffles."

Phoebe laughed, flipping on the windshield wipers as it began to sprinkle. "I'll be home in half an hour with more booty for you marauders."

As soon as she'd switched off the phone, she felt the intense pressure of a shade demanding entry—a presence immediately recognizable as Lila. Among Phoebe's rules for dealing with step-ins, one absolute was no stepping in while driving. The inherent danger of making such a transition behind the wheel notwithstanding, she had no way of knowing if the shade even knew how to drive stick.

"Not now," she said through gritted teeth. "Let me pull over."

"I don't think so, darling." Her foot pressed hard on the gas pedal as the light at the upcoming intersection turned yellow.

"Dammit, Lila, let go."

"What's the matter? We're just going for a little drive." Lila sped through the intersection, taking the next corner too fast.

"Why don't you tell me where you want me to go, Lila, and I'll drive?"

A low, throaty laugh came out of her. "You don't like it when somebody else drives, do you? At least you know this time."

Phoebe clutched the wheel, feeling like she was in a bad driver's-ed simulator, doing little more at this point than hanging on for the ride. Lila was trying to get under her skin—even though she was already inside her skin—and the more Phoebe focused on negative emotions, the less control she was likely to have.

Lila turned the Jeep around and circled the roundabout onto the Red Rock Scenic Byway, heading south.

"Where are we going, Lila?"

"To a funeral."

"Whose funeral?" As Lila spun around a curve, Phoebe was convinced it would be her own.

"Rafael Diamante's."

Phoebe's heart lunged into her throat. Had something happened to Rafe? She lost control to Lila completely for a moment until her brain reminded her. Rafael Senior. The service was today.

It was unnerving how alarmed she'd become at the thought of something happening to Rafe. It wasn't as if they had a relationship. And she'd all but convinced herself he couldn't be trusted. How could her heart have made that strangled little leap at the very idea of losing someone she didn't even have?

Lila turned onto the winding drive among the red sandstone, heading for the cemetery.

"Why the funeral?"

"Be*cause*." Lila let the word draw out long and slow from Phoebe's mouth. "I figured it would have the most impact."

Before Phoebe could process what this might mean, Lila floored the gas, jerking the wheel on the wet road as the pavement ended. The tires spun in loose gravel.

Phoebe had control of herself now, but not the Jeep. The latter went into a fishtail when Phoebe hit the brakes. And then the world was flipping ass end over teakettle, and Phoebe's head collided with something solid and sharp.

Rafe recognized the out-of-control vehicle as soon as it came to a stop. The graveside service had just concluded when the sound of screeching tires preceded the flip and roll of a driver who'd been going too fast on the paved section of the road. Rafe ran toward the wreck, realizing too late the camera crews covering the funeral were eagerly following.

Hamilton had advised him not to engage reporters, no matter what, but this time he couldn't help himself. "Why don't one of you goddamn vultures make yourselves useful and call 9-1-1?" He reached the overturned Jeep and got on the ground to look inside. Blood ran from the side of Phoebe's head, but she was semiconscious, making a disoriented attempt to unbuckle her seat belt.

"Phoebe, hold still. The paramedics will be here soon. They'll get you out. Let them check to be sure you're okay before you try to move." He reached in and grabbed her hand to keep her from releasing the button, and Phoebe curled her fingers around his. The strength of her grip was reassuring.

She groaned and murmured something that sounded like "glad you're not dead." Rafe figured she must be confused, thinking he'd been in the accident, as well.

He had little doubt the image of him holding hands

with a bleeding, upside-down Phoebe at his father's funeral would be plastered all over the internet in an hour. He shook his head. "What are you doing here?"

"Lila," she murmured.

Rafe followed the ambulance to the hospital against Hamilton's advice. The media was going to make a big deal out of it no matter what he did. He needed to be sure she was okay.

"You could find that out with a phone call," Hamilton had reminded him before giving up with a shrug.

He lied and told the emergency room nurse he was Phoebe's husband so they'd let him in to see her. Phoebe sat on the gurney, looking much more alert, while an ER attendant stitched up a gash on her head at the hairline.

She grimaced gamely as Rafe peered around the curtain. "Beaten up by my own cell phone. Can you believe it?"

"I've been trying to tell people—Skynet has become aware." Rafe stepped inside. "You okay? You had me scared."

"Just a little rattled. And embarrassed. Apparently, I'm headline news again in our little burg."

Rafe waited to ask the serious questions until the attendant finished up and left the little cubicle. "Phoebe, you said something about Lila when you were in the Jeep. Did she…step in?"

Phoebe nodded, wincing and putting her fingers to her scalp below the gauze bandage as though the movement pulled at the stitches. "She was driving. Not the first time she's done that recently. Drive me, I mean. Not the Jeep. Whatever she wanted to achieve, she said it would have more impact at the funeral." Her blue-gray eyes were apologetic. "I'm really sorry, Rafe. I didn't mean to crash your father's funeral. Literally."

"Obviously not your fault. And it had just finished, so you didn't interrupt anything. I'm just glad you're okay. It could have been much worse." Rafe studied her, struck by what she'd said, that it wasn't the first time Lila had taken her over recently. He knew Lila had tried to mess with Phoebe before, but this seemed much more purposeful and malicious. "When else has she done it? Driven you?"

Phoebe looked startled, as if he'd caught her saying something she hadn't meant to, and her complexion made an odd transition from pale to flushed. "I—I don't... I told you before."

Rafe came closer to the gurney, setting his hand on the mattress to steady himself because he was having a horrible thought. "Did it have anything to do with a compromising photograph?"

"Oh, my God." Phoebe covered her face with her hands. "Just kill me now. You got one, too."

"Last night—or I guess this morning—after I left your place. I didn't know what to make of it. But that was Lila, wasn't it?"

Phoebe lowered her hands, scrubbing one palm over her mouth. "I don't really want to talk about it here."

Before he could ask her anything else the nurse swept the curtain aside. "The doctor has cleared you for release, Mrs. Carlisle. We've got all the insurance squared away. It's probably best to have someone keep an eye on you for the next twenty-four hours to make sure there are no ill effects from that bump on your head. Looks like you have a mild concussion. Will your husband be able to stay with you?"

"Yeah, I'm on it," Rafe said before Phoebe could answer. "She's in good hands."

Phoebe eyed Rafe's profile as he led her out to the truck after they'd filled her prescription for pain meds. "Husband, huh?"

"It was the only way they'd let me in."

It was weird how that little word, which obviously didn't mean anything—just a convenience—sounded so unexpectedly sweet. She slipped into the passenger seat, triggered a bit as she buckled the seat belt. Nothing like getting right back on the horse.

Rafe was quiet as they drove along the rainy streets toward her house.

"It's really kind of you to give me a ride home. I could have called my sisters." In truth, she hadn't even let them know she'd been in an accident. She knew they'd worry needlessly, and she'd see them in a few minutes.

"Not a problem." Rafe pulled up in front of the house and sighed as if he'd been holding a deep breath. "Look, Phoebe, I don't know what's going on between you and Hamilton, but—"

"*Nothing* is going on between me and Carter Hamilton." The words came out a little more violently than she'd planned.

Rafe glanced at her. "Well, I'm not concerned about that right now, is what I'm trying to say. It really scared me to see you bleeding and half conscious in that Jeep. I've strengthened the protection spell around the house, but these shades are obviously extremely dangerous and determined. And I'm the reason they've fixed on you. And I know after how I acted last night—this morning— after everything I've done, really, you'd probably just as soon see the back of me. But I think the nurse was right. I should stay with you. If the necromancer's going to…to— whatever he's gotten Lila to make you do—I think it'll be harder for him to do it if we stick together."

Phoebe's pulse was racing. Since this much was out in the open, she had to know. "So, you didn't having anything to do with it? Not with Jacob directing you. No ridealongs of any kind."

Rafe looked genuinely taken aback. "Ride-alongs? With whom? When?"

"With *me,* Rafe. Or with anyone." Phoebe was shaking with delayed shock—and with uttering the words. "Right before my adventure with Lila, I met with a sex worker who knew Monique and she told me even more disturbing things about the ride-alongs than I'd imagined. I need to know you've never participated in that. That you're not part of some network of powerful men these trapped shades are being forced to cater to. I need to know you weren't in on…*that*…with Carter."

Rafe's knuckles went white around the steering wheel. "You think I'd do that?" He swallowed. "Of course you think I'd do that. I conjured Jacob to… Jesus. No. That was the first and only time I ever considered letting a shade 'ride along.' I didn't even know it was possible before that. I swear to you."

Phoebe opened her mouth to respond but the front door to the house flew open with a bang and her sisters came racing out.

"Phoebe! What happened?"

"Where have you been?"

"Don't let Puddleglum out!" Phoebe climbed out of the truck to face the onslaught of sisterly love. When Rafe remained behind the wheel, Phoebe spoke before he could do his usual disappearing act. "Rafe's going to stay for a while. If that's okay with you two."

Predictably, Rhea couldn't just say "sure" and leave it at that. "I guess, if you think you can keep the noise level to a minimum. Some of us need our sleep."

After she'd given her sisters the short version of her adventure with Lila and managed to reassure them she was okay, Phoebe took Rafe's hand. "I kind of need to talk to

Rafe in private." She led him to the bedroom. "And shut up, Rhea Iris."

"What?" Rhea feigned innocence as Phoebe closed the door.

Rafe stood awkwardly with his hands in his suit pockets. Phoebe wondered if it was particularly perverted to find a man dressed in a suit he'd just worn to his father's funeral that attractive.

She hugged her elbows, not sure where things stood between them. "I just wanted to tell you I'm sorry I doubted you."

"You had good reason to. I don't know why you're not throwing me out right now."

Phoebe smiled, looking down at her feet. "As much as I enjoy seeing the 'back' of you, Mr. Diamante, your front is pretty fantastic." She glanced up to find him staring at her with a quizzical smile.

Rafe took a step closer. "You're an unusual woman, Phoebe Carlisle."

Phoebe laughed. "You're a little weird yourself."

"I didn't say it was a bad thing." He lifted her chin, bringing her mouth to the level of his. "The ink on my tattoo is swimming," he murmured. "Every time I'm near you." His kiss was soft and tentative, and Phoebe moved in closer, slipping her arms around his neck, and kissed him back somewhat more aggressively.

Rafe's breathing quickened with his heartbeat, his hands sliding over her hips as he pulled them closer to his, letting her feel his desire for her.

A sudden sharp rap on the bedroom door made Phoebe jump. "Why don't you two get a room?" Rhea's voice on the other side of the door dripped with amusement.

Phoebe drew her mouth away from Rafe's. "We *have* a room. Screw you."

Rafe laughed and tugged on her belt loop, bringing her

up against him again. "I love your mouth. It's like kissing a sailor."

"That's a little weird, Rafe." Phoebe winked. "But whatever floats your boat." She reached up to meet his lips
again but whimpered against them as her head started
to throb.

Rafe searched her eyes. "What's wrong?"

"I think I'm starting to feel that bump on my head. I
should probably take a pill."

"The nurse did say to keep an eye on you, not…every-
thing else on you." Rafe smiled. "Let me get you some
water." Phoebe sat on the bed and he placed a gentle kiss
on her forehead before turning to open the door, but drew
up short.

Rhea stood in the hallway holding a fizzing glass of
sparkling water. "Did someone say 'water'?"

Phoebe made a sound that was half laugh, half groan.
"You suck, Rhe. Stay away from my door."

She could almost hear Rhea's eyes rolling in her head
from across the room. "You're welcome."

Rafe watched the sisters with amusement as Phoebe
took the pill and lay back to close her eyes just for a minute. The minute turned into a surprising several-hour nap.

She found Rafe reading by the light of her bedside
lamp—a paperback romance Phoebe had been reading in
bed the night before.

She propped herself on an elbow. "I wouldn't have
pegged you for a romance fan."

Rafe glanced at the cover with mock surprise. "Oh, is
that what this is?"

Phoebe snorted. "I think the headless naked male torso
pretty much gives it away."

Rafe shook his head. "You women. Always reducing
males to a collection of parts for your amusement."

"Some parts are more amusing than others."

"Ouch."

"Hey, I didn't say any of *your* parts were amusing." Phoebe grinned. "I like your parts just fine."

"Is that so?" Rafe set the book aside and leaned over to give her a kiss that made her toes tingle. "Feeling better?"

Phoebe smiled. "Much." She moved her hand toward his lap, but Rafe caught it in his.

"Unfortunately, I'm sworn to chastity this evening. Your darling sisters made me promise to let you recover fully before putting my filthy man-paws on you."

"Jerks." Phoebe sat up. "They said 'filthy man-paws'?"

"No, I'm embellishing based on my interpretation of an hour-long interrogation I endured."

"Oh, my God. I'm sorry, Rafe. I didn't mean to abandon you to the twin terrors."

Rafe smiled. "That's okay. They're sweet. And they obviously care a great deal about you. It must be nice to have family that devoted to you."

Phoebe studied his guarded expression. "They are now. It wasn't always that way. I was the mean big sister without the bigger-sister clout when they were teenagers. But being on our own definitely made us closer." She touched his forearm. "I'm really sorry about your father. Today must have been tough."

Rafe sighed and wrapped his arms around her, and Phoebe leaned her head against his chest. "It's hard not knowing what happened to him, or who's behind it. But speaking of that, your sisters gave me some rather enlightening information during our little chat."

Phoebe glanced up at him with apprehension. "Enlightening how?"

"Why didn't you tell me what Hamilton did to you?"

Phoebe's shoulders tensed. "They didn't. That wasn't for them to tell."

"Don't be too mad. I kind of dragged it out of them. After what you said about Lila and that photo—" Rafe's voice tightened with anger. "I'd pretty much sorted some things for myself. And I don't mind telling you, I've been having some difficulty not going straight to his hotel and beating the living hell out of him. If it weren't for the fact that I'm too worried to let you out of my sight, I would have."

"Rafe, I don't even know what he actually did. I was out cold."

"I think that's kind of his point. To make you wonder exactly what he did, to be sure you'd have to imagine the worst—to make you wonder if you could trust anyone, ever. Even me. He's a despicable, vile piece of garbage."

Phoebe couldn't disagree. "I do trust you, though. Just so you know. My paranoia got the better of me earlier."

Rafe was quiet for a while, an odd tension in the way he held her. "Phoebe, there's something I need to tell you about me. Something I've never shared with anyone."

Phoebe hugged her arms against his where they were wrapped around her. "Okay."

"When I was in sixth grade…" Rafe swallowed, as if he couldn't quite get the words out. "My soccer coach— he was a friend of the family—he got me drunk and…"

"Oh, Rafe." Phoebe turned in his arms.

"I didn't know what he'd done, either. Until he black-mailed me."

"Son of a bitch." A surge of rage went through her toward a man she'd never met. Beating the hell out of the asshole paled in comparison to what she was fanta-sizing about doing. But her anger probably wasn't what Rafe needed after making himself so vulnerable. Phoebe squeezed her arms tighter around his. "I'm so sorry that happened to you, Rafe."

"I always wondered what I did to make it happen."

"You did *not* make that happen. *He* made it happen. He betrayed your trust."

"I know. I know it now. But it messed with me for years. That's why I was in counseling back in school—the records that reporter dug up. I thought for sure it was all going to come out. I was terrified you'd find out, and that would be the end of whatever was happening between us."

Phoebe was vehement. "Not a chance."

Rafe hugged her against him in silent acknowledgment. "I even tried to cast a spell to prevent it. But the necromancer somehow tapped into my magic and messed with the spell, like he was letting me know he knew all my secrets." Rafe rested his chin on top of Phoebe's head. "And I think that's why he chose to do what he did to you. As a message to me, and to make us both feel powerless."

Phoebe let the implications of that sink in for a moment. There was only one conclusion to draw. "So you think it's him. You think Carter Hamilton is the necromancer."

"I don't see who else it could be. But if he's not, he's working for him. I'm convinced of that."

Chapter 24

Since Phoebe hadn't managed to make it to the grocery store, dinner was Chinese delivery. With her feet tucked under her on the couch while everyone insisted on pampering her, Phoebe shoveled chow mein into her mouth straight from the carton. If her table manners turned out to be a deal-breaker for Rafe, might as well find out now. At least she was using chopsticks and not her fingers.

Rafe only seemed amused. She needed to find an opportunity soon to do something other than amuse him. But that could wait.

He dished out some rice and kung pao chicken onto his plate. "So what were you telling me about your divine bloodline this morning? How does that work, exactly?"

In the excitement of the past twenty-four hours, she'd forgotten about the revelation of their Lilith blood.

Theia turned to look at her with an expression of annoyance. "That wasn't exactly for public consumption, Phoebes."

"Probably should have told me that. Besides, Rafe isn't exactly the public. He's my—" She stopped, mortified.

Instead of looking equally mortified, Rafe shrugged

and kept eating. "Her main squeeze, I think she meant to say." He winked at Phoebe.

Rhea's brows flicked upward with amusement. "Main who-with-the-what, now?"

"Her old man." Rafe chuckled. "Her gentleman caller. Her paramour."

Phoebe finally managed to make sounds with her mouth. "Oh, my God."

Theia laughed. "What decade did we just travel to?"

"What decade didn't we travel to?" Rhea grabbed another pot sticker. "You're weird, Rafe Diamante. I like you."

"See there?" Rafe winked at Phoebe again. "Official family approval. I think that makes me your steady beau."

Phoebe hunkered over her chow mein, trying not to let him see her smile. "I'm pretty sure I'm never going to live this down."

"Not as long as I'm your devoted swain."

Lying awake beside Phoebe, Rafe wondered about the divine heritage she'd referred to. His father's journal had spoken of the divine blood requiring "chalchiuatl" to awaken it, which Rafe had taken to mean a symbolic representation of blood sacrifice. But what if the blood wasn't meant to be his own? And hadn't Jacob said Phoebe was awakening the quetzal within him?

It was awake *now*—the tattoo, at least—ink undulating across his back in a gentle rhythm he'd almost gotten used to, like the susurrus of waves against a shore. It made him restless, annoying Puddleglum, who demanded to be let out of the room after Rafe had fidgeted for half the night. Phoebe, having conked out after taking another painkiller after dinner, slept soundly beside him.

Still wearing the suit he'd worn to the funeral, Rafe had stripped out of it and climbed into bed in the boxers and undershirt he'd worn underneath. Rafe was more of a boxer briefs kind of guy, and normally slept in the nude—but that hadn't seemed like a good option given his promise to Phoebe's sisters to let her rest and recover.

Although, frankly, it didn't seem to matter what he wore. He was going to be up all night in more ways than one. Phoebe's proximity was all that was necessary. He tried getting his mind off his condition by finishing the romance novel he'd started earlier, but found it surprisingly well written—enough to make him wish Phoebe were awake.

He finally managed to drift off well into the wee hours, having vague dreams of coyotes circling and howling in the cemetery.

Phoebe woke just before dawn feeling marvelously rested—and painfully full of the green tea they'd had with dinner. She slipped into the adjoining bathroom as quietly as she could to avoid waking Rafe, but he stirred as she crept back into bed.

"Sorry." She slid under the covers, propping her head on her hand. "Didn't mean to wake you."

"That's okay." Rafe rolled onto his side to mirror her pose and smiled. "I was kind of missing you in my sleep. How's your head?"

"Much better."

He gave her a sly look. "Fully-recovered better?"

Phoebe tilted her head with a little grin. "Aren't you supposed to be the poster boy for chastity this evening?"

Rafe glanced out the window. "It's not really evening anymore."

"You don't say." Phoebe's foot played with his under the blanket.

"And as your devoted swain, I think I'd be remiss if I didn't make a move at this juncture in the courtship."

Phoebe laughed. "God, I'm never going to hear the end of that, am I?"

Rafe leaned in and stopped her laugh with a kiss, and Phoebe closed her eyes, savoring the firm, velvety texture of his lips.

"I can take your mind off it."

Phoebe made a little mewling sound against him as he kissed her again. "Off what?"

Rafe grinned and pulled his undershirt over his head, while Phoebe took the opportunity to unbutton her sleep shirt and wriggle out of it. Damn, he had some fantastic abs. She smoothed her hand across them, and Rafe caught her wrist and drew her close, pulling her on top of him as he rolled onto his back. Both of them were still in their underwear. The half-undressed state and the way they were keeping quiet in an unspoken agreement to avoid waking her sisters made her feel like she was in college again, groping some guy in her dorm-room bunk in the dark.

Rafe gazed up at her as their hips ground together. She had to remember to tread carefully with him. She had a feeling her suggestion to pleasure each other the last time he'd spent the night had triggered memories of what that bastard coach had done.

"We don't have to do anything you're not comfortable with." She trailed a finger over his chest. "You take the lead. Just do whatever you feel like doing."

While pushing the covers down with his foot, Rafe slipped his fingers inside the band of her panties on either side and slid them off to bare her. Goose bumps rose on her skin from the slight breeze of the ceiling fan and from Rafe's hand smoothing over her ass. He pressed the hard ridge of his cock against her naked flesh, making her moan, and then rolled her over so that he was on top, his mouth at her ear.

"I was kind of thinking of fucking you. Sound good to you?"

"No objections," she said breathlessly.

With a quick motion, he lifted his hips and peeled off his underwear, dispensing with hers where they'd caught at her knees. "Where are your condoms?" He gave her a wink. "Just in case."

Phoebe nodded toward the bedside table. "In the drawer."

Rafe reached across her and fished one out, coming up onto his knees as he opened the packet to slide it on. He stroked the sleeve over his cock with his fist, looking down at her, and Phoebe shivered. His silhouette was outlined by the predawn glow, and she could almost imagine an aura of wings at his shoulders, as though the tattoo on his back were spreading them. He lowered his body onto her and Phoebe wrapped her legs around him as he entered her, groaning softly as the heat and hardness filled her, already familiar to her, though he'd only penetrated her once before.

As he began to rock into her, Phoebe stroked her hands over his back and felt the ink of his tattoo raised like silky scales along his spine. Rafe shivered as she followed it with her fingers, and his smooth, slow strokes became more rapid and rhythmic. The tattoo was decidedly moving. The more Phoebe followed his rhythm, the more the ink seemed to take a solid shape under her touch, as if responding to her.

She moaned and buried her face in his shoulder, distracted from the oddity of the tattoo by the stroke of his cock inside her. She was coming already, and she bit his shoulder to muffle the sound as the wave of pleasure rolled through her. Rafe stiffened for an instant before increasing his tempo inside her, intensifying the orgasm. Her teeth dug into the hard muscle of his shoulder. She couldn't help it. If she let go she'd scream like a banshee. The orgasm quickly rippled into another and Phoebe clung to him, moaning against his skin as she rode it out.

Rafe's breathing grew rapid. From the stifled groans, she could swear he was building to his own climax, but before she could wonder about that, the first light of dawn as the sun came up over the ridge of sandstone illuminated Rafe's tattoo. Phoebe gasped. The impression of a wing-like aura was no longer in her imagination. Spread across the room in both directions were the glittering blue-green wings of the tattoo come to life.

Rafe bucked into her with an almost startled motion at the same moment, burying his face in the pillow beside her and groaning with obvious release.

Phoebe let go of his shoulder. "Rafe."

"I know," he groaned, half chuckling. "I wasn't expecting that."

"Your tattoo." Though it seemed inadequate now to call it merely a tattoo. His back still rippled with the colors of Quetzalcoatl's feathery scales, though the physical manifestation of the wings was fading.

Rafe lifted his head. "What about it?"

"Didn't you feel it?"

"I felt it moving—it always does when I'm near you." He smiled. "Kind of felt like I was flying just now, though."

"Rafe, I think you were. In a manner of speaking."

His smile turned puzzled. "What manner of speaking?"

"You...sprouted wings."

"I *what*?"

"It was like you became the tattoo—or the tattoo became you."

Rafe rolled out of the bed, stripping off the condom to flush it down the toilet. In the light from the bathroom, she watched him turning about in front of the mirror, trying to see the tattoo, before he stepped back into the bedroom.

"Are you sure you didn't imagine it?"

Phoebe sat up, cross-legged, and stared him down. "You think I imagined you suddenly had an eight-foot wingspan. That orgasm was awesome, but it wasn't mind-blowing-hallucinogen awesome." She grinned. "I mean, it came pretty damn close. Don't get me wrong."

Rafe vaulted back onto the bed and pulled the covers up over his shoulders as he wrapped himself around her and tumbled her onto her back. "I might have to try again, then." He nipped at her earlobe, which seemed to be connected directly to her clit. "Although, I have to say, whether I sprouted wings or not, bringing things to a finish inside you was pretty mind-blowing. You understand that's never happened to me before."

Phoebe draped her arms over his shoulders and crossed her wrists behind his neck, curling her fingers in his tousled hair. "Yeah, I kinda got that." She grinned up at him. "Maybe I have a magic pussy."

Rafe's mouth turned up at one corner. "You're pretty pleased with yourself."

"It's not me. It's my pussy. It can't help it if it's awesome."

Rafe laughed and pulled her arms away from his neck. "I think your pussy's getting a little uppity. I'm afraid I'm going to have to give it a firm talking-to." He scooted under the covers and pushed Phoebe's legs apart, and she shoved the edge of the blanket into her mouth and bit down as he made good on his word and gave her a serious tongue-lashing.

Chapter 25

They'd managed to sleep past noon. Rafe knew there'd be hell to pay with Phoebe's sisters when they finally made an appearance, so he prolonged it as much as possible by dragging Phoebe with him into the shower stall. Which turned out not to be the wisest move he'd ever made. Seeing Phoebe slick and wet, with the soap and water slithering over her breasts and stomach and down her back into the crack of her ass, he found his cock springing to attention once more.

Just as he considered suggesting they step out of the shower and get back into bed, Phoebe dropped to her knees on the tiled floor of the shower and took him in her mouth. With a groan, Rafe braced one palm against the tiled wall and the other against the glass door, trying to keep himself upright. He'd rarely allowed a woman to suck his cock. The act was too laden with issues of dominance for him, not to mention the futility of someone trying to make him come that ultimately frustrated and annoyed both parties.

But despite the fact that Phoebe was on her knees, there was nothing submissive about the way she was swallowing him. She seemed to be relishing the taste—something he found unfathomable—and her soft humming noises left no doubt she was enjoying herself.

It couldn't hurt to let her give it a go, though he doubted even if he could come from oral stimulation that he'd be able to do it standing in a shower—and so soon after the first time he'd managed to do it with a woman at all. Then again, if she kept up that particular motion with her tongue, all bets were off.

Phoebe's hands were braced against his thighs. She slid them up along his hips, caressing his lower abs, which made his cock twitch in her mouth, and then moving them around to his lower back. The tattoo shouldn't have extended that far, but he felt it slithering under her hands, as though the ink were growing—as though the skin on his back was in fact the slippery, scaly skin of a snake.

He had the almost out-of-body sensation again as he realized he was nearing climax, the feeling of lightness, as if he could fly. With a stifled groan, he let go, letting Phoebe have it all. He wasn't sure about the protocol here. He'd never come in a woman's mouth. What if she wasn't expecting that? What if she didn't want that in her mouth? Rafe clutched her shoulder with one hand as she made it clear that not only didn't she mind, she was eager for it, happily swallowing against him as he shot into her.

He'd squeezed his eyes shut as he'd started to come and he opened them now to watch Phoebe with amazement. But in the mirror over the sink, his reflection caught his eye. Blurred by steam, the image was nevertheless unmistakable: at his shoulders, the glittering sheen of feathers marked the outline of folded wings.

"Holy shit."

Phoebe let go of him, looking up in concern. Rafe reached down and took her hands to help her up, drawing her against him.

"The quetzal." He brushed her wet hair out of her eyes with amazement. "It's awake. *I'm* awake."

The physical manifestation of the quetzal appeared to be something Rafe could control at will if he concentrated hard enough, but it was difficult to maintain. Sexual release obviously worked as a catalyst for it. Or maybe just Phoebe's touch. He wasn't sure. But he looked forward to doing some experimenting to find out.

His appearance returned to normal as he made a conscious effort to breathe deeply and focus on suppressing it. But they couldn't put off emerging from the bedroom any longer. Not wanting to walk around in front of Phoebe's sisters in his boxers, Rafe put on his undershirt with his suit pants and they exited the room, bracing for the expected ribbing. But Theia and Rhea had decided to act as if nothing was amiss.

They'd apparently gone to the grocery store while Rafe and Phoebe were sleeping, acquiring all manner of sugared breakfast cereals and milk, displayed on the breakfast bar along with scrambled eggs, bacon, sausage, toast and three kinds of pastries. Rafe tried not to blush thinking of what he and Phoebe had been doing as the twins were whipping up this feast.

Apparently he failed at that, as Phoebe rose on tiptoe and whispered at his ear, "I love it when the tips of your ears turn pink." Which pretty much turned everything else pink.

Theia had taken up residence in the papasan chair by the window—effectively designating her the Puddleglum petter—while Rhea lingered over what looked like a second bowl of Frosty Charms.

"Help yourselves." Rhea waved at the bounty. "We weren't sure what you'd want."

"Yeah, right." Theia snorted. "Rhea wanted everything."

Rhea glared at her twin before turning back to Phoebe. "How's your head? Feeling better?"

Phoebe rolled her eyes with a groan of exasperation. "Oh, just get it over with. Yes, we did it. Several times, in fact. Are you happy?"

Rhea went back to her cereal. "Wow. Over sharing."

Phoebe shook her head, handing Rafe a cup of coffee. "You two are monsters."

"Hey, what did I do?" Theia smiled sweetly. "I'm just over here...petting the pussy."

Phoebe finished pouring a coffee for herself and stirred in some milk. "I hate you, Theia Dawn." She took a sip and started loading up her plate.

Rhea filled her mouth with cereal and looked across the room at Theia. "Shouldn't she be *less* cranky after riding the hobby horse all night?"

"Well, she *is* out of practice."

"Oh, my God." Phoebe jabbed her fork in the air at both of them. "Stop it right now." The stern look was upstaged by the fact that the fork happened to have a sausage at the end of it.

Rafe tried not to laugh as he kept his head lowered over his coffee mug.

"Don't encourage them." Phoebe was still holding out the sausage and Rafe couldn't help it. He bit off the end. Ignoring her look of outrage, he bent and kissed her.

Rhea raised her hand for a high-five as Rafe straightened. "Welcome to the family, bro. You fit right in." When Rafe went in for the hand-slap, Phoebe, buttering a piece of toast, made a low growl in her throat.

She shook her head with a look of resignation. "I knew this would happen. God is punishing me for leaving the church."

Rafe watched her, leaning back against the sink as she ate her breakfast, pretending to be mad at the sisters she obviously adored, dark ponytail dripping on her shoulder. At that moment he knew without a doubt he was going to marry this woman.

Rafe almost choked on his eggs. *Whoa. Getting a little ahead of yourself there.* He tried to rein in his thoughts. *First time you come with a woman and you're picking out a damn ring.* He busied himself with his plate, trying to ignore his warming ears.

When he glanced up again, Phoebe was pressing her fingers to her temple as she set her plate on the counter.

Rafe set his own plate on the bar. "Are you okay?"

"Goddammit." She gritted her teeth. "Not now."

"Shade," the twins said together. But Rafe didn't need them to tell him a shade was here. Rafe could *see* it.

A handsome woman just beyond middle-age seemed to be sharing the space where Phoebe stood, faded red hair styled as it must have been in life, and her fingernails expensively manicured. "What are you staring at, darling?" The sultry, smoke-edged voice came out of Phoebe's mouth, but it was clearly Lila's shade that was speaking. She put her hand on her hip, and Phoebe mirrored the gesture. "You look surprised to see me. What's the matter? Not what you expected?"

He realized she'd said those last words on her own, no longer animating Phoebe, who stumbled back against the sink and out of phase with her. "How are you doing that?"

"Doing what?" Phoebe's voice was tinged with annoyance.

"Not you," he said. "Lila."

"She's gone already. Thankfully."

"Not exactly."

Lila moved toward him, lips curled in a knowing smile. Phoebe stopped rubbing her temples and looked up. "What are you talking about?"

"She's standing right in front of you."

"She's *what*?"

Rhea slipped off the stool beside him. "Dude, you're freaking me out."

Lila stopped in front of Rafe. "Tezcatlipoca will be pleased your goddess has finally woken you, quetzal." She ran an incorporeal nail down his chest, leaving a trail of goose bumps in the wake of her not-quite touch.

"What's that supposed to mean?"

Phoebe pushed away from the counter. "What's what supposed to mean?"

"I'm talking to Lila."

Lila took a step back and appraised him. "I wish I could see your wings. But perhaps he'll let us see them before he does it."

Despite knowing she had no corporeal form, he took a step toward her. "Does what?"

"Clips them, pretty bird. Thanks to my tumbling your goddess into your arms, you have what Tezcatlipoca desires to take from you. He'll have your vision and your power, as he's wanted all along."

"The hell he will." Rafe grabbed at her arm in a futile gesture as she started to fade. "Wait. Tell me one thing. Who is Tezcatlipoca? Tell me the name of the necromancer."

"His name is Tloque Nahuaque. The Lord of the Near and the Nigh." With that, she was gone.

Phoebe rubbed her arms, seeming to sense the shade's departure. "What did she say?"

"Gibberish. More stupid, arrogant games." He wasn't about to tell her Lila had led them into a trap. That consummating his desire with Phoebe had been exactly what the necromancer wanted.

"I mean about the necromancer. Is it Carter?"

Every time she said Hamilton's first name, it grated on him, though he knew there was nothing between them. "She wouldn't answer."

Theia approached the kitchen behind him. "How come you could see her?"

Phoebe's eyes echoed the question.

"I don't know."

"The quetzal," said Phoebe. "You're awake."

The necromancer might have engineered Rafe's awakening for his own purposes, but now that Rafe *was* awake, he'd have Rafe's power to deal with—whatever that power was. And Rafe had no intention of letting the necromancer win.

With Phoebe and her sisters, Rafe went over the list of enhanced abilities he was aware of: transformation into Quetzalcoatl's nagual—and possibly into the embodiment of Quetzalcoatl himself—the ability to see and hear shades, and, after some experimentation, it seemed he had enhanced strength when he concentrated on allowing the quetzal to manifest. Which might have accounted for his abilities with Phoebe in the bedroom, but he wasn't about to bring that up.

While the Carlisle sisters debated the likelihood of Hamilton being the necromancer and how they could go about proving it, Rafe formulated a plan. The necromancer must know Rafe's "quetzal" had awoken. If he hadn't somehow sensed it himself, Lila would have revealed it to him by now. If Hamilton was the necromancer—and it seemed improbable that it could be anyone else—he'd be seeking a way to take Rafe's power as soon as possible. Rafe needed to fight the bastard on his own turf, while Hamilton still thought Rafe was in the dark.

Making excuses to Phoebe about needing to change his clothes—which was true; he was incredibly tired of wearing this suit—Rafe fortified the protection around the property and headed back to his house, promising to return before dinner. Knowing Lila had only been luring Phoebe into danger to bring the two of them together, he wasn't as worried about Phoebe's safety, but it couldn't hurt to take precautions.

After he'd stripped out of the suit, he took the opportunity to test his abilities once more, invoking Quetzalcoatl at his altar. As with the first time he'd experienced the movement of the tattoo, he had to draw blood before anything happened, but this time the wings—*his* wings—manifested almost without effort. Rafe stared at himself in the full-length mirror, flexing the muscles in his shoulders and back connected to these new limbs and watching the light play on the iridescent teal of his feathers as they rose and fell with his breath.

His skin felt different on his back, as though the tattoo had grown immensely, and Rafe turned in front of the mirror. The wings were even more impressive from this angle—and his back was covered in the iridescent scales of a snake. It wasn't so much that the tattoo had grown as it was, as Phoebe had said, that he'd "become" the tattoo. The scarlet center traversed his spine, fading out into purple before becoming the blue-green of the resplendent quetzal feathers. Mercifully, there were no matching tail feathers sticking out of his ass. He wasn't sure he could have coped with that.

His phone rang and Rafe's muscles tensed, causing the feathers to extend outward, like a wild animal trying to make itself bigger in the face of an enemy. The ringtone was Hamilton's.

He walked to the bed with the wings still pennant and picked up the phone. "Rafe Diamante."

"Rafael, it's Carter Hanson Hamilton."

Rafe resisted the urge to smash the phone against the wall—not because of who it was, but because it was so goddamned annoying that the asshole insisted on making himself sound like a law firm.

"I have some paperwork I need you to sign as executor to your father's will. Can we meet in about an hour?"

It was exactly the opportunity Rafe had been waiting for, but he didn't want to seem too eager. "Can it wait? I was about to hop in the shower. I have dinner plans."

"With Phoebe? How is she?"

"She's fine. Just some bumps and bruises. Doctor says she has a mild concussion."

"She's lucky. That could have been so much worse." *Yeah, I bet it could have, you son of a bitch.* "I'm not sure this can wait, though. It's not just the paperwork. I don't want to go into it over the phone, but I think I have some information about your father's death. Something that may be a link to his killer."

Rafe had to take a few steadying breaths. Of course Hamilton had information. If he was the necromancer, he was the one who'd poisoned him. "What kind of information?"

"Like I said, I'd rather discuss it in person. But a link to your father's killer is a link to Barbara Fisher's killer. There may be light at the end of this tunnel." *Yeah, asshole, and it's calling to you to step into it.*

Rafe spoke casually. "Okay. Why don't you come over to my place?"

"Actually, I'm at your father's house. Can you drive up?"

What the hell was Hamilton doing at his father's house? Rafe had a twinge of misgiving, but the house belonged to him now. It was still his home territory.

"Sure. Be there in an hour."

It took him nearly that long to get his quetzal manifestation under control enough to dress. Rafe took his time on the drive. Let Hamilton wait. Maybe he'd start to sweat, wondering if he'd hooked Rafe, after all. Still an hour from sunset, storm clouds rolling in as he took the twisting drive made the sky appear darker than late afternoon. It was coming down hard by the time Rafe reached the planned community that consisted of less than a dozen sprawling mansions. There was really no other word for them.

He parked beside Hamilton's Mercedes and stared at the door, recalling the last time he'd walked through it.

Hamilton opened it and nodded to him.

Time to roll.

Chapter 26

Hamilton started to pour two glasses of cognac after Rafe followed him into his father's den, but he wasn't about to accept anything the lawyer offered. Instead, Rafe suggested brewing a pot of tea. His father had been almost as much of a tea snob as he'd been a whisky snob, and there were some exquisite varieties in his tea cabinet.

As he warmed his hands around a smoky cup of aged Lapsang Earl Grey, Rafe pretended to believe Hamilton's story. A sex worker had supposedly come forward to say she'd been paid to bring Rafael Sr. an expensive bottle of vintage Scotch whisky on the night he died.

Hamilton dropped a cube of sugar into his teacup and stirred it lightly. "She spoke to me anonymously from a payphone, but she had enough details about the Scotch—it was a rare vintage—that it can't be a scam. She also hinted she knew who else had been at Barbara Fisher's place on the night she was killed." He set his spoon aside and sipped appreciatively. "But she's promised to call again to discuss her terms. I'm certain we can make a deal."

"A deal." Rafe poured himself a second cup, breathing

in notes of pinewood and tobacco. "What exactly is she expecting to get?"

"She wants immunity. And before you say no, let me remind you she claims not to have known the Scotch was poisoned. Someone offered her a lot of money to deliver it, so she didn't ask questions."

Rafe reached for the cream. "And you think my father had a prostitute up here that night. That he hired her from the service Fisher worked for." It was a preposterous story, even if Rafe hadn't already been onto him. His father had never expressed anything but scorn for the idea of "paying for it."

"There were some significant funds your father couldn't account for—that's what I was driving up here to talk to him about that morning—and his financial records show a number of extravagant gifts to women he met only briefly. As a matter of fact, a scandal was about to break that he'd used taxpayer funds for some of those gifts."

Hamilton was starting to piss him off and the smug look on his face made Rafe suspect the slimy bastard knew exactly what was going on here, pushing Rafe's buttons in the lead-up to his attack. He was done playing Hamilton's game. Time to go on the offensive.

Rafe finished his tea and set the cup on the table, staring Hamilton down. "I think we both know why you really wanted me to come here tonight."

Hamilton managed to look convincingly baffled. "We do?"

"You think you're going to take what's mine."

"Yours? Rafael, if this is about Phoebe, I have no intention of coming between you two. I still don't think your association with her is wise, but once the charges against you have been dropped—which they will be, I assure you, as soon as we make this deal—the point will be moot."

"You know tha's not what I mean." Rafe swallowed. Had he just slurred? His throat felt numb. His gaze went to the ceramic creamer. If his father had kept cream in the house, it would have gone bad by now. Hamilton had brought this.

He fumbled in his pocket for his phone, thinking he could dial Phoebe and leave it connected without Hamilton knowing, but he'd left it in his coat in the kitchen.

"Looking for this?" Hamilton smiled and patted the rectangle shape in his shirt pocket. "I've turned off the ringer so we won't be disturbed." He sat back in Rafe's father's favorite chair and laid his arms on the rests. "Rafael, the key to being successful in this business is being smarter than everyone around you. And I don't doubt you're an intelligent man. But a shrewd lawyer studies his opponents long before he enters the courtroom, learns their weaknesses. And he comes prepared."

Rafe's head fell back against the cushion of his chair and he couldn't seem to lift it. Hamilton was right. He'd gone off half-cocked, so eager to take Hamilton down he hadn't made any kind of a plan. He'd been extraordinarily stupid.

"What I've given you is a kind of concentrated pulque, but with my own special adaptations."

Pulque—according to Aztec legend it was what Tezcatlipoca had given Quetzalcoatl to destroy him, getting him so intoxicated on the fermented sap of the century plant that Quetzalcoatl committed incest with his sister. Or saw his reflection distorted into an image of his own imperfection and cruelty, depending on which version you subscribed to.

"I'm sure you know the story." Hamilton smiled. "I thought it would be particularly fitting. But don't worry. It won't kill you. I need you alive—at least to perform the ritual."

"What...richal?"

Hamilton rose and came around the table, bending over Rafe to unbutton his shirt. Rafe's heart raced, his PTSD triggered by the unwanted touch. But whatever Hamilton had put in his pulque, it had rendered Rafe powerless to move of his own accord.

"I need to prepare you." Hamilton worked through the buttons. "It's nothing prurient. A ritual bath must be performed before we can begin. And, as you know, with any ritual, clothing dampens the body's energy." He began to draw Rafe's arms from the sleeves, easing Rafe forward to slump against him so he could remove the shirt.

"Fuh…cue." Rafe's cheek smashed against Hamilton's chest.

Hamilton laughed as he eased Rafe back into the chair and started removing Rafe's boots. "I admire your spirit, Rafael. If you were the weak, ineffectual man your father believed you to be, you could never have fulfilled the promise of your family legacy. And, as I said, I did my homework on you long before I arrived in this cozy if slightly pretentious little burg.

"It was sheer luck, of course, that Ione's sister, a bona fide scion from one of the most ancient and powerful bloodlines, happened to be a talented evocator, as well. All I had to do was drop a little hint to Ione that Phoebe might be able to provide you with the unorthodox assistance you needed to clear your name."

Was he really going to stand here and give Rafe the "villain" speech? The fucker was a walking cliché.

Hamilton paused to admire the wind jewel tattoo on Rafe's chest. "Nice work." He placed his palm against it and Rafe's skin rippled with a flinch though his muscles wouldn't respond further. "Very well placed. It will do nicely."

He finished undressing Rafe before stepping back and invoking Mictlantecuhtli and Mictecacihuatl, Lord and Lady of the Underworld. The air around them seemed heavy with energy, as though a host of shades was trying to manifest.

Hamilton spoke in a casual tone. "Ernesto."

The shade of a middle-aged man appeared, looking almost solid. He bowed before the necromancer who'd conjured him, his gaze going to Rafe with surprise—evidently at being seen—as he raised his head.

"Prepare a bath for the quetzal. You'll find the necessary implements in the bathroom upstairs and to the right."

Rafe gasped as the shade rushed into him with his breath. Despite his drugged, immobilized state, he found himself on his feet, walking toward the steps.

Ernesto didn't speak through him as he ran the bath and poured in the vial of fragrant oil that sat on the counter, moving like a silent, unobtrusive servant—but using Rafe's body to do it.

"'Nesto," he croaked, watching his own hands sprinkle dried hibiscus petals and a pinch of salt into the bath, as if he were having an out-of-body experience. "Why...?" He couldn't get anything else out, but Ernesto seemed to understand him.

"Why do I help Tezcatlipoca?" It was unnerving to hear himself speak without being conscious of forming the words, the shade unaffected by the pulque. "I told you before. We are his slaves." He stepped into the bath as it filled, and sank into it, the water almost scalding. The tub was as luxurious and overdesigned as everything in this house, a round, sunken marble bath with faucets on both ends to heat the water evenly, and big enough to stretch out in and submerge himself to his shoulders.

Rafe couldn't form any more words on his own. His tongue felt like lead. *But what if we protected your family from him?* As he suspected, Ernesto could hear the thought.

"There is no protection from the Night Wind. Yohualli Ehecatl sees and hears all. He is everywhere."

I protected Phoebe from his nagual with a perimeter spell. And Phoebe was able to cast the shades out and

send them packing, without my help. But you were there.
You know that.

"It doesn't matter." The words were uttered in a mono-
tone, as though the conversation were boring Ernesto. Or
perhaps it was hopelessness. "He has my bones."

Rafe had an instant picture in his head of what the
shade meant: a shrine Hamilton had set up somewhere
with a pile of bones jumbled in a large clay bowl. They
were finger bones from the look of them, but the sizes
were inconsistent. These were from several individuals.
The necromancer had somehow taken a bone from each
of the corpses of the shades he controlled—perhaps he'd
even murdered all of them. The bones of his victims. That's
how he controlled them so completely. Rafe should have
guessed.

So even if Ernesto's family was safe, the necromancer
owned Ernesto's shade. As he'd said, they were his slaves.
Unless the bones were burned or returned to their graves,
the shades were chained to the earthly plane, unable to
cross over. It was as hateful and vicious a thing as Rafe
had ever heard of—as cruel as crossing shades against
their will.

The necromancer appeared in the doorway. "I'm ready
for you." In true creep fashion, he was naked for the ritual,
except for a ceremonial wind jewel pectoral made of gold
and jadeite. Rafe wished he could vomit, but Ernesto was
suppressing his voluntary functions. He stepped out of the
tub, taking the towel Hamilton held out. Hamilton placed
a short string of beads of something like shell around his
neck.

Under Ernesto's volition, Rafe followed the necromancer back downstairs and into the foyer. Was he going
to march Rafe outside like this, with both of them naked?
Instead, Hamilton opened the door to the rain-collecting
pool. Rain was currently pouring into it. A kind of St.

Andrew's Cross stood in the center, a frame with two beams forming an X, complete with bondage restraints.

Screw you, pervert. I am not *going in there.* He tried to resist, but he was only along for the ride at this point. Ernesto led him straight to it, turning him around to face Hamilton, who stepped into the rain with them and brought Rafe's arms to the restraints at the tips of each beam of the cross to secure him, doing the same at the bottom with his ankles.

Rafe's body shuddered and Ernesto left him.

Hamilton observed him. "I imagine you're probably quite numb at this point. But it should wear off in an hour or so. You'll have your voice back near the end of the ritual, which I don't mind telling you will enhance the experience for me. By the end of the ritual, of course, I'll be in possession of all your energy. But I expect you'll still be able to scream."

Rafe could only stare daggers at him while he cursed Hamilton in his head with every swearword in his vocabulary.

Hamilton had set up one of the hutches from his father's liquor collection beside the cross as an altar, with a set of gold-trimmed hurricane lamps for the candles positioned inside. He cast the circle, calling the corners using the four "Tezcatlipocas"—which, in addition to Huitzilopochtli and Xipe Totec, included Quetzalcoatl as "White Tezcatlipoca." This highlighted Hamilton's spectacular arrogance, calling upon the very god whose avatar he now sought to subjugate.

When Hamilton picked up the dried maguey spine standing in as an athame, Rafe realized the necromancer intended to follow the legend, piercing Rafe in the ceremonial manner to let his blood. His breath quickened as he fought to move something—anything—but his body was unresponsive. If only it were also numb to sensation, but from his experience with the scalding bathwater, Rafe knew that wouldn't be the case.

Hamilton began. They were only ceremonial cuts, just enough to draw blood—from his earlobes, calves and tongue…and a jagged line down the shaft of his cock. This last cut brought out the quetzal, the wings trapped between the beams of the cross until Hamilton drew him forward to let them stretch across the width of the glass enclosure.

Rafe managed to gnash his teeth and hiss.

"Magnificent." Hamilton stroked his hand along the top of one wing. "I think these will look rather fine on me, don't you?" He turned to show Rafe his back, revealing an almost identical tattoo to Rafe's Quetzalcoatl.

That was taking the creep factor a little too far. How long had this nut-bag been stalking him? Even his father hadn't known about Rafe's tattoo. He'd gotten it after high school when he'd begun studying to apply to the Covent, a way of putting the past behind him and marking his body as his own.

Hamilton turned to face him. "When I've fully absorbed your power, the quetzal will take up residence in me. The pity is you'll never have the chance to learn to use it. But I'll give you a glimpse of what I can do before I send you to Mictlan."

Chapter 27

Rafe wasn't answering his phone. Phoebe's texts had gone unanswered all afternoon and calls went straight to voice mail.

She'd tried to tell herself she was just being paranoid. He'd probably forgotten to charge his phone before leaving the house. But the yipping howl of a coyote bold enough to come out before nightfall in the pouring rain had set her nerves on edge.

When Rafe hadn't arrived before they'd finished making dinner, they started without him. Phoebe pushed steak around her plate, listening to the baying of what were once again multiple coyotes off in the distance, while the twins kept insisting Rafe would be along any minute. But by the time they'd eaten, darkness had fallen, and they were starting to share her suspicions.

Theia cleared the dishes. "It doesn't make sense he'd be gone this long and not at least call."

Rhea nodded, chin in her hands as she rested her elbows on the countertop. "And the fact that his phone is going straight to voice mail means either the battery died and he hasn't managed to charge it since he left five hours ago, or it's off."

Phoebe handed Theia her barely touched plate. "So what do we do?"

After a quick twin glance of silent communication, Rhea spoke. "There's a little something I've been practicing that might come in handy."

"Practicing?" Phoebe glanced from one to the other. "Practicing how?"

Theia set the dishes in the sink. With her back to Phoebe, she lifted the hem of her shirt. At her sacrum was a tattoo Phoebe hadn't seen before—as far as she'd known, she and Rhea were the only inked ones in the family.

"When did you get that?" She rose and went into the kitchen to take a closer look. It was a beautifully stylized rising sun, the horizon and rays done in thin black outline with the look of fancy ironwork, an airbrushed wash of color behind it that changed in hue from a deep gold in the disk of the sun to brilliant oranges and reds as it blended into the "sky" of Theia's back. "Wow. That is *gorgeous*." Phoebe turned her head toward Rhea at the bar. "Did you design this?"

Rhea nodded almost bashfully, not a look she was used to seeing on her little sister.

"I tattooed it."

Phoebe gaped, taking a closer look at the tattoo. "Oh, my God. You *tattooed* it? When did you learn to tattoo like this?" Not that Phoebe was any kind of an expert, but it was the finest work she'd ever seen.

"Like I said, I've been practicing." Rhea got up and came around the breakfast bar to where they were. "But that's not what we wanted to show you." She put the tips of her fingers on the image. "I discovered I can sort of… well, do a 'reading' from my tattoos."

"A reading?"

Theia sucked in her breath and Phoebe put a hand on her arm. "What's going on? You okay?"

Before Theia could answer, however, Phoebe made a sharp inhalation of her own. She'd never had a vision before, but she was having one now. She watched Theia in her cap and gown accepting her diploma, while Rhea stood waiting at the steps of the platform for Theia's name to be called. This was the scene as Phoebe remembered it from their high school graduation. While they'd still worn their hair the same, her sisters had decided to do a classic "twin swap" for the ceremony just to mess with people. They'd kept it up all night long.

The vision dissipated and Phoebe realized Rhea had stepped away. "What just happened?"

"I'm some kind of conduit for the reading." Rhea shrugged sheepishly as Theia lowered her shirt and turned around. "While I'm touching my work, the person I'm 'reading' sees what I see—and so does anyone else who's in physical contact with either of us at the time. I call it 'pictomancy.'"

Phoebe shook her head. "Only you would come up with a whole new form of divination. But why did I just see your graduation?"

"I was thinking about the last time Rhe and I were sort of a 'unit.'" Theia shrugged. "We were always 'the twins,' always together in every class, everywhere we went. That night was our last hurrah before we went out into the big, wide world to be individuals."

Rhea laughed. "The big, wide world of 150 miles apart."

"So how does this help us find Rafe?" Phoebe shivered at the sound of the coyotes calling to each other.

Rhea put her hands in her pockets and rocked back on her heels. "Well, it might not work at all, but I was thinking since I designed your tattoo, I might be able to read it, even though I didn't ink it."

Phoebe blinked at her. "And then what? I see myself in law school? How is that going to help?" She knew she was being short with Rhea, but mounting fear for Rafe had her on edge.

"I don't just read memories. The subject of the reading concentrates on what they want to learn about, just like a tarot reading or a palm reading. It can be a general reading about the person and where they're going in life, or something more specific and immediate."

"She did one about my love life." Theia gave Phoebe a warning frown before she could ask. "And we're not going to talk about it."

Phoebe's curiosity was piqued but she saved her needling for later. She considered what Rhea might be able to glean from a reading of the moon tattoo. Maybe it was as simple as concentrating on Rafe's location.

"Okay, let's give it a shot." She slipped her top over her head and Rhea put her palm over Phoebe's navel. Phoebe closed her eyes and repeated in her head, *Where are you, Rafe? What's happened?* But as hard as she concentrated, no vision came.

After a moment she opened her eyes. "Am I doing it wrong? Should I be trying to picture Rafe or just thinking a question?"

Rhea dropped her arm. "It shouldn't take that much work."

Phoebe sighed. "Maybe it only works on Theia, because of your twin connection."

"No, I've tried it on two other friends I've tattooed, and the reading happened just like it did with Theia. It must be the tattooing that makes the connection." Rhea threaded her fingers through the short hair at her temples in frustration. "Sorry, Phoebes. I wasn't sure it would work."

"But if you tattooed me, would it work right then or would it have to heal first?"

Rhea paused with her fingers woven together behind

her head. "Well…right away. That's how I found out, while I was tattooing Thei."

"Then tattoo me." Phoebe put her shirt back on.

"Phoebe…" Rhea's hands dropped to her sides. "I don't have my kit with me."

"But you can go get it."

Rhea glanced at Theia and back, as if she thought Phoebe might be starting to lose it. "That's going to take hours. It's at least two each way. *Maybe* one and a half if I drive fast."

"I need to do something, Rhe. Something bad has happened. I feel it. And if there's anything we can do to find him, I need to try. Please."

Theia nodded at her twin. "Do it. I'll stay here with her and we'll call you on your cell if anything changes, so you won't have to drive all the way there and back if he shows up."

Rhea looked dubious. "Are you sure? A tattoo isn't something to get on a whim. Especially one of mine. Have you even thought about what you might want?"

"I know exactly what I want." Phoebe crossed her arms. "Just go."

Rhea shrugged and grabbed the car keys from the coffee table. "See you in a few hours, then." She gave Phoebe a hug. "I'm sure it'll all turn out to be a misunderstanding—a flat tire or something—and you'll be calling me to head right back."

"I hope so." Phoebe knew she wouldn't be.

Theia studied Phoebe as Rhea headed out. "So, what are you going to get?"

Phoebe didn't hesitate. "A resplendent quetzal."

The numbness of the pulque had started to lessen, but other effects were becoming apparent as movement returned to Rafe's limbs. Unadulterated pulque had a high that was almost hallucinogenic, but whatever Hamilton had put into his concentrated brew was seriously starting to mess with Rafe's head.

The rain had stopped falling a while ago but Rafe's skin kept rippling with sensation, as if drops were falling on it and slithering down his body. The invisible raindrops seemed to take on a translucent form, like tiny, clear snakes.

Hamilton had left him for a while, but returned periodically to observe him, as though waiting for something specific to happen. When Rafe started feeling the "snake" drops, Hamilton watched him with a smile.

"I see it's beginning. Are you having visual hallucinations or just creepy-crawlies?"

Rafe tried to open his mouth to tell Hamilton to go fuck himself, but his muscles still weren't responding to his brain.

"What you'll see, once they begin, is your true self. Like the original Tezcatlipoca, I am the smoking mirror to which you are being held up, and as you experience your true self, your power will pass through the plane of reflection and become mine."

Smoking mirror. It was the English translation of Tezcatlipoca's name. Hamilton's narcissism and presumption were mind-blowing. What he had was more like smoke *and* mirrors. Hamilton's magic was all tricks, spells he'd perfected, perhaps, but no innate power. Rafe could feel his own power in his limbs, though he couldn't yet access it. All he had to do was wait.

But something was happening in the glass around him. Hamilton had turned off the lights inside the house, and the flickering candles on the makeshift altar were throwing shadowy reflections on the surface of the glass. Instead of being reflections of what was inside the pool—Rafe on the St. Andrew's Cross—it was like a movie projection dimly seen, as though projected onto smoke.

To his left, he saw himself on his last night with his father, face twisted with self-righteous anger. There had been no reason for Rafe to bring up the fact that his father's best friend had been screwing his wife. But he hadn't been able to resist in the face of Rafael's criticism.

The realization struck him like a blow to the gut. He'd been blaming his father for what Ford had done to him, when it was Ford who was to blame, Ford who'd violated his father's trust, and his mother's—and violated Rafe. His father hadn't done anything to him, and it had been cruel to lay that at his doorstep. And worse to keep digging at him about his mother's infidelity.

But the images on the right now caught his attention. It was Gabriel's shade, on the night Rafe had forcibly crossed him. His younger brother knelt, pleading, as Rafe ignored him and continued the invocation. Around this image, other scenes played—Gabriel in middle school and high school, drinking to excess as he'd done from the first time he'd broken into their father's liquor cabinet with his friends at age twelve. *Twelve.* Jesus Christ. Gabriel had been acting out, just as Rafe had at that age. By then, Rafe had blocked it all. He was busy with college, getting his life together. And he'd left Gabriel to take his place.

Rafe's mouth and limbs might not yet be responding to his brain, but he was able to weep, and he did so, gut-wrenchingly, as he began to realize how thoroughly he'd abandoned his brother, too absorbed with himself at every turn to hear Gabriel's cries for help.

In front of him, Hamilton seemed to have become transparent. Rafe was still aware of being watched, but Hamilton had ceased to matter to him. Through him he saw the reflection in the sliding door of the enclosure—Rafe's shame and rage in his youth, his fumbling attempts to "be a man" as his father wanted him to be, which had only ended in humiliation with the women he'd desired.

Then he saw himself with Phoebe. Though he knew
the scenes were Jacob animating him, he seemed like a
predator to himself, trying to seduce her, and then nearly
allowing Jacob to consciously assist him that night at his
house, like a fool. God, he didn't deserve Phoebe. How
could she even stand the sight of him?

Another image formed in the smoky glass—Rafe with
Barbara Fisher. His heart rate accelerated as he watched
himself arguing with her. He couldn't hear the words. Then
she was stepping out of the room to answer the door while
Rafe's body sat slumped in a chair.

His soul seemed to shrivel inside him as her other visitor came into view. Rafe's apprentice, Matthew, gave the
psychic a shockingly intimate kiss. But as he stepped back,
his expression transformed—as though he'd become someone else—and Barbara stumbled away from him. She'd
been hosting a shade and had transferred it to Matthew.
And from the look of fear in her eyes, she knew why.

Rafe turned away from the vision, eyes fixed on Hamilton with hatred, as Matthew's image in the glass donned
the leather gloves. He couldn't watch any more. Hamilton
had destroyed Matthew—an eager and promising young
witch—to spite Rafe.

But in front of Hamilton's transparent form, someone
else's image took shape. A dusty-haired man in his early
twenties stood watching Rafe, hands shoved into the pockets of his jeans. His head tilted as he realized he was being
watched back.

"Hello, Rafe." The gentle twang of his voice, mildly
tinged with surprise, was familiar. Jacob's shade was addressing him, here in the present. "You can see me." He
came closer when Rafe said nothing, walking through the
rainwater pool toward him. "But you can't answer me."
Jacob glanced back at Hamilton, who showed no awareness of his presence. "I was looking for Lila. Sometimes

it's hard to track her, so I focus on Tezcatlipoca. She's never far."

Jacob circled Rafe with interest, shaking his head as he came back around to the front. "I could step in and help you speak, but not much else. He's got you strapped in pretty tight. Like a steer about to have a bolt shot into its skull."

Rafe managed to move his head slightly, trying to signal to Jacob to step in, anyway. If he had volition, even if it were Jacob's volition, he might be able to use his quetzal power to break the restraints.

Jacob didn't seem to notice the movement. "I see your lovely Phoebe finally got the quetzal to come out and play." He grinned. "Congratulations on your success, my friend."

They were hardly friends, but Rafe was in no position to refute him. Around him, the images of his true self were still playing out, but Jacob seemed unaware of them.

The shade glanced at Hamilton, who was still oblivious to Jacob's presence. "I've tried stepping into him. Thought maybe I could get him to release his hold on Lila. But I pass right through him. I think he has some kind of protective amulet that keeps us out." Jacob moved toward Hamilton and passed his hand through the necromancer's. "Probably this ring."

He wandered back toward Rafe, his scuffed cowboy boots, incorporeal manifestations of Jacob's self-ideation, unaffected by the water he waded through. "There is one thing I could do for you, though. If you'll do something for me."

There was still no word from Rafe by the time Rhea returned from her place in Tempe with her tattoo kit.

Phoebe had found a picture online of the resplendent quetzal in flight, its curled tail plume gloriously displayed, and had it printed out and waiting when Rhea arrived.

Rhea studied it after she'd set up her equipment. "Don't get mad at me, Phoebes, but I don't think you should get this."

Phoebe bristled. "What? Why? It's what I want."

Rhea looked up from the printout. "I know this is hard to hear, sweetie, but what if something happens between you two later? Do you want his symbol on your skin forever, reminding you of a fling? Hot guy or not, you barely even have a relationship—"

"It is *not* a fling." Phoebe glared at her. "We have a relationship. I don't need weeks or months to know I'm in love with someone."

Rhea searched her eyes. "Have you said that to him? You nearly swallowed your tongue last night when you almost called him your boyfriend on accident."

Heat rose in her cheeks. "No, I haven't said it. Because I'm an idiot and I was scared he wouldn't say it back."

"And what if he doesn't? Say we find him, everything's hunky-dory, you tell him you're in love with him and he says, 'Thanks, that's sweet'?"

Phoebe's eyes prickled with the sudden sting of tears. "Why are you doing this?"

"Because *I* love you, Phoebes. And I don't want you to regret this for the rest of your life. A tattoo is forever. Unless you've got a lot of money and you want to go through a lot of pain to get rid of it. And I won't take part in branding you with something in the heat of the moment that could hurt you later."

The tears spilled over. "What's going to hurt me later is if he dies because I didn't do everything I could to help him."

"Oh, Phoebe, honey, don't cry." Rhea put her arms around her. "We can find something else that isn't so personally related to him that still means something to you." Rhea studied the printout again. "Besides, this kind of detail would take hours. And I don't think you want to wait that long." Phoebe hadn't even thought of that. Of course it would.

Theia picked up the paper. "What about the tail feather?" She handed it to Rhea as Phoebe surreptitiously used the edge of her shirt to wipe her eyes. "That's less specific, more of a symbol of spiritual guidance and self-reliance. And, in this case, a celebration of your individuality, because the plume is so unique."

Rhea nodded. "That wouldn't take too long, depending on how big you want it and where. Maybe an hour."

Phoebe felt like crying again as she gathered them in a group squeeze. "You guys are awesome. That sounds perfect." She took off her shirt and turned to one side. "And I don't want it too big, just here on my right shoulder blade, extending down and angled toward my spine. Maybe six inches long?"

Rhea smirked. "You trying to find a way to personally relate it to him, after all?"

Phoebe turned back and shoved Rhea's arm as her sister laughed. She held Rhea's gaze deliberately. "Make it eight."

Chapter 28

Ultimately it took Rhea two hours to draw and ink the tattoo to her satisfaction. It wasn't elaborate, mostly shaded color within a thin outline, without the detailed definitions of the feathering. Rhea promised to work on it more at another time to do the image justice, but even the basic tattoo, Phoebe thought, was lovely. Rhea had mixed the perfect blend of jade and aquamarine to fill in her graceful, curving outline, giving the tattoo an almost wispy thinness to keep it in proportion with the length Phoebe had chosen. An actual-size plume would have been at least two feet long—which Rhea couldn't resist joking about as she worked.

Phoebe looked at it over her shoulder in the bathroom mirror when Rhea was done, already feeling a connection to Rafe—even if her sisters wouldn't approve. Still high on endorphins, she went back out to the living room.

"I love it, Rhe." She gave her sister a hug and a kiss on her cheek. "Let's read it."

Rhea stripped the latex glove off her right hand and placed her palm against the tattoo while Phoebe concentrated on Rafe's whereabouts. This time, something happened immediately, as it had with Theia's tattoo.

Phoebe saw an image of water falling against glass, like a room made entirely of windows. Then Rafe appeared, but it was a memory of him from the night she'd spent at his house—Rafe telling Phoebe his last words to his father had been a dig about Rafe's mother's infidelity. Then another image appeared—one of the Diamante Construction and Excavation billboards with Rafe's father's picture on it—before the vision dissipated.

Theia, sitting opposite her, leaned in as Phoebe opened her eyes. "What did you see?"

"Water and glass. I have no idea what that means. Then something about Rafe's father—a billboard for the business." Phoebe shook her head, turning to Rhea. "Did that make any sense to you?"

Rhea ran her fingers through her bleached-blond pixie cut. "What was the question you had in your mind?"

"I was thinking 'Where are you, Rafe?'"

"So the answer could be literal—in a glass room full of water made for Rafael Diamante Senior by his construction company."

"Where in the world would that be? Who would have a glass room full of water? What is it, a shower?"

"A rain catcher," said Theia. "I saw it on some program showcasing homes of the wealthiest Arizonans. It's in Mr. Diamante's house."

Phoebe stared at her for an instant before she tacklehugged her. "Thank goodness you watch even more TV than I do."

Rhea peeled off the other glove. "So, where's Diamante's house?"

"I don't know. But the address has to be online somewhere, right?" Phoebe grabbed her tablet from her bag and pulled up the browser.

"Not necessarily. Super-rich businessman and politician? He wouldn't exactly advertise it."

Phoebe realized Rhea was right as soon as she started searching. Maybe if he were someone like John McCain, who couldn't really hide from the public eye. But anyone less famous but equally wealthy would be a challenge. "Any ideas, Thei?"

She thought Theia might remember the street or neighborhood the house was in, but, as usual, Theia's answer was the one that should have been obvious but would never have occurred to anyone else.

"Ione. She'd have the alumni list for the Covent."

Spot-on or not, Phoebe didn't relish bringing Ione into this. She was bound to get an earful no matter what she told Ione, but if she had to tell her about Carter Hamilton, there was no telling how Ione would take it.

"Any other ideas?"

"We have to tell her about Rafe's lawyer, anyway." Trust Rhea to zero in on what Phoebe was leaving unsaid. "Everyone in the Covent is in danger from this nut-job. Even if he's not the necromancer and just a garden variety fuck-pig." No one could accuse Rhea of mincing words.

Phoebe bit the bullet and dialed Ione on speakerphone. After three rings she was afraid it was going to the machine, but Ione picked up before it rolled over.

"Phoebe." The flat intonation said she was still pissed about the Taizé service.

"Hey. It's the Three Musketeers. Rhea and Theia are here."

They greeted her in unison. "Hey, Di!"

Ione's voice became considerably more animated. "What are you two doing here? When did you get in?"

"Rhe came up to see me after finals. We just drove down on a whim." Theia's innocent-sounding answer conveniently avoided actually answering either question. Phoebe smiled to herself. She'd taught them well.

But Ione wasn't easily fooled. "And what are you doing

calling me at one in the morning? You three haven't been drinking, have you?"

Phoebe sighed. "No, we have *not* been drinking. I need to ask you for something, and it's really important, so please try to listen with an open mind before you refuse outright."

Ione's answering sigh was audible. "Phoebe, you don't talk to me for months, but when you want something magical, all of a sudden I'm really important to you. It's pretty shitty."

"You're right, and I'm sorry. But this is an emergency."

"What do you need now?"

"Do you have Rafe's father's home address?"

"Rafe's father? Why would you need his address? He's dead."

Phoebe tried to keep her voice calm. "Yes, I know he's dead. But I think Rafe is in trouble, and I'm pretty sure he's there."

"We did a reading," Theia added. "He's there."

"You did a reading?" Ione's voice was clipped. "What are you fooling around with, Phoebe? If this is more shade nonsense—"

"Ione, his life is in danger." There was no time to dance around it. Phoebe would have to come clean. "We found out who's been manipulating the shades. The man who killed Barbara Fisher, and probably Rafe's father, and my client Monique Hernandez—he's a necromancer. And I think he has Rafe." The silence that followed was so long, Phoebe thought the line had dropped. "Are you still there?"

"If you think Rafe is in danger, you should call the police."

"Ione—"

"I'm serious, Phoebe. I'm not going to give you privileged information so you can run off and get yourself killed playing detective. And Theia and Rhea with you. What are you thinking? If you want to be respected as a lawyer—

and an adult—maybe you should start acting like at least one of those things."

Phoebe's face went hot and she couldn't speak.

"Ione, it's Theia. We totally love you and respect you, but you're dead wrong about Phoebe. This guy's been targeting her, and the police aren't going to be able to handle him. I know Phoebe doesn't want to ask, but we need more than just the address. We need the Covent's help."

"Theia!" Phoebe grabbed for the phone to take it off speaker, but Theia held it out of her reach.

"You can bind his magic, can't you?"

"Bind his magic?" The low pitch of Ione's voice said she wasn't messing around. "How would we be able to bind some random necromancer's magic? How would we even know what spells he uses? You don't understand how magic works, Theia. None of you do. And you shouldn't be messing around in—"

"He's a Covent member." Rhea had interrupted before Phoebe could stop her. "And don't tell us we don't understand how magic works just because we aren't ordained into the secret society. We may not know spell work, but I know enough about it to know the Covent can bind one of their own. Which is why we need your help."

Ione's silence was full of outrage. When she finally spoke, her words were carefully controlled. "What Covent member?"

Phoebe shook her head at Rhea but Theia answered. "Carter Hamilton."

Unexpectedly, Ione burst out laughing. "I can't believe you guys prank-called me at one in the morning. You're awful. Now go to bed and we'll get together tomorrow."

Phoebe frowned. "It's not a joke." Laughter was a peculiar response for Ione. Why would she think they'd prank her about something like this?

Ione still sounded amused. "You three call me in the middle of the night—after you've obviously been drinking—to tell me my boyfriend is a necromancer. That's a good one, but, come on. Admit defeat."

Theia fumbled the phone and Phoebe grabbed it, almost hitting End Call on accident, her heart pounding so hard she couldn't think. She and Theia stared wide-eyed at each other, trying to figure out if they'd both heard the same thing or they were losing their minds.

Only Rhea retained the ability to form a coherent sentence. "I don't know who you're seeing, Di, but Theia said *Carter Hamilton*. Rafe's lawyer."

"Yes, ha, ha, you caught me and decided to teach me a lesson for not telling you I was involved with someone new. You're hilarious, all of you, now go to bed." With a little click, the phone's screen informed them the call had ended.

They were stunned speechless, staring at the black screen, until Rhea broke the silence. "Did that just happen? Is she punking us?"

"Call her back," said Phoebe. "One of you call her back on your phone. She won't answer if I call."

Theia pulled hers out of her pocket and hit Ione's number. Three rings again. Four. "You've reached Ione Carlisle. Speak your piece."

Phoebe grabbed the phone. "Ione, this isn't a joke. If you're really seeing Carter Hamilton, you're in danger. Please pick up." Ione was the only person Phoebe knew who still used her landline. "Carter is part of an organized sex trade ring that's been abusing living sex workers as well as shades. Ione…he sexually assaulted me."

The machine cut off. Whether because of a time limit on the recording or because Ione had disconnected the phone, Phoebe couldn't be sure. But she was sure she shouldn't have left that message on an answering machine anyone in the apartment might be able to hear. What if Carter was there with her? Or showed up later and played the message?

"I don't know what to do," she said to no one in particular.

Theia and Rhea answered together in true twin synchrony. "We'll drive over there."

Rhea got to her feet. "You stay here in case Rafe shows up. Keep your phone charged. We'll call you once we've talked to Di."

Phoebe had no reasonable argument. "You call the cops if Carter's there. Don't try to get between the two of them. There's no telling what he'd do."

She watched them through the screen door as they backed out of the drive, shivering as it invoked the memory of her parents driving away from Immaculate Conception. As they turned onto the road, she felt something watching her. A lone coyote sat at the property line. It made no sound and didn't look menacing, but the hair rose on the back of Phoebe's neck. The coyote stood and trotted toward her. Her hand clutched the door, but there was no way it could get inside. The screen door was heavy-duty. It had to be to keep Puddleglum in. She'd learned that the hard way.

The animal sat in front of her door, not two feet away from her, and stared at her knowingly. As it opened its mouth in a pant, Phoebe pressed her fingers to her temples against a sudden change in air pressure. A shade was stepping out of the coyote—and into her. The animal loped away.

She knew him by now. "Jacob."

"Just wanted to see if I could do that. Brain feels weird inside a dog. Feels like I'm still half dog-minded." Jacob shook her head to rid himself of the sensation.

"What do you want?"

"That's not a very nice greeting for someone who's come to help you."

Phoebe found that doubtful. "How are you going to help me?"

"I can take you to where your quetzal is being drained of his power."

Chapter 29

Rafe found his voice, just when it came in handy. Hamilton had decided to bleed him again, freshening the ceremonial cuts. Rafe roared with pain as he reached the fourth.

"Get that fu'ing athame 'way from me." Blood dripped from his tongue. The cut there had gone deep.

"You're taking longer than I expected. I need fresh blood to hasten the process. Traditionally, one would also disembowel the quetzal, the entrails spilling into the water like a litter of snakes to mix with the blood."

As Hamilton spoke the words, Rafe thought he'd actually done it. He stared in horror at his insides unraveling in a puddle at his feet. But then they slithered away, serpentine hallucinations.

Hamilton smiled. "That was just what we needed. You've become receptive to suggestion." He set the maguey athame aside and put his palm flat against Rafe's ehecacozcatl tattoo, the spiral conch shell design echoed in Hamilton's own ceremonial pectoral. "Do you feel the wind blowing?"

Rafe didn't at first, but a spiral of rain-fresh air spun down into the enclosure, lifting his hair and fluttering the feathers at the tops of his wings. He supposed the wind wasn't really there, another of the necromancer's "suggestions," but it felt real enough.

"It flows into you, increasing the oxygen in your blood."

Rafe took an involuntary breath, feeling it surge into his lungs, feeling his heart beat faster beneath Hamilton's hand.

"And now it flows out through your heart, pumped through the jewel." Blood began to seep through Hamilton's fingers. Rafe's blood, coming from the spiraling whorls of the tattoo beneath them. He was fascinated by the darkness of it. "Your blood contains the power of the quetzal. Which you are giving to me."

"No." Rafe strained against his bonds. If he had power, he needed to use it to free himself.

"You must think I'm an idiot." Hamilton dropped his hand and the illusion of blood—if it was an illusion— continued to flow from Rafe's tattoo. The necromancer tugged at the strap that held Rafe's left wrist to the arm of the cross. "These are custom made, etched with the sigils of Tezcatlipoca. You can't break them, not even—or especially, I should say—as quetzal. I took every precaution to be certain I could contain your power while I drained it from you. Which I've been doing for the past eight hours."

Eight hours? It hadn't seemed like eight hours. His arms were aching and his fingers were numb, but nothing like they ought to be after such an extended suspension. He hoped to hell Jacob was upholding his end of the bargain— even if Rafe's end of the bargain hadn't been his to make. Phoebe might not forgive him for that, but if the necromancer was dead, at least he'd have accomplished what he'd set out to do. He'd have to learn how to live without Phoebe.

Hamilton turned about. The tattoo of Quetzalcoatl was writhing, as Rafe's own had at his back...since Phoebe.

"We're halfway there." Hamilton turned to face him once more.

Halfway? Son of a bitch. "But you don't have the blood."
Rafe's tongue was easier to manipulate now, if bloodier.
"You're not a Diamante. What makes you think you can
contain the quetzal even if you manage to take it from me?"

"I have something better than Diamante blood." Hamilton came close to him again, crossing over the stepping
stones that bisected the pool. He lifted the choker he'd
placed around Rafe's neck and fingered one of the pieces
of shell. Rafe hadn't been able to look at it closely when
he'd put it on, but he had a sinking feeling it wasn't shell,
after all. "Gabriel is bound to me."

The name punched Rafe in the gut. "Bullshit. I crossed
Gabriel over. You can't touch him."

Hamilton dropped the choker with a laugh. "I've been
studying the art of necromancy since before you were
born."

The claim seemed highly doubtful. Hamilton looked no
older than thirty. Perhaps a well-preserved forty—he had
the perfect amber hue of an artificial tan, and he wasn't a
smoker or a heavy drinker; a careful regimen might have
kept his skin youthful—but there was no way he was older
than that.

"Shades are easy to call and control. They're practi-
cally begging for it. Even a petty witch like you can do it.
Spirits of the dead who've left our plane of existence, on
the other hand, require arcane magic you wouldn't know
how to handle. Blood sacrifice—personal sacrifice—and,
as with the practice of law, a great deal of studying. But,
once called, they're bound by the one who calls them. The
one who possesses their mortal coil. And their immortal
souls have a surprisingly rejuvenating effect."

Rafe wanted to put his hands over his ears, to stop the
horror of what Hamilton's words were invoking. He forced
the question out. "What 'mortal coil'? What are you talking about?"

The necromancer laughed and flicked his fingers against the beads of the choker. "What do you think?"

No. Please, no.

"Some years ago, after discovering your family's legacy, I unearthed Gabriel and distilled what I needed to command his spirit. You're wearing pieces of his vertebrae."

Phoebe debated calling the twins to let them know she was going, but the debate only lasted a moment. They'd try to convince her to wait until they came back, and she couldn't bear to leave Rafe at the necromancer's mercy a moment longer. Instead she left a note on the door telling them she'd found someone to take her to Diamante Sr.'s house near Boynton Canyon. Jacob was fuzzy on the actual address. She'd have to text it to them after she got there.

Letting Jacob drive was unnerving. He insisted giving directions would be too confusing while inhabiting her physical form. She took a back seat to him in her own head as she had with Lila, watching her body operate the vehicle. This was what it must feel like to be a ride-along. Phoebe needed to not think about that. And she needed to get more information from Jacob about what was happening at the house.

"Tezcatlipoca has given him some kind of drug." He answered her thought as he turned up Dry Creek Road in the darkness and switched on the high beams. "To immobilize him while he works his spell."

Just like Carter had done to her.

After a few minutes Jacob took a turn onto a private road, and the wheels skittered in wet earth. In her head, Phoebe gripped the steering wheel, but she had no control right now. She'd ceded her body to Jacob. She was beginning to wonder exactly how stupid that had been.

"Don't worry," said Jacob. "I'll take good care of your body. And even better care later."

Before Phoebe could worry about what *that* meant, they'd pulled up in front of a dark, sprawling edifice that couldn't possibly be a single-family dwelling. It looked more like the façade of a chic, exclusive hotel. Rafe had alluded to his father's estate being ostentatious, but she hadn't pictured anything quite like this. Dimly glowing lights designed to look like authentic luminarias—candles held in place by sand inside small paper bags—edged the walk to the entryway.

"This is as far as I go, lovely Phoebe." Jacob dropped her hands from the steering wheel after he'd turned off the engine. "This is all I promised him."

"Promised who?" The words came out audibly. She had control of her body once more.

"Some advice? Don't try to take on the necromancer by yourself." A fine thing to tell her as he left her here on her own.

Phoebe turned the lights off and slipped the keys out of the ignition and into her pocket, quietly opening the door and leaving it ajar. Her engine might have alerted him, but it seemed wisest to make as little additional announcement of her arrival as possible. She walked up the little luminaria-lit path, a good twenty yards from the circular drive, and saw candlelight flickering through the glass blocks of the windows framing the massive door. If Carter was where those candles were, she couldn't just walk in the front door.

She remembered to type the house number into her phone.

Got Mr. Diamante's address. She sent the message to both Theia and Rhea before following the brick path around the side into a secluded courtyard garden. Through a long glass wall, the candlelight was visible again.

Phoebe ducked behind the scrub brush and squinted, trying to understand what she was seeing. Carter stood naked inside a glass room—the rain catcher Theia had spoken of. Water glistened on the bottom like a small indoor pool, with little fountainheads bubbling at the corners, and something ominously dark swirled through it. But there was some structure in front of Carter that Phoebe couldn't make out, with something extending from either side that looked like wingtips. And then her brain made sense at last of what her eyes were seeing.

"Oh, my God."

Phoebe's phone buzzed in her pocket. Theia had gotten her message. Wait for us, Phoebes. Don't go up there on your own.

Yeah, she typed. About that...

The phone rang almost immediately and Phoebe quickly silenced it and clicked over to the call, not sure how much the noise might carry. She kept her voice low. "Thei, they're here. Carter has him...tied to something." She swallowed. "It looks like there's blood in the pool."

"It's Rhea. We're at Ione's. She wants to talk to you."

"Don't put her on the phone."

"Why shouldn't she put me on the phone?" Ione's terse reply came instead of Rhea's voice. "What are you doing going up there by yourself?"

"You wouldn't help. I had to do something."

"And what are you doing, exactly?" Her voice was thin, as though she'd been crying. Phoebe supposed she'd be crying, too, if she found out her boyfriend was a scum-sucking bag of dicks.

"I'm sorry about Carter. I had no idea you were seeing him."

"I don't want to talk about that right now. I'm going to call the cops and get them up there to take care of the situation, and I don't want them to find you there."

Phoebe's blood pressure started to rise, the way it always did when she dealt with her older sister. "Don't. He has friends in the sheriff's department—some of them are clients of his 'side business.'"

"Damn him." The sound of something crashing onto the ground came through the phone, as if Ione were throwing things. Phoebe couldn't really blame her. With a sigh, Ione spoke again. "They found Rafe's apprentice yesterday afternoon. At the temple. His body had been stuffed in a storage locker in the basement. He'd been strangled, just like Barbara Fisher. They think it's been there since right after the Conclave met last week."

"Oh, God."

"I let Carter deal with the sheriff because I just couldn't go down there. I couldn't face it. And he probably did it."

"I'm sorry, Ione."

"I guess I'll have to make a call to some people I trust at the Covent."

"Do you know who you can trust?"

"Yes." Ione's voice was sharp. "People I've known for years. Convincing them Carter's a necromancer won't be easy, but they trust me, too." She paused for a moment. "Phoebe, are you one-hundred-percent positive about what happened to you at his hotel?"

Phoebe bit her tongue on a sarcastic reply. "Yes. He drugged me, undressed me and took pictures of me being animated by a step-in. I can send you the photographic evidence if you need proof."

"*No.* I just…needed to ask." Ione sighed heavily. "I'm going to gather a quorum for a binding ritual, but you need to get out of there just the same."

"Ione—"

"There's nothing you can do for him, Phoebe. If he's still alive—"

"Of course he's still alive!"

"Then Carter isn't trying to kill him. He's had plenty of time. Whatever ritual he's performing apparently doesn't require Rafe's life. Once the quorum has bound Carter, we'll send help for Rafe. But I want you out of there. Now."

She wasn't in the mood for Ione's parental bullshit. "Well, you know what, Ione? You can't always get what you want." Phoebe disconnected the call with an angry jab of her thumb while Mick Jagger's voice repeated the refrain in her head.

Creeping out from behind the shrubbery, she peered inside, only to find Carter no longer in the rain catcher with Rafe. Crap. Where had he gone? Warm drops of rain were beginning to fall again, pattering against the water in the infinity pool that edged the borders of the house, and she could see little ripples on the surface of the pool inside the rain catcher as it caught it. Rafe's eyes were closed, and the quetzal's wings that had been outstretched behind his shackled arms were no longer visible. She wasn't sure what that meant—but she also wasn't sure what it meant that they'd been visible in the first place. It was silly; she'd kind of gotten the idea they were *her* thing.

She wondered if she should try to bang on the glass wall to get his attention, but thought better of it. If she banged loud enough to get Rafe's attention, she'd surely have Carter's, as well, from wherever he'd disappeared to.

Phoebe settled back behind the brush, trying to think of anything she could do besides wait. If nothing else, at least she could be there to take care of Rafe as soon as Carter was bound.

Her phone buzzed and she answered without bothering to look to see which of her sisters was calling. "Any luck?"

"Luck, Ms. Carlisle? I don't need any. I make my own." *Carter.* Well, wasn't that a kick in the pants? "I thought I'd extend an invitation to you to come in out of the rain. I've just started a fire in this marvelous fireplace. It's very cozy."

Phoebe froze, unable to collect her thoughts enough to formulate a response.

"I've left the front door open for you." Carter's voice was amused. How nice that she could entertain him.

"I want you to let Rafe go." Which he was sure to do now that she'd said so.

"Come inside and we'll talk about it." Carter hung up.

Phoebe stared at the phone. She didn't have a lot of choices here. She could sit outside in the rain, waiting for Carter's power to be bound, knowing he knew she was there, or she could sit inside, maybe find out exactly what he was doing to Rafe and try to stall him from doing anything worse.

With a sigh, she stood and shoved her phone into her pocket before making her way around to the front entrance. As Carter had said, the door was wide open. The glass-encased rain catcher was stunningly displayed in the center of the foyer, with Rafe as the centerpiece. And beyond him, in a great room worthy of a world-class hotel lobby, Carter sat in front of a crackling fire, as promised, wrapped in an expensive silk robe.

Carter smiled. "Care for an *añejo*?" He held up a liqueur glass of pale amber liquid. "Aged tequila. You'd be surprised how smooth it is."

"As if I'd drink anything you offered me." She peered in at Rafe when she came close to the rain catcher, palms pressed against the glass while rain snaked over it on the other side, hoping for a sign he was aware of her presence, but his eyes remained closed. Only the steady rise and fall of his chest kept her from losing it completely.

"There's nothing in the *añejo*, I assure you. Though I suppose I can understand your hesitation." Carter patted the sofa cushion beside him. "But, please, come join me."

Phoebe moved away from the rain catcher and stepped into the great room, keeping her distance. "I'll stand, thanks." Rainwater dripped from her ponytail onto the terra-cotta tile as she faced him down. "What are you doing to him?"

"Nothing, at the moment." Carter finished his *añejo* and set the glass on the table beside the sofa. He looked eminently pleased with himself. "I've acquired what I intended to."

Phoebe's stomach sank. "You have his power."

"I have the manifestation of divine energy you awoke in his blood." Carter rose and shrugged off the robe. With a roll of his shoulders, the brilliant blue-green wings that belonged to Rafe fanned out behind him. A hot flood of outrage warred with a gut-twisting stab of anguish inside her. "I possess the quetzal and all its attendant power. I am the human embodiment of Quetzalcoatl."

"So I guess we don't have to call you Tezcatlipoca anymore," Phoebe snapped, trying to use her anger to keep back the tears. "Or any of those other absurd cultural appropriations you're so fond of."

"Appropriation is just another word for conquest. To the victor belong the spoils." He smiled, as though he thought he was adorable. "Call me a conquistador, if you will."

"I'll call you something, all right." She gave him a derisive up-and-down look, and her gaze was unfortunately drawn to his rather enthusiastic erection. She closed her hand in her coat pocket around the can of pepper spray on the keychain Theia had given her after learning what had happened at Carter's hotel.

The smile became slightly chagrined. "An unintended side effect of the quetzal's activation. Don't be alarmed. I have no plans to molest you in any way."

Phoebe's lip curled in a sneer. "Oh, well, that's good to know. I'd hate to think you *planned* drugging and assaulting me the other night."

Carter shrugged. "I did plan that, yes. You were upsetting my thralls. I had to teach you a lesson and put some healthy fear into you. But I didn't harm you, so you're welcome."

A harsh laugh escaped her, echoing inside the great room. "You want a thank-you for not penetratively raping me while you had me unconscious and naked?" She felt like pepper-spraying him just for being a dick. "And what about my sister? What lesson have you been teaching her?"

Carter picked up the silk robe and shrugged it over his folded—*stolen*—wings, but left the sash hanging loose. "Ione is a beautiful and passionate woman. Who happens to share the blood of your auspicious ancestry—I assume you've figured that much out, given your impressive little display with my nagual. She's my insurance policy, in case the quetzal needs 'maintenance,' so to speak."

Phoebe tried to relax her thumb so she wouldn't accidentally activate the trigger in her pocket. "Well, too bad. Your policy has just expired. She knows everything."

"And I possess power over the souls of Mictlan. All I need to keep her in check is a little help from Lila or Barbara or Monique, or any of an endless number of souls now available to me." He made a gesture with his right hand. "Lila." His eyes were focused between them, as though he could see her.

Phoebe took a step back, trying to steel herself against possession, but Lila charged her like a psychic bull and physically knocked her on her ass with the force of her step-in. The can of pepper spray rolled out of Phoebe's pocket.

With a slight smile, Carter picked it up and slipped it into his own. "But since you're here and Ione is not, I'd like to try something. Lila, bring her."

Phoebe tried to resist, but Lila's shade had always been overwhelming. Under her direction, Phoebe rose and came to stand before Carter. She glared up at him in defiance as Lila lifted her arms to his shoulders.

"It's just a kiss, Phoebe. Don't act like I'm stealing your maiden virtue."

Phoebe's arms wrapped around his neck and she tilted forward onto her toes, her mouth obediently seeking his. She wanted to bite off his lip, shuddering as his tongue brushed hers.

Carter breathed in sharply, pressing his hands against her shoulders to move her a step back, and disengaged their mouths. "That's what I thought." He eyed her with new appreciation. "You're like a shot of adrenaline."

Phoebe spat on the floor beside him. She'd been aiming for his face, but she was surprised Lila had allowed her enough autonomy to do it at all. Perhaps Lila didn't care for nonconsensual tonsil hockey with Carter Hamilton any more than Phoebe did.

Carter's eyes narrowed, apparently at the same thought. "Go sit down," he snapped. "I'll let you know when I need you again."

As Phoebe sank into the chair opposite, her pocket vibrated. Lila took out the phone. Ione had texted her.

Lila read it aloud with Phoebe's mouth, in the husky tone only Lila could manage to wring from her vocal chords. "'We've run into a snag. My friends at the Covent sympathize with Rafe's predicament, but since he's officially a warlock, they've voted against assisting him magically. Carter will be dealt with through a formal convention of the Conclave. Phoebe, promise me you'll get out of there now. We'll meet up at your place and figure this out.'"

Carter strode toward her and yanked the phone out of her hand. "You got her to poison the Covent against me." He threw off the robe once more, flinging out his wings and raising them in an apparent display of dominance. "It won't matter in the long run, because I don't need the Covent, but in the short run, it's goddamned inconvenient. And I don't like to be inconvenienced." He stormed toward the nearest doors on the rain catcher and yanked them open, flinging the phone into the pool.

Rafe lifted his head, rain pouring over his face.

Carter leveled his gaze at him. "I'd considered sparing you, Rafael, but loose ends always unravel. And blood will make my transformation that much stronger."

Chapter 30

Rafe folded onto his knees in the pool like a rag doll after Hamilton unfastened the straps at his wrists and ankles. He felt lifeless. Soulless. He'd opened his eyes briefly, thinking he heard Phoebe's voice, only to see her kissing the necromancer. He'd been an idiot not to see he was being played. Phoebe had been Hamilton's secret weapon from the beginning, the perfect trap for a wounded quetzal: desiring and being desired; the promise of love.

Ernesto's unobtrusive shade sidled into him when Rafe didn't move at Hamilton's order, lifting him to his feet and walking Rafe across the stepping stones through the glass doors, out of the rain at last. He'd almost forgotten what it was like not to have rain falling on him. The hammer and crack of thunder and lightning was muted. His father had designed the pool to be air- and water-tight. The entire house had always seemed a dulling of the outside world, turning rain into a decorative fountain, and the panorama of rugged, iron-oxide-infused stone and gray-green desert brush in all directions around the house into a pretty, high-definition painting.

"I'm sorry," Ernesto murmured through his mouth, and

Rafe wondered why until he found himself lying back on the large, round, wood-on-stone coffee table in the great room. Ernesto maintained possession of him while Hamilton stretched Rafe's limbs over the sides of the table and bound him to the legs. Phoebe wasn't anywhere in his range of vision, though it was admittedly limited.

He looked up at Hamilton, flaunting Rafe's quetzal wings, and pondered how it would feel to tear the bastard's heart out of his chest with his teeth. Imagining the blood running down his throat got his heart pumping enough that he was able to jerk against his bonds and make a sort of growl in his throat when Ernesto stepped out of him.

Hamilton was unmoved by his ineffectual struggle. He stood at Rafe's head, a clay bowl held high in one hand and a knife in the other—no makeshift maguey athame this time, but a hand-carved obsidian blade with a heavy steel handle. "Mictlantecuhtli, Lord of the Land of the Dead, I offer you the blood of a scion of Quetzalcoatl, that it may drip down into Mictlan upon the bones of the dead and release their spirits to me."

"Hope you choke on it," Rafe snarled.

Hamilton's lofty ceremonial mien faltered for a moment, his face twisting with irritation. With more spite than ceremony, Hamilton slashed the side of Rafe's throat with a stinging, shallow cut, placing the bowl on the table beneath the wound to catch the blood.

"You're not very good at this human sacrifice thing, are you? This is going to take all night."

Hamilton dipped his fingers in the trickling blood and drew something on Rafe's chest. "I need to collect your blood to paint the glyphs before I send you to Mictlan, and I don't care for messes." He dipped again, and took his time finishing his drawing. "But your mouth is beginning to annoy me. I liked you better when your senses were dulled." Hamilton brought the knife to Rafe's throat once more. "Phoebe can clean up the mess." This time the knife went in deep, and dark venous blood began to splatter into the bowl.

Rafe turned his head away, black spots dancing before his eyes as Phoebe came into view.

Hamilton handed her the knife. "Why don't you do the honors?"

Phoebe gripped the handle in both hands and raised it over her head, staring down at Rafe with an expression devoid of passion.

"A firm plunge between the breastbone." Hamilton's voice seemed to come from far away, and Rafe's eyelids were heavy. "Like you're deboning a chicken."

He wanted to say something to Phoebe, but his mind had stopped making sense.

Phoebe closed her eyes, engaged in a desperate internal argument.

Let go of me, Lila. He just gave us his weapon. We don't need to do what he says.

Maybe you *don't.*

Why do you? *What's he going to do to you? The only reason you obey him is for his lame promise to let you be with Jacob again. Do you seriously think that's ever going to happen?*

You don't know what you're talking about. I'm bound to him. I can't resist his orders.

But I can, if you just let go of me and let me stick this knife in his gut.

You can't kill Tezcatlipoca. Jacob will be lost to me forever.

What if I promised to let you be with him—through me?
Phoebe knew she shouldn't be making promises Rafe's body would have to keep—if he lived. He was still breathing, but blood was pouring out of him at an alarming rate.

But she seemed to have gotten Lila's attention. The struggle to keep the knife from plunging lessened.

You would do that? After what I've done to you?

If Rafe lives, yes. And that was beginning to look doubtful, whether Phoebe drove a knife into his heart or not.

She felt Lila relinquish control. *The bones around your Rafe's neck—they give Tezcatlipoca the power of the quetzal. Destroy them, and he loses everything he's worked for. I can't help you beyond that.*

Carter frowned. "What are you waiting for?"

Phoebe plunged the knife, but Lila had released her. Instead of burying the blade in Rafe's chest, she slipped the knife under the choker and yanked it toward her, severing the cord. The choker dropped into her hand.

Carter gripped her other arm. "What the hell are you doing?"

Before he could stop her, she turned and flung the choker into the fire. Carter made a snarling roar like a caged jaguar and leaped on her with similar force, knocking her into the table as he grabbed the knife from her. Seeing the blade flash as it descended toward Rafe's heart, she did the only thing she could think of and threw her body across his. The blade slammed into her back like a vicious punch. Carter swore and yanked the knife out, and Phoebe heard herself scream as if from a distance.

"Get out of the way, Phoebe."

Phoebe ignored him, pressing her fingers against the fountain of blood still burbling out of Rafe's jugular, trying to keep it in.

Carter tried to yank her away, and she rolled onto her back, her arm twisted at a painful angle as she struggled to keep pressure on Rafe's wound. She could feel blood seeping through her shirt against Rafe's clammy skin.

Carter's eyes were dark with fury. "Thanks to your little stunt, I now need Rafael's bones as well as his blood.

You've bound him to this plane forever as my slave." He ripped open the buttons at the front of her shirt. "I'll have to make do with you as the blood sacrifice. I would have preferred to keep you around. But your sister will suffice." He lifted the knife and raised his voice in invocation. "Mictlantecuhtli, I give you the blood of my enemies!"

The knife plunged once more, but Carter faltered inexplicably, stumbling against the table, and the weapon fell from his hand onto the stone as if someone had struck his wrist with a sharp blow. The wings were no longer visible at his back. Instead they extended once more from Rafe's shoulders as Rafe's chest rose beneath her with a deep breath, the cut at his throat somehow closing on its own as her hand slipped away.

Rafe's voice was a soft rasp in his chest. "Don't you die on me, Phoebe."

The room spun dangerously but she managed a weak laugh. "On you. Literally."

With a powerful jerk, Rafe broke the bonds at his wrists and sat up, cradling Phoebe against him.

Carter staggered back, the loss of the annoying erection he'd been sporting reflecting his profound defeat even more than the dumbfounded expression on his face. "How did you do that?"

"I didn't." Rafe touched his fingers to the blood smeared on the wind-jewel tattoo. "I think she did."

Phoebe tried to focus on his face, shaking her head. "I didn't do anything."

"Your blood." Rafe held out his fingers. "Where it mixed with mine."

Carter reached for the knife but Rafe moved faster, closing his hand around Carter's wrist as he snatched the knife out of the necromancer's grasp. The snarl on Carter's curled lip was cut short with a howl as Rafe severed

Carter's ring finger, dropping both finger and ring to the ground.

"Ernesto." Rafe spoke as though the shade stood before him. "Get something to stop the bleeding. And see that he stays put."

With a sharp intake of breath and a look of surprise, Carter picked up the robe and wrapped the fabric around the bleeding stump of his finger before he sat abruptly on the couch. "I do as you will me." His accent was one Phoebe herself had spoken before. "I am the slave of the quetzal."

"Not for long, you're not. I have no interest in keeping you bound here. But I appreciate your help right now."

Phoebe was having trouble keeping her eyes open. She let her weight sink against Rafe's chest.

His arms tightened around her. "Stay with me, Phoebe."

"Not going anywhere," she murmured, slightly annoyed he was keeping her awake. She just needed a little nap.

As she let her eyes close, running footsteps sounded outside the open front door, accompanied by familiar voices.

"Phoebe!"

"Oh, my God."

"Sweet baby Jesus. He's got wings."

Chapter 31

"We have to stop meeting like this." Phoebe smiled at Rafe as he came around the curtain into her little cubicle in the ER, but he wasn't smiling back.

"I thought you were going to bleed to death."

Phoebe shifted gingerly against the pillow propped between her and the raised bed. "I think that's supposed to be my line. Thankfully, your amped-up blood seems to have accelerated my healing as well as your own. More stitches this time, and it hurts like hell, but they're giving me the good drugs. Want a hit off my IV?"

Theia got up from the chair beside her gurney. "I think I'll go see what's taking Rhe so long with those lattes." She and Rhea had ridden with Phoebe in the ambulance, filling her in on the binding ritual Ione had led them in after her friends at the Covent turned her down. What Theia called the "Lilith bond" had given it the strength to work against Carter's magic even without the Covent's influence.

Rafe frowned when Theia had gone. "I'm serious. You threw yourself in front of a knife."

"And you're very welcome, Mr. Cranky Pants."

"Phoebe—"

"Your jugular was bleeding like a fountain and that necrofreak was about to take your heart. I wasn't going to just watch him do it. You would have done the same for me, wouldn't you?" Phoebe narrowed her eyes. "You'd better say yes."

"Of course I would have, but that's different."

"How is it different? Because you have a penis? Were you planning to use it to block steel? Because I have news for you—your cock is amazing, but it's not *that* amazing."

Rafe made a half-strangled laugh and then looked angry about it. "Not because I'm a man. Because I'm quetzal."

"Which you've been for all of twenty-four hours. And, again, you're welcome."

Rafe sighed and sat in the seat Theia had vacated. "Point taken." He took her hand. "I just don't ever want to be that scared again."

"Okay, well, I'll make you a deal. You don't get tied to any more sacrificial altars by a power-hungry dick-bag who wants to cut your heart out of your chest and offer it to the god of the underworld, and I won't throw myself in front of any more knives."

A reluctant smile tugged at his lips. "Deal."

"Speaking of the power-hungry dick-bag, what are we going to do with him?"

"I'm trying to work that out. Ernesto's holding him for the moment. Apparently it's the bones Hamilton possesses from each of his victims that enable the shades to retain such complete control when they step in. Seems like you're the only one who's been able to successfully throw them out. But we can't keep Ernesto inside him forever."

"Can we throw him into an active volcano?"

Rafe's laugh was cut short by the arrival of Ione at the partition.

She gave him an awkward nod as he stood. "Rafe. Glad to see you're none the worse for wear. I'm sorry about the

Covent—" She stopped in surprise as Rafe enveloped her in a bear hug.

Phoebe tried not to laugh. Ione hated hugs.

"Screw the Covent. You and your sisters saved our lives, plain and simple."

Ione tucked her hair behind her ears in a nervous gesture when he released her. "Well, I'm glad it worked. I'm just sorry I wasted so much time." She glanced at Phoebe. "I should have listened to you."

"Hey, you had a perfectly good reason not to want to believe it."

Rafe bent to give Phoebe a kiss on the forehead. "I'm going to go see what's taking your sisters so long with those lattes." He winked and stepped out.

Ione sat beside Phoebe, looking defeated. "My ego almost got you killed."

Phoebe wanted to laugh but her back hurt too much. "I hate to have to point this out, but that's a pretty egotistical thing to say." The shocked, hurt look on Ione's face wasn't what she'd been going for. "I should also point out I'm on an awful lot of Dilaudid and I don't think that came out right."

"I was trying to apologize to you, Phoebe."

"I know. I just meant you don't have to. You didn't do anything wrong. He used both of us."

Ione sank against the chair. "But I brought him here. I pushed Rafe to let Carter represent him instead of you. In my mind, you're still my rebellious kid sister, and I told myself I was just looking out for you, when the truth is, I thought I knew better than you. I wasn't even honest enough with myself to give you the respect you've more than earned over the past ten years."

Phoebe glanced at the Dilaudid drip to see if it had accidentally gotten turned up. Those were words she'd never expected to hear Ione say. She put her IV-taped hand on

Ione's. "You didn't bring him here. He's been planning this for years, waiting for the perfect opportunity. He just wanted you to think it was your idea.

"He knew Rafe had the potential to become quetzal, and he murdered Barbara Fisher to set Rafe up. And then encouraged you to recommend me to Rafe to help with the shades, because he knew about our ancestry. Seducing you was just a spiteful cherry on top of his twisted sundae. He actually said he was going to use you as an insurance policy to 'top off' his quetzal power if it started to wane."

Tears slid down Ione's cheeks as she listened without speaking—something else Phoebe couldn't remember her ever having done before.

Phoebe handed her a tissue from the box on her "invalid tray."

"Make sure you get as much use out of that as you can. They're charging me ten dollars a tissue." She managed to make Ione laugh—would the day of firsts never end?

"So, Rafe…" Ione sniffled and wiped her nose. "He's really this 'quetzal'? What exactly—?"

"He's the embodiment of Quetzalcoatl, his 'nagual'—a sort of shape-shifting expression of the divine. And, God, is he good in bed."

Ione smiled. "I think the Dilaudid is talking again."

Phoebe shook her head, lying back against the pillow. "No, ma'am. He is fucking fantastic. And I made him come so hard he sprouted wings."

Her sister covered her mouth with her hand, laughing into the expensive little tissue until the tears started to flow again. Maybe it was a *wee* bit of Dilaudid talking.

While Phoebe recuperated, Rafe had one last bit of business to take care of with the shades. The altar Ernesto had revealed to him had to be destroyed, the bones, like Gabriel's, burned to release the shades and spirits the necromancer had enslaved. Hamilton, it turned out, had been using Rafe's father's house since his arrival in Sedona, and the altar was there—in Gabriel's bedroom.

The shades assembled around him in the great room as he set up his own altar, all of Hamilton's victims—all except Ernesto, who'd promised to remain within Hamilton until he was dealt with—watching as Rafe pricked his tongue to let the blood drip into the bowl over the bones.

"With the blood of the quetzal, I release you. You are no longer bound to the false Tezcatlipoca, or to me. You are free to leave this plane or stay as you please. Go where you will." He emptied the bowl into a wooden box that held Hamilton's supplies and placed it on the fire, watching the flames lick over it, taking quickly to the dry wood.

Weeping openly, Barbara's shade gave him a cool, spectral kiss on his cheek as she faded. The others acknowledged his gift with less personal goodbyes. Matthew, whose bones hadn't been here, Rafe never saw. It seemed Hamilton had simply killed him to keep him from revealing what he knew.

Jacob, in his jeans and shit-kickers, watched him from a spot apart from the others, leaning against one of the column supports that framed the open architecture. "You made me a promise."

Rafe sucked at the blood on the tip of his tongue. "I did, and I mean to keep it." How he was going to break it to Phoebe that he'd made such a promise without her consent, he wasn't sure.

"I mean to hold you to it, quetzal." Jacob walked in the direction of where Lila had last been standing and dissipated.

Rafe returned to his brother's bedroom with the bowl, not knowing what else to do with it. As he set it on the bureau, something caught his eye in the mirror. He whirled to find Gabriel seated on the bed, watching him.

"Gabriel…" He took a tentative step toward him, afraid the ghost would spook. "Phoebe released you. How are you still here?"

Gabriel tucked one foot under his leg in a gesture that made Rafe feel he'd stepped back into the past. "I know. It turns out spirits who've crossed can visit whenever they like." An almost-smile touched his lips. "You didn't do anything so terrible to me, after all, crossing me over."

"Gabriel…" Tears choked him as he recalled the ritual when he'd turned a deaf ear to his brother's pleas for mercy.

"I've wanted to tell you that, many times, but you've never been able to see me."

"I was wrong," Rafe choked out. "I ignored you—I ignored you while you were still living, when you needed my help. I could have protected you."

"You had to protect yourself. It's okay. It all seems different on the other side. I wish I could explain, but it's something you have to experience yourself. I just wanted you to know I'm okay. You can stop grieving."

Rafe shook with emotion, unable to speak.

Gabriel rose and came close to him, brushing him with an embrace he could almost feel, though Gabriel's limbs floated through him. "I'll visit again sometime. You can tell me all about Phoebe." His smile this time was warm and genuine as he dissolved into the ether.

Rafe lay on the bed—untouched except by the cleaning service since Gabriel had last slept in it—hugged the pillow to his chest and let himself sob for the first time since Gabriel's death.

It was while he lay drying his eyes that he thought of the absurdly simple solution to the problem of Carter Hanson Hamilton.

Chapter 32

"You really think this will work?" Phoebe reclined on the couch on her first night home from the hospital while Rafe laid out his plan.

"All we need to do is make sure Ernesto can do a convincing impression of a pompous douchebag." He smiled. "I've been working with him. If he slips into his own accent a little, they'll just chalk it up to affectation, part of Hamilton's obsession with appropriating my culture."

"What about afterward?"

"Ernesto has agreed to stay with him until Hamilton is sentenced and behind bars. We'll provide a confession in Hamilton's handwriting and Ernesto will swear in court as Hamilton that he wants to plead guilty to the murders of Barbara Fisher, Matthew Palacio, Monique Hernandez and my father, and that he wants you to represent him."

"Why would anyone believe he'd want my representation? He's smarter than that."

"Because he had an attack of conscience after becoming involved with your sister and this is his way of making it up to her. Besides, he doesn't need an experienced trial lawyer since he's pleading guilty. All you have to do is walk him in there and hand him over and Ernesto will handle the rest."

There was a little more to the process than that, but she had to admit, it was a good plan. "Using necromancy against the necromancer. I like it."

Carter's surrender to the police went smoothly, earning Phoebe a rather more satisfying fifteen minutes of fame.

The compromising positions in which she and Rafe had found themselves of late took on a different significance when Carter revealed in his confession that he'd engineered the secret photography and leaks to the press to throw suspicion on his own client for the crimes he himself had committed. Phoebe was even reinstated with the Public Defender's Office, although plenty of offers were flowing in from private law firms wanting to cash in on her success.

The most satisfying moments, however, were in private consultation with her "client," when Ernesto, with Phoebe's leave, gave Carter the temporary freedom to express his true feelings on the matter. His impotent rage, silenced when Phoebe ordered it, almost made up for the memory of being drugged by him. Payback was a bitch.

After celebrating "Phoebe's" victory once Carter was safely behind bars awaiting sentencing, Rhea and Theia announced they were heading home.

"You don't have to do the drive tonight," Phoebe protested. "Get some sleep and leave fresh in the morning." She tried to help them tidy up in the kitchen but Rafe steered her back to the couch as they insisted she stay put and give her back a rest. They could be pains in the butt, but she was going to miss them when they were gone.

Ione leaned on her elbows on the back of the couch when Rafe excused himself to use the restroom. "Honey, shut up. You're going to give that poor sweet boy a case of blue...feathers. He's been looking at you like lunch in front of a dog that's been ordered to sit and stay since you got home from the hospital. Just get laid and enjoy it while the rest of us live vicariously."

Phoebe blushed, but she couldn't help grinning. "Jesus, Di. You're as bad they are."

"Yeah, well, turns out we're all related." Ione winked.

"Hey, what do you think about their theory, by the way?" She'd forgotten about it in all the excitement that had followed the revelation. "About the Lilith blood?"

Ione straightened. "Some other time." She smiled as Rafe returned from down the hall. "Hey, my warlock friend, we're going to take off. Think you can get this one tucked into bed?"

Rafe laughed. "Yeah, I think I can manage."

Ione swung her purse over her shoulder. "You know I can talk to the Covent about your standing. After everything that's happened, I'm willing to bet they'd reconsider."

Rafe tucked his hands in his pockets. "That's okay. I think my beliefs have evolved a bit beyond Covent doctrine these days."

"Understandable." Ione turned to the twins. "So, you two are hitting the road, aren't you?"

"Nice hint," said Rhea.

Theia tossed a dishrag at Rhea's head and the two of them came over to give Phoebe their parting hugs.

"Use that tantric position I sent you on Facebook," Rhea whispered loudly. "Keep you off your back."

Phoebe rolled her eyes. "Go away now."

The twins gave Rafe his own goodbye hugs. Rhea cupped her mouth against his ear and apparently left a parting nugget of Rhea wisdom with him, as well.

Phoebe grinned as Rafe colored to the tips of his ears.

Damn, that was hot. It made her want to say inappropriate things to him in mixed company all the time.

As the house got quiet in the wake of the Carlisle clan's departure, both Phoebe and Rafe found themselves temporarily tongue-tied.

"So." Rafe rocked on his heels. "Guess they're gone."

"Guess they are."

"Guess I'm supposed to put you to bed."

Desire rose inside her like an uncoiling snake. With all that was going on, she'd put the thought of intimacy with Rafe on the back burner, and Rafe had kept his distance while her back healed. The stitches had come out yesterday, but she and Rafe hadn't really had any time alone since the morning she'd woken the quetzal—not even to explore in the abstract what might be between them.

"Guess you are." She started to her feet, but Rafe stepped in toward the couch and swept her off them, lifting her in a smooth motion with both hands beneath her ass while she caught herself against him with a gasp, arms wrapped around his neck and legs around his hips.

"Your back okay?" His dark eyes were heavy with desire.

Phoebe nodded, unable to take her eyes off his.

"You want me to—"

"Yes." Phoebe didn't care what he was asking. Any of it. All of it. She brought her mouth to his. "Do what you want with me," she whispered against his lips.

He made a noise deep in his throat and dove for her mouth with his, drinking her in like she was ice-cold water and he was a man who'd been adrift at sea for days. He made a soft humming noise into her mouth and Phoebe echoed it, her panties damp inside her cotton shorts as his jeans swelled against them. She worked his T-shirt up his abs, and Rafe drew his mouth away from hers long enough to pull the shirt over his head before unbuttoning her thin cotton-and-lace cami. He lifted her higher to bring her breasts to his mouth, sucking a nipple through the rough lace of the bra cup until Phoebe was whimpering against him.

Rafe somehow held on to her with one arm at the small of her back while he tugged open the drawstring of her shorts and shimmied them down her thighs. Phoebe released her legs from his hips long enough to let the shorts fall to the ground with her panties, wrapping her thighs around him once more with a moan as he jerked open the buttons of his fly. A condom packet appeared like magic from a pocket, the foil between Rafe's teeth for an instant as he tore it open with an animal growl. Phoebe clung to him, shaking with desire while he rolled it on, and then slid down over him, soaking wet, and groaned as he pulled her in close and hard.

Her bra had slid up on her breasts and Rafe tugged it higher to free them from it as she rode his cock, a groan of relief escaping him as if he'd needed to see them. He held on to her waist and thrust into her hard, rough, panting noises of encouragement following each rising moan she emitted as he rocked her toward orgasm.

Phoebe threw herself against him, clinging tight to his neck, breasts slick with sweat against the rock-hard terrain of his pecs, and wailed aloud, unapologetically, as her whole body tingled with the rush of her climax, made even sweeter when Rafe's hips picked up speed in response.

He stilled and almost stumbled back with the force of his own climax, his fingers tugging hard on the hair at her nape as he came inside her. And then his quetzal wings sprang from his shoulders and spread over them both with the outburst of sound he ended on.

Phoebe let her body collapse against him, twitching with aftershocks, and realizing after a moment that tears were streaming down her face.

Rafe must have felt them against his shoulder. "You okay, love?" His voice was a soft whisper of concern.

Phoebe nodded against him, her heart leaping at that little word. "Yeah, I am." But okay wasn't anything close to what she was. She sighed against him. "I'm absolutely perfect."

Rafe laughed softly. "Yeah, you are." He hoisted her up for a firmer grip, still inside her, and carried her to the bedroom. This man was a god.

"I think we scared Puddleglum." He tucked his wings back like it was second nature already as he sat on the bed with her in his lap. "Think I should go check on him?"

Phoebe began to laugh, the motion causing little tingling waves of fleeting contractions deep inside her. "God, I love you," she gasped, trying to get her laughter under control.

Rafe lifted her chin and met her eyes with a hopeful smile. "Yeah?"

Phoebe giggled. "Yeah."

He grinned. "Well, that's a damn relief, because I love you, too." He kissed her, holding her face with both hands, and Phoebe squirmed in his lap, rising up on her knees, already wanting him again.

He chuckled as he let go of her mouth. "I might need a little time."

"That's okay." She sighed and softened into him. "I'll be right here."

After a moment Rafe rolled with her onto his side and held her gaze like he had something important to say. "I should probably take off my pants. And my shoes."

Phoebe laughed again, collapsing into semi-hysterical giggles as Rafe extricated himself and slid his pants down to his ankles before realizing they were too narrow to go over his boots and he'd have to take them off first.

"You seem to be finding this awfully amusing."

She grinned up at him. "You're like this insanely hot dork. It's adorable."

"I'm not sure I want to be adorable." Finally naked, he climbed onto the bed and reclined beside her with his head propped in his hand. Phoebe moved up beside him and he gave her a soft kiss. "Maybe I can make you stop laughing at my 'adorkableness.'" He kissed her throat then eased her onto her belly.

Phoebe turned her head and rested it on the pillow. "What are you doing?"

"Getting rid of unnecessary things." Rafe slipped the straps of her unbuttoned camisole top sensuously down her arms and tossed it on the floor before moving to undo the bra strap. As it came away, slid gently from beneath her while he cupped her breasts, Rafe stopped with the bra dangling from his hand. "Phoebe...what's this?"

"What's what?" She turned her head but couldn't tell what he was looking at.

"When did you get this tattoo?"

"Oh." She'd almost forgotten. Phoebe crossed her arms under her cheek. "This is going to sound weird, but—Rhea did it that night while you were..." She shrugged at the unspoken end of the sentence.

Rafe was silent for a moment. "You got a tattoo while I was being tortured by that asshole?"

Phoebe rolled onto her back. "I told you it would sound weird. Rhea's taken up tattooing and she does a sort of pictomancy with it."

"Pictomancy?"

"She reads the ink of the tattoos she's done, like a psychic reading. I didn't know how to find you, and she showed me how it worked on Theia, so I thought it was worth a try."

Rafe's brows drew together. "You had your sister tattoo you—to find me?"

"I didn't know what else to do. And it worked. Somewhat. We knew you were at your father's house, but we didn't know the address. That's when I tried to get it from Ione and found out she was dating Carter. She hung up on me, thinking we were pranking her, and then wouldn't answer her phone. Luckily, Jacob came along and showed me where the house was."

Something flickered in his eyes, but Rafe didn't say anything, just nudged her to roll over. "Let me see it again."

Phoebe turned onto her stomach once more and felt Rafe's fingers moving over the soft, newly healed skin. "Good thing the knife missed it." The fresh scar was just to the left of it. "I would have been pissed if he'd messed it up."

"Not to mention he would have punctured a lung." Rafe traced the outline. "Is this—is it a resplendent quetzal tail feather?" His tone was somewhat incredulous.

Phoebe smiled and nodded. "Rhea will be pleased you recognized it. She's really pretty amazing. She's going to do some more detail on it later."

"*You're* pretty amazing. I can't believe you did this for me."

"I was going to get the whole bird, but Thei and Rhe convinced me not to." Phoebe turned her head and looked up at him with a shy smile. "In case you didn't feel the same way about me as I felt about you. They didn't want me to regret it."

Rafe wrapped his arms around her, resting his weight on her, and kissed the top of the tattoo. And the scar beside it. "About Jacob. There's something I should have told you."

Phoebe did her best to give him the stink-eye from beneath him. "You'd better not say he's been inhabiting you since that night and you're not really you."

Rafe laughed and it sounded suspiciously like nervous laughter. "No. No, I'm all me. I'm not about to allow him in without my permission. I'm the necromancer now, remember. Not that I want to be. But I can see the shades, as well as spirits that have crossed. And I could compel them if I were a jack-hole like Carter Hanson Hamilton." He uttered the name with all due contempt.

Phoebe lay back on the pillow. "Then what did you need to tell me?"

"Yeah." Rafe swallowed. "That. I may have promised Jacob he and Lila could, uh…consummate…their unfulfilled love affair. Please don't leave me," he added hurriedly. "I was a little desperate and high on pulque at the time."

Phoebe breathed a sigh of relief and couldn't help breaking into another mini fit of giggles.

"Now what's funny?"

She swallowed the laughter and caught her breath. "I may have promised Lila the same thing to get her to help me. I wasn't sure how to break that to you."

"Wow." Rafe relaxed against her, resting his cheek between her shoulders. "I think we may just deserve each other."

They lay quietly for a few minutes, enjoying the novelty of being alone together, until Phoebe felt her ears pop with the changing air pressure of a shade's presence. "Um, speak of the devil. I think Lila's here."

Rafe nodded against her. "She is. And Jacob."

"Should we…?"

"I'm not sure I can accommodate Jacob quite yet, but…" Rafe paused, and Phoebe felt him become rather firmly accommodating against her. "Apparently, Jacob can take care of that."

Head pounding with Lila's insistence, Phoebe sighed and let down her defenses against her, letting Lila rush in. "Just this once." Phoebe was firm. "That was the deal."

"Don't worry, sweetheart." Rafe's voice was modulated

with Jacob's slow and sensuous intonation. "I'll make it one to remember."

Lila deepened Phoebe's voice. "You had better be talking to me."

Jacob closed Rafe's hands hard around Phoebe's breasts. "Of course I'm talking to you, my love." He eased back a moment and flipped Phoebe's body over with Rafe's powerful musculature, dark eyes glinting with hunger as he hovered on all fours above her.

Lila reached for him, dragging Phoebe's nails down Rafe's chest. Phoebe could feel her own desire for Rafe tangling with Lila's need for Jacob, making her heart beat rapidly. The sense of having been denied the one she loved for so long was overwhelming, even though Phoebe herself had just been intimate with Rafe.

"You were a fool to leave me." Her husky voice was a mixture of scolding and sorrow.

"I know. But I have been with you every moment since my death—until your own. And then I haunted your shade, trying to connect with you, but Tezcatlipoca kept you from me."

As Lila reached for him, Jacob grabbed her wrists and held them against the bed, teasing her with his mouth. He took his time, tasting her from the tips of her breasts to the apex of her sex, until Phoebe was moaning and writhing along with Lila and begging to be entered.

As Rafe's body lowered onto her, Jacob's desire was potent in his eyes. "You bargained with me once, quetzal, to bring things to a swifter close. This time I intend to prolong them."

As if with the lingering essence of the coyote she'd recently inhabited, Lila let out a primitive howl as they came together.

Their coupling was frantic and wild, and yet fraught with deep passion and tenderness, until at last Phoebe's body surrendered to a shattering release, though it was clearly Lila's, long held and finally granted her.

They kissed as Jacob's release followed, and Jacob held Lila in his arms, crooning and lightly rocking her. "You are my love, my only love, and I will never leave your side. Whether heaven or hell tries to come between us." Once more, Phoebe found tears running down her cheeks. With a sigh of satisfaction, Lila was gone.

Rafe pressed his lips to her throat. "Everything all right, love?" It was definitely Rafe again.

Phoebe wrapped her arms around him, hugging him against her, every inch of her skin between them feeling the warmth of his.

She smiled and breathed in his petrichor scent. "Absolutely perfect."

* * * * *

REQUEST YOUR FREE BOOKS!

2 FREE NOVELS FROM THE PARANORMAL ROMANCE COLLECTION, PLUS 2 FREE GIFTS!

YES! Please send me 2 FREE novels from the Paranormal Romance Collection and my 2 FREE gifts (gifts are worth about $10). After receiving them, if I don't wish to receive any more books, I can return the shipping statement marked "cancel." If I don't cancel, I will receive 4 brand-new novels every month and be billed just $24.76 in the U.S. or $27.96 in Canada. That's a savings of at least 29% off the cover price of all 4 books. It's quite a bargain! Shipping and handling is just 50¢ per book in the U.S. and 75¢ per book in Canada.* I understand that accepting the 2 free books and gifts places me under no obligation to buy anything. I can always return a shipment and cancel at any time. Even if I never buy another book, the two free books and gifts are mine to keep forever.

237/337 HDN GLDY

Name	(PLEASE PRINT)	

Address		Apt. #

City	State/Prov.	Zip/Postal Code

Signature (if under 18, a parent or guardian must sign)

Mail to the **Reader Service:**
IN U.S.A.: P.O. Box 1867, Buffalo, NY 14240-1867
IN CANADA: P.O. Box 609, Fort Erie, Ontario L2A 5X3

Want to try 2 free books from another line?
Call 1-800-873-8635 or visit www.ReaderService.com.

* Terms and prices subject to change without notice. Prices do not include applicable taxes. Sales tax applicable in NY. Canadian residents will be charged applicable taxes. Offer not valid in Quebec. This offer is limited to one order per household. Not valid for current subscribers to Paranormal Romance Collection or Harlequin® Nocturne™ books. All orders subject to credit approval. Credit or debit balances in a customer's account(s) may be offset by any other outstanding balance owed by or to the customer. Please allow 4 to 6 weeks for delivery. Offer available while quantities last.

Your Privacy—The Reader Service is committed to protecting your privacy. Our Privacy Policy is available online at www.ReaderService.com or upon request from the Reader Service.

We make a portion of our mailing list available to reputable third parties that offer products we believe may interest you. If you prefer that we not exchange your name with third parties, or if you wish to clarify or modify your communication preferences, please visit us at www.ReaderService.com/consumerchoice or write to us at Reader Service Preference Service, P.O. Box 9062, Buffalo, NY 14269. Include your complete name and address.

REQUEST YOUR FREE BOOKS!

2 FREE NOVELS
FROM THE SUSPENSE COLLECTION,
PLUS 2 FREE GIFTS!

YES! Please send me 2 FREE novels from the Suspense Collection and my 2 FREE gifts (gifts are worth about $10). After receiving them, if I don't wish to receive any more books, I can return the shipping statement marked "cancel." If I don't cancel, I will receive 4 brand-new novels every month and be billed just $6.49 per book in the U.S. or $6.99 per book in Canada. That's a savings of at least 18% off the cover price. It's quite a bargain! Shipping and handling is just 50¢ per book in the U.S. and 75¢ per book in Canada.* I understand that accepting the 2 free books and gifts places me under no obligation to buy anything. I can always return a shipment and cancel at any time. Even if I never buy another book, the two free books and gifts are mine to keep forever.

191/391 MDN GH4Z

Name	(PLEASE PRINT)

Address	Apt. #

City	State/Prov.	Zip/Postal Code

Signature (if under 18, a parent or guardian must sign)

Mail to the **Reader Service:**
IN U.S.A.: P.O. Box 1867, Buffalo, NY 14240-1867
IN CANADA: P.O. Box 609, Fort Erie, Ontario L2A 5X3

Want to try 2 free books from another line?
Call 1-800-873-8635 or visit www.ReaderService.com.